# SAVE HER FROM ME

McRae Bodyguards - #2

Jolie Vines

WWW.JOLIEVINES.COM

*To all you lasses who've simped over a hot guy and listed all
the ways you could use him.
This is for you.*

# BLURB

*He's her bodyguard and her brother's best friend. She's a virgin with a spicy wish list.*

*Ariel*

Someone's out to get me, forcing my car off the road and me into hiding.

When my brother recruits his Scottish best friend to protect me, though the brooding bodyguard drives me nuts, I can't refuse his help.

Or hide my crush.

As a distraction, I create a spicy wish list and have only one man in my sights to share it with.

What better way to spend my time locked in a house with the man of my dreams?

*Jackson*

I shouldn't want this lass so much, but my best friend's younger sister is under my protection and my skin.

Hooking up with her is off-limits. I can't risk losing my job. Without it, I'm unemployed and homeless.

But Ariel offers a deal I can't resist, even if I'm the last man she should take to the sheets.

While her enemy hunts us, she's using my body for more than just protection.

I vowed to keep her safe, but what if it's my secrets that are the real danger?

--

Save Her from Me is a close-proximity wild ride with a steamy deal between a determined woman and her brother's best friend. Scorching scenes. Flaming cheeks. Guarding bodies never looked so good.

This is a standalone in the McRae Bodyguards romantic suspense series with crossover characters and a gorgeous Scottish Highlands backdrop.

Jump in now and discover Ariel's list for yourself!

# READER NOTE

Dear reader,

Thank you for picking up Save Her from Me, the second in my series about the McRae Bodyguards team.

The audiobook featuring Aaron Shedlock and Addison Barnes is delicious.

Please note a trigger warning for a depiction of murder (a story told), stalking (active), and historic sexual assault (brief).

Like with Touch Her and Die, there's a hidden code in this book. Join my Jolie Vines Reader Group on Facebook or go to the acknowledgements at the end for more information.

Love hot Scottish heroes? I have five series of them. Once you're done reading this smutty story, check out the full works and reading order at the end of the book.

There's also a map of the McRae lands you can download for free here: https://www.jolievines.com/mcrae-estate-map

Love, Jolie x

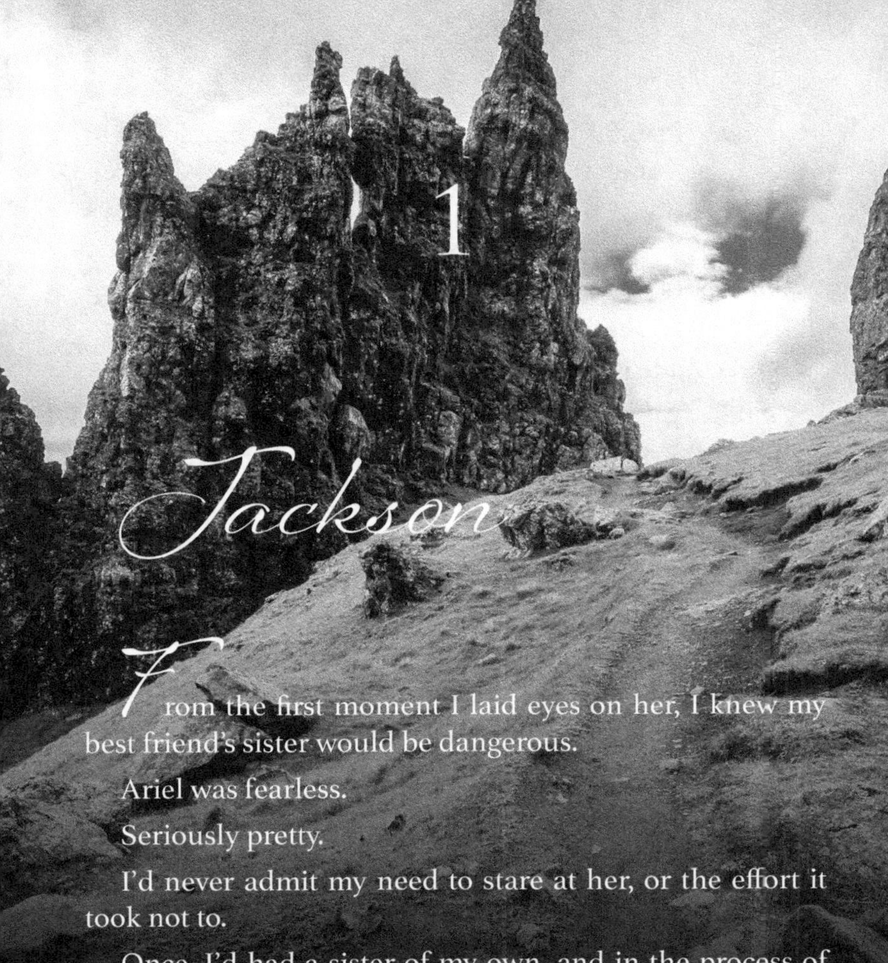

# 1

## Jackson

From the first moment I laid eyes on her, I knew my best friend's sister would be dangerous.

Ariel was fearless.

Seriously pretty.

I'd never admit my need to stare at her, or the effort it took not to.

Once, I'd had a sister of my own, and in the process of her life being ended, my instincts for keeping women safe had been blasted then broken.

Obsession was the real danger, and I would never, ever succumb.

On any normal day, I steered clear of Ariel Gordonson, but not today.

I stared at the smashed-up Mini, her car, abandoned by the side of the mountain road near a village in our remote corner of the Scottish Highlands.

I'd passed here a minute before, returning from duty at

Inverness Hospital where the rock star I was employed to protect had brought home his wife and new baby. I'd been fully focused on providing an escort, but now we were back and the family safe, I'd retraced my steps to Ariel's car.

She could have stopped to take a call. Been meeting someone for a date. None of my business.

But I couldn't shake my sense of foreboding.

And her car had been intact then.

In the time it had taken me to turn around after dropping Leo off, someone had crashed into it then taken off, not stopping at the scene of the accident.

My mind raced, and I flung open my door, my boots crunching through a frosted layer of snow.

Her front road-side headlight had been taken out and the bonnet crumpled. Glass twinkled on the frosty ground. Her door was open, but there was no sign of the woman herself.

"Ariel," I shouted.

Nothing.

I circled the vehicle.

Ice spread through me that had nothing to do with the winter's night. Ariel's possessions were scattered by the open door.

Her keys.

A shoe.

The worry lurking in the back of my mind activated into full-blown alarm, and my heart pounded.

Recently, I'd helped to protect Daisy, Ariel's closest friend, who'd suffered a kidnap attempt in the US, and we'd worked out that the man involved was someone who'd been overly interested in Ariel when the two women had been in school together.

Ariel, not Daisy, though he appeared to be on the payroll of Daisy's family.

Ariel had relocated here in secret.

She'd left her old life behind entirely, vanishing into smoke.

On the surface, it looked like I was pulling together loosely related facts, but my skill set involved a detailed understanding of how twisted a mind could get. I knew all too well that fanatical men didn't get over their fixations.

What if he'd come after her?

Monitoring one woman in the hope she'd lead to the other?

I got it together enough to perform a fast check of the scene, just to be sure she wasn't lying across the back seat or in a ditch, but then I was taking action.

I snapped up my phone, pacing back to my Toyota.

"Group call, urgent," I ordered. "Ben, Raphael, Valentine."

I had a second to make a decision, but it had already been taken.

I was new to the bodyguard job, but not to dealing with sick men. That was ingrained in me.

"Ben," my boss announced, joining the comms line.

"Valentine," reported the newest recruit to our team.

"Raphael here," Ariel's brother said. My friend. He didn't work for the bodyguard service yet as he was in pilot training, but he would soon. "I just touched down. What's happening?"

"Backup needed," I snapped. "I'm out on the road by the village."

Movement sounded at their ends of the line where the

men were hustling.

My boss was first to speak. "Halfway to my car. What's going on?"

"It's Ariel. Her car's abandoned by the roadside. It's been hit in the past few minutes. There's signs of a struggle. I think she's been taken." I glowered at the icy road lit by my headlights, black night and the surrounding hills swallowing any taillights ahead.

No other sign of life haunted the road.

After I'd passed the Mini, another car had driven my way. I'd barely paid it any attention, but had that been her attacker? Were they on the move or hidden nearby? Had she fought or was she playing it calm?

"Fuck," gritted out Raphael.

I knew his pain.

Had felt it when it was *my* sister as the subject of a report. The anxiety and panic steeled my muscles and sharpened my mind for all that was to come.

But this time would be different.

History was not going to repeat itself.

If it killed me, I'd find her.

# 2

# *Ariel*

An icy wind blasted me, sweeping down the foothills to where I trudged through the snow. If my stupid car hadn't broken down, I would've driven this in minutes, delivered the warning message I had to give, and been on my way home. My cosy tower apartment called to me, with a hot shower after a hard day at work, but I had no choice in what I needed to do.

The telling-off I had to give to one of my students.

At the end of my final lesson this afternoon, a boy in my class had sidled up to me outside the snowboarding centre's slope entrance. With a sheepish expression, he'd asked if I'd seen the video with my name on it.

I hadn't.

He'd shown me.

For six years, since I'd been in hiding in Scotland, I'd kept a low profile, never putting my face online. Not all risk could be eliminated, but phones were banned on the slopes, and the kids in my class knew me as Ari, rather than Ariel, apart from a few who lived nearby.

Like Bridgette, the menace I was on my way to see.

The pixie-haired fourteen-year-old had taken a sneaky video of me in the staff locker room and another on my snowboard. In the first, I'd shrugged on my skiwear over a sports bra. In the second, I'd wiped out while trying to correct the course of a nervous youngster.

She'd made it sexy and funny.

She'd used my full first name, an unusual one that made searching for it easy when paired with Scotland.

It had gone fucking viral.

Muttering, I stowed away my fear and stomped on. After what had happened to Daisy when she'd escaped her family of criminals, I'd had a surge of worry that I hadn't felt in years. Scotland was safe. My wannabe-Mafia father hadn't found me, and with my brothers, we'd even started talking to him again, over a secure line, trying to keep a relationship with other family members. So why did I feel so weirded out over this slip?

At the low wall to Bridgette's home, the last house on the street, I marked the fact there was no car outside—disappointingly, her mother wasn't home—then swung onto the path and up to the house. Thumped on the door with my fist.

After a few moments, it opened a crack. The girl herself peered out.

She spied me, beamed, and threw it open wider. "Hey, Ariel."

I gritted my teeth. "Can I come in?"

"Sorry, I'm not allowed to let anyone inside when Ma isn't here. Well, apart from my boyfriend." She pressed her lips together, amusement plain. "Finally saw my post then. Made ye famous."

"Bridgette, that video is not okay."

I patted my pocket for my phone, belatedly realising I'd left in the Mini.

The girl squinted, then reached for her jeans and brought out her phone, the case with bunny ears springing from the top. "Seriously? Did ye even read the comments? You're hot. People actually typed that."

I had read the comments. Teenage boys were scoring me out of ten. Grown-ass men older than my dad wrote what they wanted to do to me. That wasn't the biggest crime, though. It was the fact that Bridgette had several other videos that gave away too much information. The car park of the snowboarding centre, me in the background getting into my car. Her dancing at school in her uniform, the badge visible and the school name clear.

It led directly to the tiny corner of the UK where I'd been squirrelled away.

I didn't want to leave.

If I acted fast enough and got the video offline, perhaps it'd be okay.

Bridgette scanned her screen, the video playing. "It hit the big views two days ago but it's still climbing. Ma makes cooking videos, and this beats down on anything she's posted. I'll show ye how I made it. Are ye even online? I couldn't find an account."

"I need you to take it down."

She gasped and widened her eyes. "No way."

Pretty much the response I guessed she'd give. In a flash, I grabbed the phone from her and wheeled around, pacing down the iced-over path while I jabbed at the settings.

The DELETE option appeared.

I hit it.

"What are ye doing?" In her socks in the snow, Bridgette yanked on my arm, pulling me around.

I held out the phone, and she snatched it back, her expression one of pure outrage.

"You can't post videos of people without their permission," I scolded, trying to keep a handle on my emotions. I wasn't in the habit of mugging teenage girls, but this was cause for an exception. "And for the love of all that's holy, you shouldn't put your face and the name of your school on there either. Don't they teach you anything about internet safety?"

She shot her gaze from the app to me, her cheeks reddening. "Ohmigod. Ye deleted it! I can't believe you'd do that."

"When you started in my class, I told you no videos of me. That's for a reason."

Tears lined her eyes. "You're such a bitch. I'll just post it again."

"Do that and I'll have the police come talk to your mom. Then say goodbye to your phone as she'll know you can't be trusted with it."

She scowled at me, her bottom lip trembling, then stormed inside and slammed the door.

I exhaled a long breath, overheated from being forced to play the bad guy. But I'd done what I needed to do.

Slowly, I headed back to the street and the long, cold walk home. When I got to my car, I'd retrieve my phone. Maybe one of my brothers would be free to come pick me up to save me the forty minutes' stomp around the icy water of the loch to the castle.

Overhead, a helicopter tore up the air, the beat of the

rotor blades bouncing off the mountains all around. I couldn't see the craft itself through the low cloud cover, but I instinctively searched for it. Both Gabe and Raphael, my brothers, flew.

It could also be the mountain rescue service or even the bodyguard team who used helis on occasion.

Unwittingly, my thoughts slid to a particular member of the bodyguard team who seemed to have a permanent camping spot in my mind.

Jackson was my brother's best friend. They'd met at university, and though Jackson was older than Raph, they'd become close. So much that, prior to them both finishing their degrees, my brother had invited him to stay on several occasions, sometimes for weeks on end over the holidays. Raphael and I shared a tower apartment at Castle McRae. It was a good size for the two of us, but three was a crowd, particularly when the third was ridiculously attractive and sleeping on our sofa.

Jackson was the stuff of red-cheeked daydreams and midnight twisted bedsheets.

Dark hair, dark eyes, easy-going, but also kind of serious. He had some kind of family tragedy in his past, the details of which I knew nothing about and hadn't pried, not willing to indulge my fascinated mind more than it already was.

I couldn't ignore the little details that made up the man.

Strong hands and forearms that moved past my vision when he'd accepted a beer from Raph. Forearm porn had been a new one on me. The way he listened intently when anyone else was speaking. More than once, I'd got caught up in a vision of him bringing me in close with those arms, his steady gaze flicking down from my eyes to my mouth, lips taking mine...

Despite the weather, I shivered in hopeless lust.

The guy was catnip in a six-two bottle.

Not for a second would I admit my crush, though. Even after he'd given up our sofa for a bed in the hangar's bunkhouse. I'd be humiliated. Only two people knew: Daisy and her boyfriend, Ben. Ben was the head of the bodyguard service and Jackson's boss, but also a long-term family friend, and I knew he had my back.

I blew out a breath of frosted air. The problem was that tomorrow, I turned twenty, and I had almost zero experience with the opposite sex.

The only person to have ever touched me was a creep in high school. The same asshole who'd tried to kidnap Daisy.

Even Bridgette had a boyfriend.

My exasperation turned into a snort of a laugh. When I was Bridgette's age, my father had attempted to marry me off to a business associate. Only six years separated me from that incident, but I'd grown up fast because of it.

I approached the end of the dark street, the main road that skirted the village beyond.

Tonight was a wake-up call. Maybe the fact that I hadn't dated anyone was the reason for my intense crushes.

The next time I liked someone who liked me back, I'd take the initiative.

My unrequited little heart craved for that to be Jackson though he'd only ever been polite to me. If he showed any sign, if I caught any ripple of emotion in him, if he called my name...

I rounded the corner.

A tall figure sprinted down the middle of the road.

"Ariel!" he shouted.

It was Jackson, his expression troubled. Compelling.

And he was coming straight for me.

# 3

## Jackson

"Ariel," I yelled again, relief filling and fuelling me.

Putting on a burst of speed, I ran faster, taking in every inch of the woman, scanning for injuries. But in a ski jacket and snow boots—not a single shoe like the one discarded by her car, she moved okay.

I had the whole crew out on a search. Ben had assumed command and taken off in pursuit of the car I'd seen, dividing Raphael and me up between the local roads and the village. Others were on their way to join our hunt.

I'd been furious at my assignment but had to accept it. I'd been certain the kidnapper had her in a car, but I'd been wrong. Here she was. I'd found her within minutes, and pure shock spurred me on.

I closed the distance and grabbed the lass into my arms, bringing her close with my hand to the back of her head, my fingers digging into her soft hair.

I turned us, still looking for the threat.

My heart in tatters and my mind scrambled.

There was just the two of us on the road, the village quiet, and the only sound my harsh draws of breath.

"Jackson?" Ariel said, muffled against my chest.

I centred my gaze on her.

She peeked up at me. "Are you all right?"

I wasn't. Not on any planet. Not in any way. I forced my limbs to unlock and my grip to relax. But I didn't let her go.

A beat passed, and awareness of what I was doing settled. We'd never touched like this and somehow still weren't close enough. I should've released her, but I couldn't. She held my gaze, her hands against my jacket, her warmth permeating through to me.

*Raphael's younger sister,* I reminded myself.

Not mine. Not kidnapped either.

"No," I managed. Then I added, "Wait."

I spoke into the open line on my phone. "Target located. I'm in the village. All okay."

Replies came, but I barely heard them.

Ariel's eyebrows furrowed. "Who are you talking to? What was your target? Did I just walk into an exercise?"

A lock of her dark-brown hair fell over her forehead. With my thumb, I pushed it aside, my heart rate falling enough to let a degree of panic ease.

"No, I was looking for ye. I'll explain," I started.

Still wasn't letting her go.

Somehow, I was stuck on the look in her eyes. Like she was now holding me rather than the other way around. I'd panicked her. Infected her with the fear I'd built and carried.

Yet even if I'd overreacted, her car had been hit and ransacked, for fuck's sake. That part was fact. She wasn't safe.

Again, I tried and failed to speak, battling demons that had long held me in their grip.

History hadn't repeated. The scenarios I'd conjured while in pursuit didn't come to pass. I'd been down this path before with the opposite result, and the impact had left me stunned.

"I just had to find ye," I finally released.

Ariel took a rushed breath.

Then she pushed up on her toes and pressed her lips to mine.

Soft lips met my cold ones. In shock, I leaned in rather than pulled away.

I hadn't kissed anyone in a long time, and in a heartbeat, I only needed more. I angled my head and kissed her back, part in relief that this had ended well, and part because I was on autopilot and driven by emotion.

The brief, hot kiss floored me. Her mouth was fucking delightful.

Ariel gave a soft whimper... And lightning struck, my brain rebooted.

I let go of her and staggered back. "Shite, that was bad," I mumbled.

A car took the corner fast and zoomed down the road, the engine loud despite the blood pounding in my ears.

"Ariel," Raphael called through the open window. "Holy fucking hell. What happened? Where were ye?"

Ariel swung her attention to her brother, her hands going to her mouth. "What do you mean?"

"We've all been trying to find ye."

"Why?" She peeked at me, her expression uncertain.

Her cheeks flamed red.

A burst of energy snapped tight in me, soaring off that inappropriate attraction, and now, at long last, aimed in the right direction. I found my words and addressed Ariel in the way I should've done the moment I came across her.

My informality fled, the strange behaviour behind me. She was unharmed. That was all that mattered.

"On my way bringing Leo home, I passed your car left abandoned on the road."

She dipped her head. "I broke down on the way here. I still don't understand the drama."

That made sense to the state I'd seen it in on my first pass. Empty but not damaged.

"I came back to check on ye. In that short space of time, your Mini had been broken into and ransacked. I thought…"

I sensed the weight of Raphael's stare on me.

My overreaction felt all the bigger now. If I'd just driven around, I would have found her and saved a lot of hassle. Even so, I didn't regret it.

"Ransacked?" Ariel repeated.

Her concerned expression darkened, and she glanced around.

"Smashed up, too," her brother said. "Get in. I'll take ye back to collect your stuff, then we'll talk it out at home."

She nodded and climbed into his car.

He turned to me. "Jax, are ye with us?"

I shook my head, needing space. A minute to breathe. "I'll drive myself back. Keep her out of sight."

"See ye at the tower. Ben will join us there."

Then they were gone, and I watched their taillights sail into the distance.

Left behind, I clamped my hands at the back of my head and let the emotions roll. Alive. Fucking hell. But all I could recall was that kiss.

It would never happen again, but God, that had felt good.

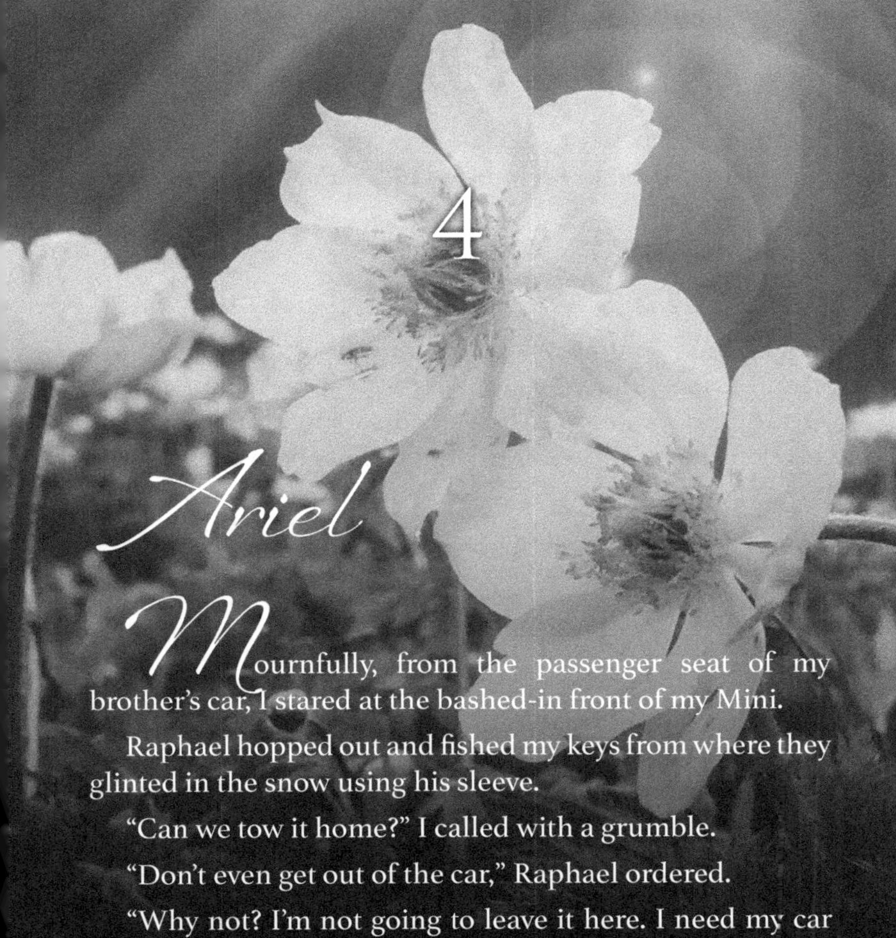

# 4

# Ariel

**M**ournfully, from the passenger seat of my brother's car, I stared at the bashed-in front of my Mini.

Raphael hopped out and fished my keys from where they glinted in the snow using his sleeve.

"Can we tow it home?" I called with a grumble.

"Don't even get out of the car," Raphael ordered.

"Why not? I'm not going to leave it here. I need my car for work."

"It's a crime scene."

"Is it?" I peered closer. "Could've been that someone hit black ice and slid into it, then opened my door to look for owner's info."

If it wasn't for Bridgette's video, I could've been convinced of that conclusion, but I'd already been on a paranoia jaunt this evening and doubt crept in.

My brother collected my shoe and the spilled papers from the ice. "Stay low in the seat, just in case you're being watched. I'll secure the car, and I won't touch the handle or the frame in case it has a print. It isn't roadworthy with that damage. We need to get it towed to a garage for repair."

I muttered thanks and sank lower, my mind jumping elsewhere.

*That was bad.*

Jackson's summary of my poorly thought-out kiss haunted me. Ridiculously, I'd thought he'd run to me because he wanted me. It seemed so stupid now, and his reaction showed me exactly what he felt about my act.

Didn't it?

He'd kissed me back. Then told me it was bad.

*Asshole.*

Raphael circled the car. "Nothing else to see. We'll head home."

"Wait," I said. "Can you grab my phone? It's in the cupholder. At least it should be."

God, what if the person who hit my car had taken it?

A strange and uncomfortable sense washed over me. Someone had been in there. It didn't feel like my safe space anymore.

Bending into the Mini, Raphael whipped the device out, brandishing it.

"Thank fuck for that," I whispered.

He snapped photos of the scene, then closed up the car with his elbow. "It'll fry the electrics if we just leave it open to the elements," he explained. "This way we can show the police how Jackson found it."

If my brother noticed my slight quiver at his friend's name, he didn't comment.

We returned home in silence.

Our tower apartment sat on the right-hand side of Castle

McRae, the imposing ancient structure owned by a family friend. Jackson had beat us back and was out of his vehicle, flagging us down outside the main entrance.

Raphael wound down his window.

Jackson spoke low, his gaze flitting over me. "Just in case we're being watched, drive around the back and go in the rear entrance."

I shivered at the subterfuge, shrinking lower in my seat while my brother did as asked. We parked up in the shelter of the heavy retaining wall, out of sight of anyone looking on, and entered via the kitchens. The castle was divided into several different apartments, but we managed to cross through the large, communal kitchens and the echoing great hall without seeing anyone. A narrow passageway at the back led to our tower door.

Up the spiral staircase we climbed, me at the front not thinking about the man who followed after my brother.

When we'd reached the top, a holler came from below.

"Ariel?" Daisy said.

"Come on up," I called back, a little wobbly in emotion at hearing her.

Ben had obviously rang her, and she had a spare key for the external door.

I'd barely taken off my coat before my best friend was bustling in and wrapping me in a tight squeeze.

"Holy shit. You okay? What happened? I need details." She drew a look up and down me.

I answered her first question by flinging my arms around her again.

I sank into the much-needed hug.

Daisy rubbed my back, her floral perfume filling my

nose. It was familiar and comforting, and also reminded me how I hadn't yet showered after a sweaty day of work on the slopes. Still, I needed the comfort for more than one reason. I had tea to spill, but it wasn't the same as I'd share with the rest of the room.

Ben joined us a minute later, pursued by Valentine, the newest recruit to the bodyguard service. Valentine had long black hair back in a man bun and a frame so tall he had to stoop to get under our doorway. He and Ben were brothers, though I didn't think they were all that close from what Daisy had told me.

I received a one-armed hug from Ben, who grumbled something about thanking fuck I was okay, then I curled up on the sofa that curved around the tower's interior wall, waiting for everyone else to take a seat. There were too many bodies for the snug space. Or maybe it was just that one whose presence took up too much room in my head.

I summoned a smile. "Thanks, everyone, for going out to search for me tonight. Nice to know you all care, even if it was a false alarm."

Jackson snorted, setting down a dining chair he'd taken from our kitchen. "That was no false alarm."

I stared at his nose, not willing to either make eye contact or focus on his mouth. "Aside from my car being hit, nothing happened."

"Someone crashed into your car and then searched it," he retorted.

"Or it was an accident and they were hunting for driver ID."

His jaw tightened. "Don't minimise this."

I bristled, suddenly annoyed by him, and overheated in the thermal wear I hadn't stripped off yet. He was right, but irrationally, I didn't want him to be.

"Was I kidnapped?" I snipped back. "Did you happen across me wrestling some creep?"

His expression dropped, revealing a flash of something unexpected.

A vulnerability my words had exposed.

Just as quickly, it was gone, and Jackson was all business again. "No, but that doesn't mean any of us should be flippant."

Ben cleared his throat. "Hold up. There's a bigger picture. For the benefit of a proper debrief, Ariel, walk us through what happened. Jackson, you'll get your say."

My head buzzed with too many thoughts. "I left work and drove to the village to see one of my students, but my Mini broke down on the main road, so I finished the journey on foot. Next thing I knew was Jackson finding me in the street and telling me what had happened to my car. It had been fine when I'd left it."

I avoided any talk of my insane kissing act but needed to connect the dots on Bridgette's video. It had been live for three days.

Long enough for someone to come after me.

Jackson was going to love this.

He watched me, his jaw still tensed and his expression pissed off. "Question," he said before I could continue. "Did ye lock your car?"

I pressed my lips together, a little chagrined. I often didn't bother because of how remote we were here. "Probably not."

"Did ye even take the keys out of the ignition? They were in the snow."

"I can't remember. But wait up before you start judging

me. There's something else to tell first. The reason I was in the village was to get my student to take down a video she made of me. It went viral online and included my name and face."

There was an uproar of questions. Earlier, I'd saved a copy of the video, so I played it for everyone to see. They passed it around, the same annoying R&B song playing on repeat. Jackson viewed it last. While he grimaced, presumably at the sight of me in my underwear, my brother tapped my knee.

"I don't like this," he said.

A chill ran down my spine.

Raphael had uttered the same words to me in the past, right before our father tried to sell me off. My brother had been secretly communicating with Gabe, who'd already broken away from the family business. On Raphael's warning, Gabe had rescued us both.

"The video panicked me," I admitted. "But it doesn't necessarily mean that someone's after me."

"Seriously?" Jackson's voice cut through the hubbub of the others talking and drawing their own conclusions.

I brought my gaze to his.

He raised a hand to count on his fingers. "Worst-case scenario is someone who wants to do ye harm has an alert out on your name and saw the video. They find out the area where ye work and the car ye drive. They proved that by showing up and getting in a lucky hit. It's no big stretch from there to finding out where ye sleep at night."

There was nothing of heat or any kind of recognition of what we'd done in how he looked at me. Why the hell had I kissed him?

It made me want to be argumentative.

I cocked my head. "So many guns being jumped. Following that logic, he doesn't actually know where I work. There are three ski and snowboarding centres around here, and Bridgette's video doesn't show which. Next, my car isn't registered to the castle, so he can't find out where I live."

"Daisy was almost kidnapped. A man came after her who once was interested in ye. Landon Larson. Employee of an organised crime business." Jackson's gaze bored into me.

Ben took Daisy's hand, the reminder presumably affecting him.

I shrugged. "Right, so let's say Larson pieced together the clues and came here. If he had any skills, he wouldn't have blown his only lead."

Jackson paused like he was considering my point. "When I drove past, I couldn't tell if there was anyone in your car. It was too dark."

For a moment, everyone went quiet.

Well, shit.

The picture he painted was pretty scary. Some guy out hunting for me spotted my car and crashed into it, with only bad intent.

"Then the trail goes cold for him. I'll be careful at work," I said slowly. "Make sure I'm not followed home."

His forehead crinkled. "Why put yourself in danger at all?"

"You mean cancel my lessons?"

"Exactly. Stay out of sight until we've worked this out."

I knew something he didn't. Well, I suspected something. My employer at the snowboarding centre was Effie, my older brother's wife. A few months ago, Gabe had said something in passing about kids that made me think he and Effie were trying to get pregnant. Then last week, she'd cleared her schedule of the more challenging classes and gave up the chance of a rare winter paragliding trip, despite the conditions being perfect.

I was pretty certain that soon, they'd make their announcement.

I'd be an auntie.

There was no way I'd leave her high and dry and forced into a bigger workload. I'd also never steal their thunder or guess in front of an audience. Their secret was safe with me.

"I can't just quit based on this. Your scenario was the worst case. There could be a hundred other explanations."

"Luckily, information gathering is our bag," Ben interrupted. "Jackson, what did ye see of the other car?"

His employee flattened his lips. "Next to nothing. I was focused on getting Leo home. Couldn't even be sure of the colour."

Ben drummed his fingers on his knee. "But you'll have dashcam footage."

Jackson took in a sharp breath then leapt to his feet. He exited the room, my brother jogging after him. Daisy said something to Ben about some kind of safety routine for me, but I inched forward to peer out of the living room door. In the octagonal hallway, the two men were speaking. Jackson's hostile demeanour had dropped, and pure emotion played out in his expression. Raph said something to him that made him shake his head, a hand to his eyes.

Then my brother hugged him.

Jackson accepted it, then turned away without a word and left.

What was that about? Why did he need comforting?

There was more to my incident tonight than met the eye. And I suspected that the missing factor wasn't anything to do with me.

# 5

## Jackson

Outside the tower, I crunched the gravel under my boots, stomping back to my car, the black Toyota Hilux pickup my refuge.

Ben caught up with me. "Wait up."

Embarrassment washed over me. Raphael had already informed me that my trauma was showing. I'd snapped at Ariel, jumped to conclusions, and he'd instantly known I wasn't okay.

And the reason why.

Now my boss was presumably going to order me to fix my head as well.

I wheeled around. "I know how this looks. At my interview, ye made the point about me overreacting when it came to the safety of women. I swear I've got this."

Ben furrowed his brow, his dark-blond hair messy where he'd been running his hands through it. He had a few years on me but was a thousand times steadier.

I wanted his respect and to keep this job.

"Is that why ye thought I came after ye? It isn't. I agree that we should be treating this as a worst-case scenario, even if Ariel doesn't want to hear it."

I closed my mouth, relieved that it wasn't just me.

Ben offered a grim smile. "In that respect, I consider your instincts to be your superpower. I employed ye because of them. I trust that history won't cloud your judgement and only came out to say I want timely updates. Daisy's mixed up in this, too."

My embarrassment lifted. "We should do more. Get a list of exes from Ariel. Anyone with a grudge. She needs a protection protocol. We should organise a patrol."

He held up a hand. "Leave that with me. You seemed to get her back up with your questioning." He tilted his head. "Did the two of ye have a fight?"

If only. I would never reveal the real reason. "No."

"Huh." Ben accepted my answer and moved on. "I'll go back upstairs and get that list, though my money is on our previous suspect. Raphael's talking to the police, and we'll have a couple of people drive around tonight to keep an eye on things. Go get to work."

He clapped me on the shoulder then returned to the tower. Valentine passed him at the door and jerked his chin at me.

"Heading back to the hangar?"

Valentine and I had recently both started living in the bunkhouse—a space made out of huge, metal shipping containers that had been constructed under the cover of the aircraft hangar and made into a temporary home. It provided comfortable, if a little chilly in February, accommodation for us, the pilots who were training at the helicopter school, and the occasional overnight mountain rescue team member. In the days we'd been staying there, though, it had been just us.

I confirmed my destination, and the two of us drove convoy out along the river, passing the second castle on the estate, and through the forest to the open moor where the wide aircraft hangar sat, bright lights marking its presence in the landscape.

The drone of a helicopter returning to base and the clunk of something mechanical within the structure had become familiar now, just as the scent of engine oil was my homecoming.

Before I left my car, I downloaded the dashcam footage from earlier, then sent a quick message to Leo's father-in-law, Gordain, to ask him to do the same from Leo's car which had been ahead of mine. I didn't want to disturb the rock star himself. He and Viola had better things to do, like looking after a newborn.

Armed with one set of footage on my phone and the other on its way, I travelled through to the bodyguard team office, waving greetings to the folk still working around the huge open-fronted building. Valentine kept pace with me.

The big man drew up a chair next to mine and pulled at the band that kept his hair tied back. I uploaded the video to our data storage then cued it up on a monitor, talking him through the process. He'd barely been here a week and had a military background, rather than any protection experience. I'd worked with Ben on Daisy's case but barely had more than that myself. Clearly Ben, and the service owner, Gordain, had seen something in us they liked.

Onscreen, my headlights picked up the car ahead and the dark road, the early fall of night hampering visibility. I spooled through, recognising when we turned onto the loch road by the occasional glint coming off the water.

Ariel's abandoned car appeared, and my heart thumped. I'd slowed, so Valentine and I were able to take a good look as the recording proceeded. The dashcam sat right at the top of the windshield, and even from that angle it wasn't possible to identify anyone inside her car.

I sped back and forth in the video, confident I hadn't missed anything.

"The guy was coming from the other direction, right?" Valentine asked.

I grunted agreement. The video played on.

We both leaned in. Headlights appeared on the other side of the screen, emerging from the gloom and growing bigger and brighter until the vehicle passed.

"Speed's about the same as yours," Valentine surmised. "From my grand experience of living here for a week, people bomb along that road, even on ice. It's a long, straight run with few turnings, little traffic, and no speed cameras. No reason to cruise along it."

He was right. "Unless you're hunting for something. Or in our case, carefully driving a new baby home."

Skipping back, I played the video at a slower speed, pausing at intervals.

"Those full-beam headlights are a bitch." Valentine squinted at the screen which was blown out with white light. "Most newer cars automatically dip their headlights when they pick up another vehicle. It suggests this one is older. Can ye make out the model?"

I nodded. "It's a VW Golf. Probably the most popular car brand here. Either dark blue or grey."

"Can't see shite of the driver or the number plate."

I couldn't either. The headlights obscured both.

A message arrived on my phone, Gordain sending the

second lot of footage along with a text.

*Gordain: Heard about Ariel. You on the case?*

I tapped out a response.

*Jackson: On it now.*

*Gordain: Let me know if you need help. I'll take a patrol overnight.*

I set up the video he'd sent.

Valentine's foot jumped, like he was as anxious as me to discover something. "Ben told me Gordain used to run this team, but he's semi-retired."

I snorted a laugh. "Gordain set up the team after ultra-famous rock star, Leo, married his daughter, Viola. He's in his early sixties but is probably fitter than any of us, and he rarely misses an event, despite Ben being in charge. Especially if Viola or his grandson, Finn, are attending. Some people never retire. Pretty sure he's one of them."

The footage from Leo's car played, the angle different from mine, and with the background sound of a tiny baby crying and Viola's gentle soothing. The offending car neared, and this time, I picked out the shadowy outline of the driver.

My pulse thrummed.

That was him. Larson, it had to be. Fucking arsehole.

"Partial plate," Valentine crowed, sounding just as excited as me.

I hitched my breath and wound back, pausing each frame until I saw what he had.

He was right.

*SV04 9.*

Try as we could, the last two letters were too obscured to make out, but still, we had something.

Valentine gave me a hard, celebratory shake, fisting my shirt at the shoulder. "What do we do with it now? Tell me we have a contact who can run a plate."

I shoved him off me with a grin. "We can do it ourselves, but assuming this car isn't registered to someone who lives in the US, my guess is it's stolen. We need a police insider to help with that. Luckily, we have one of those, too."

"Ye seem dead set on the suspect's identity."

I shrugged. "Path of least resistance. We don't need to prove a court case, only protect our client. Ben is going to talk to Ariel about anyone else who might have reason to break into her car, but this guy, Larson, already has form. First, he tried to grab Daisy from the street into his truck. He was masked up, but we worked out who he was because he'd been hanging around her roommate previously and she was able to ID him, then I discovered he was on the payroll of her family. They wanted her back, so it wasn't a stretch to work out that they'd sent him. After some digging, I was able to track his passport which showed he'd followed her here, but he gave up the hunt after her family's business imploded. I guess they recalled him because we tracked him right back out of the UK. But, here's the kicker. Larson, Daisy, and Ariel were all in the same school together in California. He was a teenage pervert who assaulted Ariel. Felt her up."

A rush of pure outrage poured through me. Though I didn't know the details, it enraged me. This was exactly why the 'boys will be boys' defence needed to be locked in the past with the 'What were you wearing?' question. Kids who weren't checked when they were young only went on to be worse.

I knew that to my bones.

"Fucking little punk," Valentine muttered. "So he was

paid to find Daisy but is now after Ariel?"

"That's my gut instinct." Ben had called it my superpower. I wasn't so sure. "If that car was stolen, I'll feel a lot better about my working theory."

Repeating the lesson Ben had given me not all that long ago, I walked Valentine through how to access the number plate database. The system spat out a list of potential hits which we narrowed down by the model and colour of the car until there was a single vehicle left. It was registered to a woman who lived in Inverness.

Valentine tapped his pen on the pad where he'd made notes. "What's the odds that Terri McArthur reported her reliable old Volkswagen as missing earlier today?"

"Let's find out. First I need to get approval from Ben because this will cost."

We waited for a moment until Ben's okay came through, then I dialled a number.

The police systems specialist took the details and promised a call back soon. We could've just waited for an officer to be assigned once Ariel had reported the incident, but that would be slower.

Then I sat back and breathed out for what felt like the first time since I'd recognised Ariel's car.

It was cathartic working through the process. At least now I'd done something. She was safe. I just had to force my muscles to unlock.

I sensed Valentine's gaze on me. "What?"

He wrinkled his nose. "Are ye and Ariel...something?"

"No," I said, too fast and too hard. "Why do ye ask?"

"Just picked up on tension."

I liked Valentine. He had the same openness as Raphael

and the hard-work ethic I admired in Ben. Maybe in time I could trust him enough to confide about personal shite, but we weren't there yet.

Instead, I gave up a different truth. "No, it was my fault for rubbing her the wrong way with my questions. Ben's going to take over on that front. The two of us can research other areas."

He gave up the scent easily. "Such as?"

"Put yourself in the mindset of a man who pursued her here from California. We don't know his motive, but we know he has a lead which gave him a location. Where do ye go from there?"

Valentine lifted his phone. "I'd look more at that lead. That teenager had other videos on her account."

I raised my fist for a bump. "Perfect answer."

"Can we research over food? I'm starving. That pub over in the village does a mean ribeye."

Come to think of it, I was hungry, too. I agreed, and we left the hangar, both of us piling into my car to head out.

It didn't hurt that we'd be travelling the road where Ariel's car had been ransacked and entering the village where she'd walked. Someone would already be on patrol, but it would make me feel better to be out and active before coming back and getting stuck into research all evening.

And I fully intended to. I'd investigated Landon Larson once before, but I'd go over every single step.

On the main road, a tow truck from a business I recognised was hooking up the Mini.

I paused alongside and rolled down my window. "Police check this over yet?"

The tow truck driver acknowledged me. "They couldn't get here tonight so gave it the okay for pick-up. They'll dust it at my garage. Better for it to be there than out here."

I thanked him and moved on.

If Ariel's would-be attacker was watching, he'd see the car being taken away. I had the feeling he'd fled the scene once he'd realised she wasn't in the car, though. He'd missed his chance, and getting caught would throw off his plans.

Still, he could be nearby.

I sent a quick message to my friend.

*Jackson: Did Ariel get out of your car when you took her to see the Mini? Could he have seen her?*

*Raphael: Negative. She stayed inside. Can't rule it out, though.*

I didn't like that, but even if he followed her brother's car to the tower, finding her in that huge, ancient, well-protected building was high risk to him. If we could trace the licence plate leaving the area, I'd be a lot happier.

In the village, we entered the cosily lit pub, shucking off our jackets the moment we got inside the warm space. A log fire burned, a group of old boys and their dogs lounging in front of it. Valentine found us a table, pointing out the chalked-up menu on a blackboard across the room while drawing more than one lass's attention his way. The big man was apparently eye-catching.

"I highly recommend the steak. I'm going to order a couple plus a few of their sides."

I lifted my eyebrows. "A couple?"

He threaded his way through the tables to the bar, patting his belly with a grin. "Growing boy. I'll order the same for ye."

"You're good on a date," I called after him.

It earned me a bigger grin, and I relaxed into the wooden seat.

A message pinged in from Raphael. A photo.

It was a painted dragon. A little model.

*Raphael: This dude's cute. How about him?*

Once, I'd confided in him that, as a geeky teenager, I'd had a hobby painting characters from movies.

I'd amassed a whole collection, but that was in the past, and it had long been destroyed.

Even in the middle of his family's drama, he was trying to do something nice for me.

*Jackson: I'm ten years on the wrong side of finding dragons cute.*

*Raphael: No one's too old for a hobby.*

I pursed my lips and shot him back a change of subject.

*Jackson: What sound does a 747 make when it bounces?*

*Raphael: Eye roll. I don't know.*

*Jackson: Boeing. Boeing. Boeing.*

A reply landed of a fist with the middle finger raised. Each time he offered me dragons, I served him bad pilot jokes. Felt like a fair exchange.

Valentine returned with our drinks.

In an hour, we'd consumed a healthy amount of charred meat, steak-cut chips, and various vegetable and deep-fried dishes. Alongside that, we scoured Ariel's student's videos, seeing what else Larson could have gleaned from them.

A locker room, snowboards, snowy slopes, the girl's Scottish accent, her school badge, identifying the senior school ten miles south of the estate.

Valentine groaned, resting his hands on his belly. "He's doing the rounds of the snowboarding centres and nearby housing estates at the end of the working day, hunting for Ariel's car. That's my bet. Fuck, I ate too much."

"Agreed. Now we need to work out how to better trace the man himself."

My phone rang with the police contact's number. I answered.

"The car was reported stolen at ten past two this afternoon by its owner," she advised. "So far, not recovered, though the number plate was recorded by one of our cameras about an hour ago."

"Where was that camera?" I asked, my heart skipping a beat.

She gave a location in a town south of us. He'd driven away. Thank fuck for that.

The woman continued. "In most cases like this, it's a joyrider. We'll find it trashed and abandoned in a day or two, no doubt. Joy rides are usually short-lived."

"Can ye let me know when it's found and if ye pull a print?"

"I'll see what I can do."

I thanked her and hung up, relaying the information to Valentine while simultaneously tapping out a message to Raphael.

*Jackson: The car that hit Ariel's was stolen from Inverness. It's not been picked up yet but was tracked heading south. She's safe in the tower. Keep her inside?*

She'd hate me for it, but better safe than sorry.

Something was bothering me. I addressed Valentine. "It's a tight timeframe."

He steepled his fingers. "Ye were there shortly after four, which gives under two hours from the car being taken in Inverness and him getting here. What's that, an hour's drive?"

Slowly, I inclined my head. "Suggesting he wasn't wasting any time in getting around the sites. We're about forty minutes from the next snowboarding centre."

"Very precise. Like someone on a time limit or a contract. Your description of the man blurred the lines between professional and personal in terms of what he might want from Ariel. Maybe this is an indication that it's more the former?"

He had a point.

I knew from Raphael that he and his siblings had all lived in the US, despite being Scottish, but had run from their father. They were in hiding. The picture was getting murkier.

We left the pub, and I dialled Ben on the way back to the car, giving him the update.

"Raphael will take her to and from work," he confirmed. "We're all off-site tomorrow, but we can pick this up once we're back. Make sure your head is in the game, aye?"

I gritted my teeth, not liking the diversion, even though that was my actual job. We were carrying out a risk assessment of a TV studio in Edinburgh ahead of Leo interviewing there. A much-needed training session for Valentine and me.

"It would be better if she didn't leave the tower at all," I griped.

"She made her choice. If needs be, we'll take her on as a client. But until that moment, we can only give her advice. See ye in the morning," my boss concluded.

I breathed out clouds of frosted air, frustrated. Ariel wasn't just another client. She wasn't a client at all yet.

Right now, all I wanted was to be standing in front of her, providing the protection I believed she needed.

Either that or tasting her perfect lips again.

Both would be ideal.

Fuck.

# 6

## Ariel

The falling of fat snowflakes softened the world around me, muting the squeals of excited kids and the shouts of older thrill-seekers on the slopes. I'd just escorted a class of kids back to their bus. The local schools employed our company to provide skiing lessons which the kids could take instead of regular PE.

Usually, snow season was a joy.

The youngsters would start shakily and knock-kneed, but after a few weeks be able to hold their form and take on the beginner slopes. We only had a few short months of good snow in the mountains before the melt came and we shifted our offer to other outdoor sports. Mountain boarding, orienteering, trail biking, paragliding, and even guided walks in spring through to autumn.

I loved being out in the fresh air, but all day I'd sensed someone watching me. Likely my imagination, and I'd even gone inside to change my skiwear, swapping out the neon blue for a brilliant pink.

I still couldn't shake the feeling.

It stalled me in my plan to take on the slopes myself. Usually, I'd be getting in a few decent runs before my next booking, but what if someone sideswiped me? Took me out and somehow spirited me away? I'd never once been afraid out here before, and the sense was new and deeply awful.

"Hey, birthday girl." Arms wrapped around me from behind.

I twisted into my sister-in-law's hug. I hadn't seen her all morning, though she and Gabe, my brother, had talked to me on the phone last night, both worried about what had happened.

Not how I'd anticipated turning twenty.

Effie released me. "All okay?"

I shrugged. "Normal as. No one's tried to smash up my snowboard, at least."

She dipped her head at the snowboarding centre. "Lennox has been keeping an eye on the slopes. He'll pounce on anyone suspicious."

I followed her gaze to the wraparound windows of the centre's top station café. Earlier, the huge, gruff owner had waved to me from a booth by the glass, his laptop open on the table in front of him. I figured he'd chosen to work there for the day, but now I knew different.

I turned back to Effie. "Did you ask him to watch me?"

She shrugged. "He messaged this morning to say he'd be there."

I was going to fake complain about everyone being overprotective, but Effie's hand drifted to her belly. Someone called her name, and she twisted to respond.

I had the sudden, stark instinct of getting her away from me.

If I was a hazard, I couldn't put her in danger. My sister-in-law was tough. She had a sleeve of awesome china-blue tattoos and feared nothing. She'd protected me in the past, and I'd done the same for her. But everything changed if there was a baby involved.

A gaggle of youngsters left the centre, a few peeling away from the group to approach me.

The ringleader was Bridgette, my teenage nemesis. Thankfully not mine to handle today.

"Oh look, it's Little Miss Famous," she uttered with a curled lip.

I planted my hands on my hips. "Glad I saw you. If anyone messages you to ask who I am or where that video was taken, don't reply. And take down anything with your school badge on for both our sakes."

"Are ye really trying to tell me what to do? I came over to say that ye owe me."

"Owe you what?"

She pouted. "That account is monetised under Ma's name. Deleting my video literally cost us money."

"Yeah," jibed one of her friends. "Pay up, bitch."

Effie whipped around. "Hell no. Who are ye girls with?"

Instantly, Bridgette's pack scuttled back to the group, the injured party herself giving me one last glare before turning up her nose and joining them. Effie started in pursuit, but I paused her.

"Don't mind her. She's just butthurt that I told her off. Listen, I'm going to relocate my birthday celebrations to my apartment. We'll have cocktails, or mocktails, and celebrate there."

She tilted her head, giving me an appraising look, probably at the mocktails comment, but then smiled. "I'll pass around the message. See ye tonight."

She left, and I made a mental note to talk to Bridgette's mother. But before then, I had work to finish up and a party to relocate.

Several hours later, I was sticking lights up around the tower's living room, Daisy holding the chair I was standing on. Raphael had left shortly after she'd got here and once the little pastries he'd made us came out of the oven. He'd made them as an apology for skipping out on my birthday. For the next week, he was booked in for night flights as part of his training.

He'd wanted to cancel, but the day had passed without event, and Daisy had offered to stay the night so I wouldn't be alone. As it was, the party had become a women-only deal. Originally, we were going to take over a local pub, but the tower meant cutting back numbers, so for now, I'd see in my twenties with my local girlies.

I was lucky to have a tight group of good friends, most of them married and with kids, and a mixture of Scottish, English, and American. An excellent group to sound off against any life problems I had.

Like random car attackers, who I definitely didn't want to talk about.

Like really wanting to kiss someone and laying it on the wrong guy.

"Before anyone shows, I have something to tell you." With a hand on Daisy's shoulder, I climbed down from the chair and switched the strip lights on. They pulsed in time to the music thumping in the background, filling the round tower room with an instant party atmosphere.

"Do I need a cocktail in hand?"

"Probably. I definitely do."

I followed her into the kitchen and sucked up my courage.

"Last night, I kissed Jackson."

The vodka Daisy had just started pouring slopped over the side of the cocktail shaker. She set down the bottle and stared at me. "Shut the front door."

I palmed my cheek, heating up. "I'm so embarrassed. I'd been thinking about him, stupid crush and all, and he came running down the street calling my name."

My best friend widened her eyes. "You went into horny beast mode and leapt at him? Badass."

"Worse. Horribly mistaken."

She winced. "He dodged?"

"No, not exactly." I cringed. "He kissed me back. But then he pulled away and said something like, 'Oh no, that was bad.' I'm mortified."

Sympathy spread over her face. "It was brave of you, particularly for a first kiss. Don't let this put you off."

I hadn't liked dwelling on the fact that Jackson's mouth on mine really had been the first time. For all my crushes, I'd never once pursued anyone before.

"If it's something to do with Larson," she went on.

I didn't want to go there. We'd talked it through to death. In middle school, Landon Larson had followed me around like a rabid dog, undeterred by teenage-me rejecting him, then trapped me in a corridor and put his hand up my shirt. He was the only male to have ever touched my body in that way.

If it was him who'd smashed my car, I was going to kill the fucking creep.

My phone alerted me to a message—people downstairs, waiting to come up.

I gestured to the array of glasses and cocktail umbrellas on the kitchen counter. Colourful mixers. A half-chopped lemon where we'd run out of prep time.

"I'm going to let everyone in. You rack 'em up. Then we're going to shit-talk men but naming no names."

Daisy mimed zipping her lips and throwing away the key.

I trusted her with all my secrets.

I needed to trust myself to find a way through this mess.

Two hours and several drinks later, I was on my back on the sofa, sobbing with laughter, tears streaming down my face.

My friends had brought the fun to me, considering I couldn't go out to find it myself. I'd told them I'd had a bad first kiss, and they'd been swapping outrageous first-date stories. Anything was better than dwelling on whoever had hit my car.

I'd had a message from the police saying they'd dusted for prints and found nothing other than mine, which they'd ruled out because they were all over the Mini. They recorded the incident as a hit-and-run, not a robbery as nothing was missing that I could remember, and informed me that I could now do what I liked with my car.

If anything, I didn't want the Mini back yet. It had been my lifeline. Without it, I had a killer hike up the mountain to work. It was also a fluttering flag, indicating my whereabouts to whoever had hit it. I didn't want the safety of my home to be compromised.

"Okay, okay, my turn," giggled Effie from her sprawl on the rug. Against her black jeans and a simple black halterneck, her blue tattoos stood out down her arm. She was so pretty.

"I'm switching to chat-up lines because this one kills me. Let me lay out the scene," she began, in her slightly cocky Scottish brogue. "I was rock climbing and halfway up a cliff face. It was a new location for me, and I'd gone solo to scout it out as a potential jump site. But the weather changed, and hail started battering the rocks, zinging off my helmet and trying its best to bruise me. So naturally, and because I don't have a death wish, I paused, debating whether to finish the climb and abseil, or just descend. Another climber appeared to my left and stopped. I gave him a little wave, assuming he was thinking the same. Weighing up the is-it-worth-it odds. I was nineteen and used to the adrenaline junkie alpha bros, but this guy took the biscuit. He dead-ass looked me in the eye and, instead of making any reference to the sport or the conditions, said, 'Were ye born on a farm? Because ye know how to raise a good cock.' Then the dude just kept on climbing."

A peal of laughter came from Daisy, echoed by the other women.

I clutched my stomach in silent mirth. "He didn't even

wait for a rejection?"

"Nope! And in there is a lesson. Some guys, no matter the circumstances, will only see women as a potential conquest. Ye could be the expert in the room, or tasked with saving their life, or in my case hanging from a rope hundreds of metres above the ground, and they can't help but make it known that their shrivelled sausage is available." She put on a deep voice. "Just fall this way, madam, legs open, I'll do the rest."

I dropped my head back. "I've heard some pretty average chat-up lines, but that one wins."

"Wait up," said Rory. She'd settled here from the US and had a son with her husband, Maddock. "I have one that could beat it. I was in a store, I mean a supermarket, when a guy sidled up to me and asked if I worked in Subway."

Someone groaned like they already knew the cheesy line.

Rory continued. "I didn't immediately answer because I assumed he'd just mistaken me for someone else. That illusion was ruined two seconds later when he grabbed his unimpressive crotch and said, 'cos I've got a foot long, just for you.' Then he winked and walked away." She gave a snort of disbelief, waiting out our laughter. "Seriously, who does that? I don't generally feel sorry for average men, but can you imagine constantly feeling the need to offer your man meat to strangers?"

"Man meat? Ew. That's worse than shrivelled sausage. Here's one," Daisy said. "I Googled it because no one ever tried a line on me, but it's kinda cute, 'I've lost my teddy bear, can I sleep with you?'"

I shook my head. "Pretty sure I'd want to stab any man who came up to me and said that. How any of you found a good guy amongst all those waiting dicks is beyond me."

"Is that what ye want? A boyfriend?" Effie asked.

I hugged a cushion, remembering the feel of Jackson's lips. He hadn't been like the men with their cheesy lines. Zero want shown beyond the fever of the split second he'd kissed me back. "Maybe."

"That's new."

"Will this be your first boyfriend?" Cait asked carefully, her Scottish accent gentler than Effie's. She was a beautiful fair-haired mother of three who'd married the head of the mountain rescue service. Recently, she'd chopped her hair into a chin-length bob, and it suited her so much.

My cheeks warmed. "Yep. I've never done anything. Which I know sounds weird on my twentieth birthday."

"No, it doesn't. Not at all," she said firmly. "I was never interested in sex or relationships until I met Lochie at age twenty-three. There's nothing wrong with waiting until you're ready, just as there's no shame in playing the field."

My best friend poked me with her toe. "She's right, and you're not missing out on much based on my teenage experiences. Men over boys every day of the week."

"Same. A grown-up hunt will be much more fun," Casey chimed in. Another American, she was married to two Scotsmen, one being Effie's brother, and the other the son of the man who owned the castle we were in, so she was family. "I found two so they're out there, hidden among all the rabid one-eyed trouser snakes."

"Rabid what?" I lost it for a moment. My happiness turned into a sigh. Already, I was disillusioned with the idea of dating before I'd even started. Fear of disappointment in what I'd find mixed with a belief I'd held since childhood that most men were a waste of good oxygen.

My father had created that view, and probably Larson

and other boys at school who thought sexual assault a normal Friday afternoon. I didn't believe it now, but I still had defences a mile wide.

"What if I'm overthinking this?" I mused. "I just want to not be a virgin anymore. To feel and not restrict myself, you know?"

Everyone made sounds of agreement.

Daisy tilted her head. "What if you found a safe person to try out sex with?"

I pursed my lips, considering it. "Intriguing."

"I did that exact thing," confessed Cait, her pale cheeks bright red, though that could have been the alcohol. "Just between us, before we were a couple, I offered Lochie a no-strings-attached deal."

Effie sniggered. "Bet he leapt on that."

"Actually, no. He turned me down." She paused for effect. "The first time I asked."

We all laughed again.

Casey groaned. "I volunteer for his mountain rescue crew. I'm never going to be able to look at him the same way."

I warmed to the idea Cait had suggested. "So I just come up with the things I want to try and ask someone if he'll do them with me? What goes on that list?"

A flurry of answers flew at me.

"One at a time," I yelled over the excited voices.

"Me first," Casey said. "I vote for as many positions and experiences that we can think of and that interest you. It's hard to know what your turn-ons or kinks are until you've done them. Or at least considered them and got a little hot."

I picked up a pad and paper from under a half-eaten

bowl of Doritos on the coffee table. We'd long ago polished off Raphael's delicate pastries. My brother was a good cook.

"Start me off."

"Off the top of my head, get losing your virginity out of the way with straight-up missionary position. People call it vanilla, but it can be hot as fuck with kissing and deep pressure. All that full-body contact is delicious, particularly if it's the middle of the night and you're half asleep. Next, try blowing him, him going down on you, and finally sixty-nine each other. Tell him what feels good and ask him to do the same so you start to develop a technique."

Heat flooded my cheeks, and I scribbled furiously. "You talk during sex?"

"Yep!" Casey said brightly. "Take the image you've seen in porn out of your head and throw it away as far as you can. This is deeply personal one-on-one time with someone you trust. Communication is hot."

"So hot," Rory agreed, lifting her dark hair to fan her neck. "Get used to doing it, because then you'll be able to ask him to try stuff whilst you're in the middle of it. Give me that pad. I'm going to write you a list of positions."

Everyone started talking at once again, giving Rory things to note down.

My phone buzzed with an incoming call, Viola's name on my screen, alongside a couple of messages from my brother which I dismissed. I put her on loudspeaker.

"Hey, everyone. Sorry I'm late to the party," she said.

I grinned. "You just had a baby. We weren't expecting you."

She yawned. "While pushing a whole human out of my body is a great excuse, I'm feeling pretty good. The few days in hospital were oddly relaxing, I—" She took a rushed inhale. "God. I'm so slow. How are ye, Ariel? I heard about your car."

"Fine. Pissed off. Wish I knew who did it."

"Anything more from the police? Leo told me something, but I've napped since then and my brain is goo."

"There were no prints. They said they'd call if there was any more information, but I get the feeling they're not going to prioritise it."

After a couple more gentle questions, Viola let me change the subject. "Catch me up on what we're talking about."

"Ariel wants a fuck buddy," Daisy helpfully supplied. "We're giving her a list of sex positions."

"Ooh, dangerous for a woman who just spent hours screaming through the consequences of just such a list. Item one, good contraceptive," Viola quipped.

"Got that covered." I'd been taking the pill since I was sixteen.

"Smart woman," the new mother commended.

The ladies returned to their task of scrawling out my sex list.

Snuggled against the cushions where Jackson had slept, I conjured him in my mind, trying out these scenes with me. As my most recent crush, he was easy to imagine in the role.

He'd never in a million years agree if I asked.

I pictured his expression. Dark, glowering, grumpy, no doubt. That was probably the reason I liked him—his total lack of interest in me. I almost wanted to ask him just to see the look on his face.

"How do we find you a guy?" Daisy asked eventually.

I took the pad and scanned the list which helpfully

ended in 'repeat all this using toys'. Some of the items, like reverse cowgirl, I wasn't sure how to do. Someone had listed a couple of websites to further my education.

"Any obvious candidates?" Effie said.

A sound came from elsewhere in the apartment.

I cocked my ear.

Maybe I was just jumpy. God knew I had the right.

"How about the new bodyguard," Casey said. "Jackson? I've seen him around but I don't know anything about him. Daisy, is he good enough for our girl?"

"He's the serious type rather than a playboy," Daisy chirped back. "I don't think he'd mess her around. Ben would fire him if he did."

"Who else is single on the estate? What about the other new guy, Valentine?" Effie prodded.

"Surnames?" said Viola down the line.

"Valentine Graham and Jackson Reid," Daisy supplied.

"Researching them now." Her fingers tapped on her phone.

"Ben's brother's a gentle giant from what I know of him," Daisy continued. "They aren't super close, so I'm making it my job to bring them together. I can now add a second task in checking out his credentials as a friend with benefits for Ariel. Jackson's more of a mystery."

"Found an engagement announcement," Viola crowed.

I slapped my hand to my mouth. Not for a second had I considered that Jackson had someone. He was engaged? What had I done?

Viola continued. "It says here that Valentine's going to marry a woman named Kelly."

Cait made an *ooh* face. Casey raised her eyebrows. I

pressed my palm to my thundering heart.

*Not Jackson.*

Daisy waved a hand, not that Viola could see. "Ancient history. Kelly was using him, and they broke up. Ben told me some of that story, including how Valentine was heartbroken. Aw, see, now I want him to have the love of a good woman."

"Ariel?" Viola said with all the amusement gone from her voice. "There's a newspaper article that mentions Jackson. Several, actually—"

Distracted and very overheated, I stood from the sofa. "Hold up. Before any of you decide on me propositioning Jackson or Valentine for sex, let me—"

The door swung open.

My words dried up.

Jackson stood in the frame, his spare keys to our apartment in his hand and his dark gaze fixed on me. Valentine waited behind him, but all I could see was my brother's best friend.

From his expression, he'd heard every word I'd just said.

# 7

# Jackson

Ariel stood in the doorway, a group of women in the room behind her, leaning to peer out at us. One of them muttered *holy fuck*, and another stifled a laugh.

For a moment, the lass's eyes crinkled with embarrassment, but then she took a breath and lifted her chin in a defiant pose.

I'd heard what I'd heard.

There was no denying it.

"Hello, men," she said as if that was a dirty word. "Do you often crash parties you weren't invited to, or were you just standing out there listening?"

My blood pounded in my ears. "Neither. We were heading home from work when I got a panicked call from your brother. He's been messaging your phone, but ye didn't answer. As I had news to share anyway, I said I'd check in. No one answered my knock, so I let myself in."

"Sounds reasonable," said one of the lasses in the audience.

Ariel, though, seemed only more irritated. "I've been on the phone to Viola."

"Hey, sorry," trilled Viola's voice from the phone in her hand. "Is that ye, Jackson? Baby Torran says hi."

I allowed a small smile. In the hospital, I'd mostly stood guard outside of the private suite, but Viola and Leo had called me in for the terrifying act of holding the baby. As he and his big brother, Finn, were top of my protection list, I'd memorised his wee face. "How's the lad doing?"

"So good. He's already lifting his head, and this morning... Oh wait, Ariel probably has something to say to ye. Shutting up."

Ariel's glower fixed on me. "If you'd have just called, I would've seen someone was trying to get hold of me and there would've been no need to stumble in."

I shrugged, a little infuriated. "I don't have your number."

"Definitely swap numbers," Viola breathed.

The other women made similar noises, Daisy included.

Our eye contact intensified. Neither of us spoke. Utter heat zapped me, and I breathed out through my nose like a fucking bull, my chest rising and falling.

That damn mouth of hers. She'd stained her lips a dusky rose colour, which matched her lacey top. The delicate piece of fabric had thin straps I could wrap around a finger. Peel down her arms.

"Anyway," Valentine said from behind. "While the two of ye brand each other with your eyes, how about this party? How are ye all doing, ladies?"

Daisy gave up a laugh. "Everyone's spoken for, so save your flirting."

He barged past, rubbing his hands together. "Nothing wrong with practice. Is that tequila shots? Got one for me?"

Someone laughed and set him up with a shot. I couldn't drag my gaze from the woman in front of me. Despite being shorter than me by almost a head, she carried a weighty presence.

"Ariel?" Daisy called, breaking our staring competition.

"What?" Ariel muttered.

"Jackson said he came with news. Want to find it out?"

I took the prompt and ran with it. "I've been away all day but that doesnae mean I neglected your case."

"My case," she scoffed.

I set my hand on the doorframe next to her head. "Aye, your case. Our police contact gave a description of the man who stole the car that hit yours. A witness rang it in. Male, five eleven, sandy hair, very slim build. Sound like Larson?"

She swallowed.

Daisy appeared behind her, her eyes wide. "Exactly like him."

*Shite.* Then I was right.

A sense of dread chased my brimming lust.

If I'd had any doubt, it fled.

I kept going. "I ran another passport trace, the results of which should be back by morning. I know Ben planned to ask ye about any other person who might have a reason to wish ye harm. An ex, maybe."

"There's no one," she said faintly, her hostility melting to something closer to fear. "No ex. No one else I know who matches that description. So it is him."

"I'm certain of the fact. Which means we need to sit down and discuss all ye know about the man. Put in place a real protection protocol."

Another woman moved closer, her older brother's wife,

tattoos down her arm. "I'll rearrange your shifts or cover them myself."

Ariel shot her gaze to her boss. "No, Effie, I don't want you to do that."

Effie frowned. "I heard what he said. Daisy's would-be kidnapper is here and looking for ye. Going out on the slopes again would be nuts."

I was glad she'd said it as it earned a nod. I would've got a rebuke.

Fresh emotion came over Ariel's expression. Some kind of anxiety over giving up work which I didn't understand.

"I can help with lessons," a fair-haired woman offered.

Effie twisted around. "For real?"

"I taught there before, and my three are now in school full time. It'll be fine temporarily as we're trying for another baby, but I just got my period so we're good for another month." She pulled a face. "Sorry for period talk, people here who aren't female."

Valentine huffed. "Men can talk about periods. No squeamish boys here."

Laughter followed, and Effie retreated to discuss the offer with the helpful lass, leaving me with Ariel and Daisy. The latter tapped out a message on her phone.

"I'm asking Ben to formally take on your protection," she whispered.

Her phone rang, and she walked away to take the call.

Then it was just the two of us.

Ariel sighed. "Give me your number."

I plucked the pad and pen from her hands, scribbling my digits across the top of her note. Then I spotted what was written mid-page below.

The words in front of my eyes stole my every thought.

*Deep throat him with his hand fisting your ponytail.*

*Meet somewhere semi-public and get off fast and hard before anyone sees you.*

My mouth dropped open.

I jerked my focus to Ariel.

She had the most defiant, devilish gleam in her eyes. "Like my list?"

"Yes," I confessed without meaning to say a word.

"Want to help me with it?"

How the fuck could she say that without faltering?

How could she be so cool, with only the faintest hint of pink on her curved cheeks?

It wasn't a real offer. Couldn't be.

Suddenly, I was picturing her in a hundred different ways, all dirty. Her naked and on her knees, legs spread. Or on her back with my hips moving between her thighs. My dick buried in her to the hilt, her tits bouncing with every thrust.

I'd never wanted anyone so badly.

Then my mind supplied a fucked-up detail. We'd walked in on her considering who to ask.

It hadn't been just my name she'd said.

"No," I snarled, and I forced myself to walk away.

*O*utside, I paced to my car. The door thumped behind me, and I whipped around.

Valentine strolled after me.

He smirked big. "Wishing I was a certain someone whose name rhymes with...schmariel? What the fuck was that denial when I asked if there was something between ye?"

"There isn't. She's just my friend's sister," I snapped.

"So you'll be fine with me asking her out?"

Whatever expression I'd sunk into had him choking on laughter.

"God, man. I'm messing. I like 'em curvy, so she isn't even my type. Stop trying to murder me with your eyes. Rein it in and drive me home, lover boy."

Back at the hangar, I paced through the interior of the soaring structure to the bunkhouse, ignoring shouts of my name. Dimly, I heard Valentine greeting people and making plans for the evening, but after a day in the field, I needed to spend time in the office.

If I didn't take the edge off my mood first, I'd explode.

The unlocked bunkhouse door gave way to a living area complete with teal-coloured sofas and a wood burner. There was even a bookcase stuffed full of novels. I bypassed that and headed straight to my room. With only two of us staying here, I had the entirety of the men's dorm—a long and sparsely furnished space with six bunks, lockers, and a side table with a lamp. Valentine had the identical women's dorm on the other side of the living room, and there was one big communal bathroom.

I flicked the lock on the door behind me and tossed my jacket on the bed next to mine. Then I dropped onto my mattress and stared into the dark.

A few weeks ago, when I'd been sleeping on the sofa in Raphael and Ariel's tower, I'd accidentally startled the lass when she'd come home from work one afternoon. She hadn't been expecting me and had stripped to almost completely naked on her way to the shower.

I'd walked out of Raphael's bedroom, and she'd panicked and kicked out at me.

I'd fought to keep my gaze off her body, but the image remained burned into my brain. Pink nipples on perfect tits, thick thighs, presumably from her active job, a backside that I wanted to fucking bite.

When I jacked off to get to sleep, it was always to memories of her.

Closing my eyes, I let my thoughts roam up Ariel's legs to the underwear I remembered her having. Then I vanished that from my imagination.

It got me hard in an instant.

My jeans were in the way, so I kicked them from my body, freeing my dick from my boxers.

I pumped my shaft, imagining getting to explore her with my tongue. I wanted to know how she tasted. How she sounded. For her to order me around in a breathy tone so I got it right for her.

She'd twist her fingers into my hair. Urge me on, grinding against my face.

I shouldn't think about her like this, but it was pure fantasy that made me sleep better, or like now, just to be able to concentrate on anything other than her.

Gripping myself harder, I picked up the pace.

My mind shifted to her list. I wanted to read the full page. All the acts she'd written down. Or someone else had written it down for her? There had been different handwriting and two pen colours.

Some had been underlined, and I needed to know if that had been by her because she wanted to try them first.

There must've been a lot of laughs at her party while the women made suggestions.

Had she raised my name first or was it one of the other women, hence why she uttered it right when I showed up? Maybe that was why she was so pissed off with me. I'd featured in her fantasy and embarrassed her by magically appearing.

My blood rushed faster, my dick only getting harder. I skimmed my palm over the end, hissing at how good it felt. None of this would compare to a real-life encounter with Ariel, but that remained firmly in the never-going-to-happen box, so this was all I had.

With my free hand, I tugged on my balls, imagining her mouth on me. Hastily, I grabbed the hem of my shirt to pull it out of the way of my belly.

*Or maybe she'd wanted Valentine.*

I blinked open my eyes, jolted from my fantasy.

What the fuck? No one else had ever intruded on my alone time before.

My mind supplied an image of Ariel propositioning my long-haired housemate in the way she had me.

I sat bolt upright, my approaching orgasm fizzling out and my erection wilting. Fuck, no.

I hated the idea. Hated how he'd teased me about it, too. Even though I'd refused her and probably set her on the path to hating me.

My phone buzzed, flashing bright in my jeans on the floor. With a groan, I peered to look at the screen.

*Ma,* it read.

If my errant thoughts had messed up my jacking-off session, this killed it stone dead. I slumped back on the bed, letting the call go to voicemail. I didn't want to hear whatever she had to say. There would be some demand, some chiding of me, all based on something I couldn't forgive. My mother had made her choices, and I'd made mine.

Feeling no better than before, I unlocked the door and headed to take a shower, finishing with it on icy cold in the desperate hope that it might make me feel better. Spoiler—it didn't.

Then back in my room, dressed to armour myself, I gave in to the inevitable.

I hit 'play' on my mother's message.

"Jackson, pick up the phone," she demanded, her little dog yapping in the background. "I want ye to come to the house. I need your help with something important. I know what you're going to say, but stop being stubborn. My son holding me hostage. It hurts me that you're refusing to be involved. Come this Saturday for dinner. I'll keep calling until ye answer and accept."

Unhappiness replaced the last of my feelgood emotions.

*Refusing to be involved* made me assume she needed me for something I'd never do. Another court case or a parole hearing. Fuck that.

How had I become the villain? I hated the life she'd made for herself, or more specifically with whom she'd made it, but what kind of son refused to see his mother? I was her only child since Lisa-Marie had died.

If I saw her, it meant a refusal of what she wanted from me, and therefore a fight. Maybe even physical if her bastard of a husband got involved.

For a moment, I desperately needed a soft body to hold. To bury myself in so I could forget the pain.

I wanted Ariel.

But I was alone, and that would never change.

# 8

## *Ariel*

The thud of the apartment door shutting broke my sleep. Daisy slumbered peacefully on the other side of my double bed.

My dreams had been plagued by a tall, dark, and handsome bodyguard. Probably the fault of alcohol, which I'd consumed more of after he'd left. In each of my dream scenarios, we were interrupted before he could touch me, which was a good thing considering I wasn't alone in bed.

Besides, he'd said no. He'd flat out rejected me, it had inexplicably hurt, and I didn't want the reminder, not even in my sleep.

A faint whistling told me the incomer was Raphael, home after training all night in his helicopter. A minute later, the microwave beeped. If he was reheating food instead of prepping something fresh, my brother had to be exhausted.

I climbed out of bed, stuffed my feet into slippers, grabbed my fluffy dressing gown, and quietly crossed the room.

"What time is it?" Daisy asked.

I peeked around. "No idea. Sorry I woke you. Raph just got home."

She sat up, stretching her arms out, a huge yawn splitting her face. "I need to get up anyway. I've got cleaning jobs back to back all morning."

She repeated my routine—slippers, thick hoodie, slight shiver in the chilly morning air—and we left the room together.

"Wish I had a busy day," I grumbled.

She nudged me in solidarity and trudged upstairs and entered the kitchen. At the table, my brother waved a fork in greeting, chowing down on a ready meal, still in its plastic container. One of mine. He'd never usually buy or eat junk food. For reasons best known to himself, he'd chosen to work while also doing an escalated training programme, pushing himself to the limit to become qualified in the shortest time possible.

Dark circles ringed his eyes.

"Looking good there, Grim Reaper," I said with a smirk.

The hand holding the fork inverted so he could give me the middle finger.

Daisy rolled her eyes at us, putting on a pot of coffee. "Training going well?"

Raphael swallowed his mouthful and gave her a long and mind-numbing answer about flight hours and units. I zoned out, already familiar with his fascination with all things flying.

I came back to earth, leaving yet another unfortunate Jackson-shaped daydream, when Daisy said my name.

"If you're bored later, you can come and hang out with me at the cottage. I'm interviewing a woman who wants to join my cleaning business, and I could use a second person there. I never interviewed anyone before. Ben and I can smuggle you away from the castle on the back seat of our car."

Ben had rented the prettiest home for him and Daisy to share. They were in the slow process of moving in, acquiring furniture and getting used to the idea of living together. I was beyond thrilled as it meant my friend was staying in Scotland.

I was also part of her business plan as the technical owner for two reasons—she couldn't legally work here yet and didn't want to avoid paying tax.

"Are you kidding? Deal," I accepted immediately.

Raphael took his plate to the sink. "On that note, I'm going to bed. Before I forget, either Ben or one of the other bodyguards will be over later to talk through the safety procedures ye should be following until the situation is resolved. Wake me if I'm needed."

He left, and soon after, Daisy was picked up by Ben, who gave me a wave but didn't stop.

Returning to the living room, I slumped on the sofa.

It was early morning in the middle of the week. I should've been up at the snowboarding centre, prepping for a class. Or taking on the slopes before my students arrived. But instead, I was stuck inside because of the actions of some jerk.

I didn't handle downtime well, and definitely not if I was alone. I stared into space, fed up but safe, and with nothing to think about apart from how I'd behaved with Jackson last night.

Also the list that I'd torn from the pad and hid in my bedside table's top drawer.

The two were forever linked in my mind.

Why did the guy antagonise me so much?

Physically, I could not be more attracted. I'd tried to get rid of my crush, but it had only gotten stronger, to the point where I was pretty sure only banging him would save me.

That was off the cards. He'd practically laughed in my face when I'd offered, and I was never one to make the same mistake twice. The hurt of rejection swelled again, and I forced it down. I was not indulging in that. He didn't owe me anything.

I needed to reset things with him, which meant some kind of apology or explanation.

On quiet feet, I padded back to my bedroom, hearing only Raphael's light snoring. I eased my drawer open and fished out the list, returning to the living room with my contraband.

Printed across the top in bold characters was Jackson's phone number.

I grabbed my phone, saved him as a contact, and sent a message.

*Ariel: This is my number, so you have it.*

Then I cursed myself, because who knew how many times he'd given out his number recently, and sent a quick *It's Ariel, by the way* as a follow-up.

The messages showed as read.

Then dots appeared to indicate he was writing back. My heart skipped a beat. He didn't keep me waiting long.

*Jackson: Got it, saved it. Good timing, I have things to share with you.*

*Ariel: I'm home now if you want to come over.*

My pulse skipped along faster still. I could've just told

him to call me, but if he visited, I'd be able to have the conversation face to face. Calmly. Reasonably. No influence of alcohol.

The dots appeared. Then disappeared.

I wanted to break my phone.

A few minutes later, a message finally materialised.

*Jackson: On my way.*

Now? Like a startled cat, I leapt from the sofa, scanning the room. After last night's party, Daisy and I had cleared up. The recycling had been taken downstairs, the kitchen cleaned, and surfaces wiped down.

Next came me. I'd showered but done nothing with my hair. Nor did I have on the tiniest bit of makeup.

Hurrying back to my bedroom, I stripped, snatching up a long-sleeved, aubergine-coloured cropped top from my wardrobe. It hugged me in all the right places while leaving inches of my belly exposed. I paired it with black leggings, then drew my silver locket necklace off the little fox figurine on my bedside table and clipped it around my throat.

In the bathroom, I finger combed a dollop of curl product through my hair, ready to move on to my makeup last. As a young teen, I'd been obsessed with my appearance being perfect, but Effie had helped me see that I'd been doing it for the wrong reasons. Now, I just liked to own my look.

I dabbed on concealer, a smattering of blush, then mascara'd the fuck out of my eyelashes. If I had longer, I'd use the concealer to outline my brows, add a bright under-eye, and a deep glossy lip.

My phone dinged in my pocket. A text message.

*Jackson: I'm here. Is it safe to enter?*

A smile curved my lips, and anticipation buzzed through me.

*Ariel: You're learning. Come on up.*

A dab of nude gloss later—no need for finesse—and I scooted to the hall. The door thumped below, and footsteps drummed. Jackson emerged up the spiral staircase, and I took a step back, trying to centre my thoughts.

Just an apology, simple words to find a new way to move forward with him.

His gaze flicked over me. Dark, curious, and with more interest than he'd ever previously shown, lingering over my inches of exposed skin.

My heart pounded like I'd mainlined coffee.

I put my finger to my lips to indicate my sleeping brother and led Jackson up and to the living room. I sat on the sofa and curled one leg underneath me.

"Drink?"

He gave a single shake of his head and sat across from me.

The air between us seemed to hold still. Strung tight, like I was.

"About last night," I started.

"I need to apologise," he beat me to the punch.

I closed my mouth. "That was my line. I was two cocktails on the wrong side of out of line. Something about you gets under my skin."

The corner of his mouth tweaked. He reclined, his body looser. His plain black T-shirt stretched across his broad shoulders, and I had to fight my wandering gaze to keep it on his face.

"The feeling's mutual," he said.

I got under his skin? Was that flirting?

Jackson pressed on, taking advantage of how I'd

momentarily lost my words. "Let's talk protection protocol first. Our working assumption is that we know the would-be assailant but cannot locate him. That's a temporary problem which means we'll need to be more cautious until it's resolved. This tower is a safe space. Leaving adds risk."

"Are you saying I can't go out?"

"Ye can, but take care not to be seen. Either leaving this building, in transit, or entering another around here. In addition to that, it would be better if you're not alone at all, including overnight, and that we add additional security to your home, like cameras at the entrance, and for you personally."

"Me personally? What does that mean?"

He took his phone from his pocket and held it up. "I'm in the process of setting up one of these for ye. It works anywhere regardless of signal and has an enhanced tracking system that can't be disabled or hacked. Daisy uses one. We can also consider a tracking bracelet that's welded in place so can't easily be removed."

I knew the purpose: so I could be found if someone had grabbed me, yet instead of feeling apprehensive like a normal person, I got stuck on how Jackson would always know where I was. He'd check in on me. I liked that.

What the hell was wrong with my brain?

"I'll take the phone. We'll talk about the jewellery later," I replied.

His gaze touched mine. "What if I call it a late birthday gift?"

I was ready with a quip about expensive presents and making sure it was pretty, but Jackson's phone rang on the coffee table, interrupting us.

I couldn't help but see the name on the screen. His

mother was calling.

Instead of answering it, he stared at the device, unmoving aside from a muscle ticking his jaw. The call rang out, and he exhaled in apparent relief.

"You could've taken that," I said, a little too late to be useful.

"No, I couldn't."

"You don't want to talk to your mom?"

A fleeting grimace crossed his features. "No."

Well, that was intriguing. "I don't talk to mine either, but she never calls."

For a moment, we watched one another, but there was none of the hostility of last night. Instead, a more tentative consideration played out, like he was attempting to read me. But whatever questions he had didn't materialise, as he cleared his throat and got back to business.

"Let's go on to the motive for Larson. We haven't yet had the passport trace come back, but the description is good enough for me. What do ye remember of him? Is there any way we can link this to your father?"

"That kiss was a mistake," I blurted.

Jackson paused.

I hurried on, horrified by my mouth running away with itself but committed now. "First time I've ever done that, so I just wanted you to know I'm not insane."

"First time you've ever made the first move?"

Hot energy rippled through me, waking up certain parts of my body. "Kissed anyone."

His focus on me intensified. "Ever?"

I shrugged. "It's no big deal. Like I said, I'm sorry for what I did. I know you aren't interested, and it won't happen again."

He stared, trying and failing to start a sentence.

I liked this look on him. Rattled by me.

"What about that list of yours?" he gritted out.

"What about it?"

"Is it real? You're going to work through it?"

"Not with you. That ship sailed."

He swore and echoed my position, planting his elbows on his knees and steepling his hands.

I gave an incredulous laugh, amazed by the sharp turn the conversation had taken. "Regretting your choices over there?"

His gaze travelled over me, something so compelling, almost desperate in it that I shivered.

"No."

A burst of unhappiness let loose in my chest. Just like last night, he'd turned me down, and even though I hadn't been offering, it doubled down on the rejection I was attempting not to feel.

That deeply unpleasant sensation I'd had since childhood.

I wanted to curl up in a ball and protect myself from him. Worse, I couldn't stop it or contain it. It stunned me to silence.

In my twenty years and one day on the planet, I'd never gone on a date, never asked anyone out. So being pushed away wasn't familiar, except from being a child with shitty parents.

I swallowed, working it through in my head and trying to regain control. He'd been a test only. Nothing more. I could use that.

"Can I ask you something?" I managed, calmer. "When I kissed you, what did I do wrong? I mean, in terms of technique."

"Christ, woman. It wasnae bad."

"I disagree. You told me so."

"I liked the kiss, Ariel. If I'd known it was your first, things would have been different."

"Tell me how I could've been better," I whispered.

"No."

"Why not? Considering all that's happening to me, I really could use something good."

"Ye don't want me."

"You're right. I don't. Not now. But I still want to improve at what we did together."

He watched me, then slowly sat back, his legs wide and his body open. Something switched in his expression and posture, like he'd lost an internal war. "If ye don't believe me, I'll show ye. Come here."

I held my breath, waiting for him to give up the pretence. The dare he was hoping I'd fail.

But I never backed down and didn't intend to now.

Cautiously, and on shaky limbs, I stood. I'd thought myself the confident one, but now I wasn't so sure. Equally, he watched my approach with a mix of trepidation and utter want.

What the hell should I do? Straddle him?

I couldn't do that. Instead, I knelt on the sofa next to him. Put my hand on his arm, my heart racing at the small touch alone.

With an impatient grumble, Jackson took hold of my waist and lifted me, setting me down on his lap. Then he cupped my cheek and brought me in.

Holy hell. I was going to give my brother's best friend a second first kiss.

My eyes shuttered closed.

Our lips met.

I shuddered, bracing myself with both hands to his solid chest. From nothing to being pressed against him, my knees on the cushions, utterly scared to do more. Heat scalded me. I gave up a little gasp and kissed him again.

He made a low sound and changed the angle, this time, parting his lips. Automatically, I did the same. His tongue slid over mine.

*Fuck.* My brain melted.

His taste added to the entirely erotic overload. Something masculine and delicious.

Still holding my waist, his fingers skimming my bared flesh, Jackson drew me closer, working my lips in a thorough seduction. It was all I could do to hang on. I'd wanted to surprise him. I couldn't even match him. My ability to think had left the building, and all I knew was this perfect, soul-stealing kiss.

It was more than I'd dreamt about. And God knows I'd put in the practice there.

After a few moments of establishing how to breathe and stay conscious, I moved in sync, finding a rhythm with each pass building towards something I really needed to reach. I wanted his hands to roam. To relieve the pressure at my breasts and between my legs.

Suddenly, I became aware of the hard ridge I was riding.

I broke away and opened my eyes, my lips parted in shock. This wasn't just a lesson, or a do-over. He was into this.

As if he understood, Jackson brushed his thumb over my lower lip, his eyes half-lidded. "I told ye I liked the first kiss. I liked that one, too."

Quaking, I raised a shoulder in fake nonchalance. "That wasn't the impression you gave."

This earned me a fleeting smile. I watched his mouth, hypnotised by the image of him being happy.

"I'm not boyfriend material, but that doesn't mean I'm unable to appreciate ye."

Not boyfriend...? I hadn't been offering a relationship. I wanted to reply the same, but actually, I wanted more kissing. This temporary moment of insanity couldn't last. Sooner or later, we'd snap back into our normal mode of mostly ignoring each other. Or in my case, staring when he wasn't looking.

I tentatively touched his face and brought my lips back to his. Jackson gave up that same, delicious deep sound of want and kissed me in return.

The air seemed to press in around us.

A door thudded in the apartment.

We both froze.

A footstep landed on the stairs.

I scrambled off Jackson's lap and retreated to the opposite sofa, smoothing out my hair and setting the backs of my hands to my burning cheeks. Jackson grabbed a cushion and held it to his lap.

Right as my brother entered the room.

# 9

## *Jackson*

Raphael dropped onto the sofa next to me and nudged my shoulder. He rubbed his eyes, bleary from apparently just waking up. "Thought I heard the door but I was fighting sleep. I wanted to hear what ye had to tell Ariel."

Holy fuck. What I had to say to his sister wasn't for his ears.

I pulled myself together, keeping my gaze off the lass. And willing my erection to go away.

"I was asking about Larson's motive," I said honestly, if through a wall of distraction made from a perfect kiss.

Ariel hugged her arms around herself, her cheeks stained red. "Larson. Right. From the way I see it, he's either after me because he's had a years-long obsession and is literally insane, or he's working for our father who hasn't given up the idea of selling me."

"Tell me about the first option," I asked. "How did ye first encounter him?"

Her eyes flashed with emotion. "It was in middle school

and I was maybe twelve when I first became aware of him. He started following me around. I had no problem telling him to go away, but he'd lurk in my eyeline or sit next to me if we were in the same class because he was that level of weirdo. No conversation, just always watching. I only wanted him to leave me alone. His attention was embarrassing, and I already had enough kids who hated me because of my family." She swallowed, paling further. "Then things escalated. Not long before my fourteenth birthday, he followed me down a corridor and told me I needed to listen to him and stay away from other boys. I laughed in his face. He pushed me against the wall, smothered me with his palm, and shoved his other hand up my shirt."

"Shite," Raphael muttered.

Pure anger tightened my muscles. Larson needed to hurt for that.

"It was like I wasn't even a person to him, just a thing with no feelings and opinions he could ignore. Next thing I knew, he opened a door and tried to push me inside. I slapped him and finally managed to scream, and someone heard me and came running. He let me go. After that, I never saw him again. Dad decided to give me away in marriage, so I didn't return to the school."

"I'm so fucking sorry," Raphael said.

Ariel climbed to her feet. "Don't. It's no one's fault but his. That's really all I know. Nothing about his family, friends, enemies, or anything else. That one line of conversation before his assault and nothing more. I thought all about this when we suspected him of attempting to kidnap Daisy, and I've racked my brain. I've got nothing else useful to say because I didn't want to know anything about him so I ignored his existence." She padded to the door and paused in the frame. Lifted her focus to me. "I'm done when it comes to men trying to ruin my life. I call the shots now, and whatever he's doing won't change that. I'm going to the bathroom. Back in a minute."

She left, and Raphael sighed.

"I was only a year above her in school, but she didn't like to acknowledge me in the corridors—typical siblings—then I'd moved on to the high school when it happened. I didn't know half of those details. Only that he grabbed her and she yelled. Even that became lost in what happened next with our dad. No kidding, she's done with being fucked around. She's lucky to be alive." He scrubbed his eyes. "Fuck, sorry. This must be triggering for ye, considering what happened with your sister. If it makes things easier, I'll ask Ben not to involve ye in my family's problems. He can assign Valentine."

"No," I said fast, then took a steadying breath. "No, I'm good. I want to help, and God knows I'm better placed. Can I ask what your father did with regard to selling Ariel off?"

Raphael dipped his head. He'd told me a brief version of this in the past, explaining why sometimes he had an American twang to his words, though faded now. His sister's was stronger, and I guessed that was part of her sense of identity. But beyond Raphael's short telling, there hadn't been the cause to go into detail. Just like I'd never confided the worst of what happened to my family.

It didn't make for easy chat.

"Our father took our family from Scotland to California after establishing links with organised crime groups there. He owned a successful logistics company with an arm on the West Coast and transported illegal products under the cover of his legitimate business. But, he was desperate to be an insider, and not just a contractor, because that was where the trust was and therefore the big money, so he tried to achieve that by marrying in.”

“Using fourteen-year-old Ariel,” I confirmed, my stomach sickening.

Raphael raked back his brown hair, still mussed from sleep. “Gabe had already left after Dad tried the wedding trick with him. We were banned from ever talking about our older brother, but he and I kept in contact. The minute we suspected something was going on with Ariel, Gabe extracted us in the middle of the night by helicopter, taking us far from our father’s reach and keeping us hidden. For a long time, Ariel didn’t trust Gabe. Or anyone, aside from Effie who took her under her wing.”

“Lucky that Gabe and Effie married,” I mused aloud.

Raphael cracked a smile. “For them, but also for Ariel. It’s the reason she doesn’t want to give up work. We’re both pretty certain that Effie’s pregnant.”

I exhaled, a bigger picture forming in my mind. That was why she’d resisted my suggestions for her to quit work.

Raphael nudged me. “Don’t judge her too harshly. I know she seems standoffish, but she’s been through a lot.”

“Wasn’t judging her,” I muttered back, though that had been the opposite just a short while ago.

Ariel returned, her cheeks their normal colour now and her poise resumed. “I thought of something we should try.”

We both waited on her.

“Larson was friends with Justin, Daisy’s ex-housemate. He might be able to give us some clues, if we can squeeze them out of him. Daisy and I are hanging out together later at her place, so we can make the call then.”

Raphael gritted his teeth. “We should also talk to Dad.”

The siblings shared an expression of apprehension.

"In both cases, I want to listen in," I said.

I wanted a reason to be around her. To talk to her and share her space. I'd misjudged Ariel Gordonson, and my insane act today of kissing her had become mixed up with an equally strong need to protect her.

Ariel shrugged like it didn't matter. "We're interviewing Daisy's candidate at four. I'll check she doesn't mind, and if so, we could do it after? That'll be mid-morning in California."

Her brother pressed his lips together in a grim smile. "I can't be there. I need to sleep then cram in some final reading. Gabe's working, too."

She wrinkled her nose. "We'll just tackle the housemate, then. Leave Dad until you're both available. He never really talks to me anyway."

All the more reason to suggest he'd seen her as disposable. Or usable.

I knew the reason Raphael and his siblings kept in touch with their father was because he'd had a fourth child—their younger sibling—with his new wife. But also to keep track of the man. He claimed to be sorry for what he'd done but he didn't strike me as a man who was good to his word.

Raphael agreed, and with that, we had a plan. I needed to get back to the office, and my friend clearly needed more sleep.

"I'll see ye out," he said.

I stood, packing away all the things I wanted to say to his sister, and gave her only a short nod because anything else I said would be nowhere near enough. Then I followed Raphael down the spiral staircase and to the front door.

There, he paused me. "I want to thank ye for helping to protect my sister, but also, I need to ask a favour. I've got a problem. The final block of my training starts midweek. It was booked and paid for ages ago, but it's offsite with a specialist trainer. I'll be staying over with a group of pilots, training for a few days and nights, then taking our exams at the end. Getting to this date is the reason I've been cramming in the hours. It brings a close to all I've been working towards."

"But then all this happened with your sister," I said slowly, seeing his dilemma.

The number one item on our protection protocol was her never being alone.

"I won't go if it exposes Ariel to risk."

"Will she go with ye?"

"Doubt it. Besides, I'm not her keeper, and she would hate me if I treated her like that."

My blood rushed. "You're looking at your solution."

His short intake of breath and the expression of hope in his eyes showed me exactly how he'd agonised over this. "For real?"

"Do ye even need to ask?"

Raphael's shoulders sagged. "If she has someone overnight, she can find other company for the daytime. I know it's a lot to ask, but ye can have my bed, and the tower's a fuck ton warmer than the bunkhouse."

"You'd need to ask her first," I said, my mind spinning off in multiple different directions.

I shouldn't have kissed Ariel. It blurred the lines when it came to protecting her. I couldn't explain myself, except that I'd been rattled by the requests from my mother and the memories that brought with it.

I'd lost my sister, and now, I had the chance to protect someone else's.

Raphael shivered in the cold, his plaid pyjamas and grey T-shirt no match for the icy draught. "Of course I will. I just wanted to have a plan before even considering going ahead with it. I'll let you know once I've spoken to her. You're a good friend, ye know that? There's no one I'd trust more with my family than ye."

He opened the door for me, and I stepped outside, the daylight bright and the winter air the right degree of cold to wake me up.

I'd been anything but a good friend, but right now, I couldn't bring myself to regret a single second spent alone with his sister.

Or even comprehend nights locked away in her tower.

# 10

## Ariel

"You asked Jackson?" I repeated. My voice came out strained.

Raphael leaned heavily on his bedroom doorframe. "Is that okay? The timing is shite, but I wouldn't ask if I didn't trust him. He's better trained than me and he'll keep ye safe."

I tapped my lip, a confusing scene opening before me.

The kiss my brother interrupted had been mind-blowing. I had no job to go to, an empty apartment, plus a list of things I wanted to try and a man I'd asked to do them with me. If he'd said yes, then talk about making lemons into lemonade. But Jackson had rejected me.

Then kissed me. This was a bad idea.

"What did he say?"

Raphael yawned big. "He agreed as long as it's okay with ye."

I couldn't say no, not when my brother had worked so

hard. Nor could I explain my hesitation. Instead, I just nodded. If things got weird, I could always bail and stay with Gabe and Effie. "When will you leave?"

He slumped in apparent relief. "Tomorrow night. I'll have time to talk to Dad with ye before then."

"We'll call him before you go. Go get some sleep."

He gave me a salute and then retreated to his bed.

I skipped back into my room and closed the door. Taking up my phone, I fired off a message to Jackson before I lost my nerve.

*Ariel: Hey, babysitter.*

*Jackson: Good to know you said yes for your brother's sake.*

I grinned and tapped a reply.

*Ariel: Having you around is going to make it difficult for me to move on with my list #cockblocker*

*Jackson: I tried to forget what was on it. It was causing me to be a hazard at work.*

*Ariel: Want a reminder?*

For several minutes, he didn't reply. Then a single-word answer, *yes*, popped up on my phone.

A thrill shot through me, catching alight the lust he'd kindled earlier. I took a photo of the page then blurred all but the top two lines and sent it to him.

*Lose virginity fast with straight-up missionary. Full-body contact. Moving slow.*

*Get on your knees for him. Have him go down on you. Sixty-nine until you're both on the edge.*

Almost instantly, my phone buzzed.

But it wasn't Jackson calling, it was Daisy.

"Hello," I crowed.

"Hello to you, too. About later, I'll be done by three, so Ben and I will come get you. He'll have to return to work, but if you sneak out the back of the castle, dive into the car and hide, we'll get you to the cottage safely."

"Deal," I said, not even trying to hide the smile in my voice.

"What's got you purring?" my friend enquired.

"Tell you when I see you. Oh, by the way, Jackson's coming over after the interview so we can call your old housemate. Is that okay?"

"To question him about Landon? Good idea. See you soon."

We hung up, and I lay back on my pillows, reliving every second of that kiss.

Jackson didn't reply, and I wondered if I'd broken him.

A few hours later, I was finally out of the house, trundling through the countryside in the back of Ben's car.

"Tell me about the woman who's coming for the cleaning job," I asked from low down on the seat.

Daisy replied without twisting around. "Her name's Mia. She's a single mother, and she sounded so sweet on the phone. Ben's checked her out, so I know she's who she says she is. Get this, it sounds like someone's done a number on her self-esteem. One of the first things she said to me was not to judge her by her appearance."

"What about her appearance?"

"She said I shouldn't consider her lazy because of her weight." Daisy gestured up and down her ample and beautiful plus-sized frame. "Wait till she gets a load of me."

Ben muttered about some men not knowing their arse from their elbow and drove us on. At the cottage, he jumped out to open the garage door then reversed in. Once safely hidden away inside, I climbed out and stretched my legs, happy to see anything other than the inside of the tower.

With us delivered, Ben gave Daisy a kiss and me a parting warning about staying away from the windows, then left us to it. I swept through the rooms, taking in all the changes they'd made in the past few days. Daisy had hung pretty floral curtains on newly installed iron rails. The walls downstairs had been painted a warm cream, which offset the dark-wood staircase and door surrounds. It was the prettiest place, and my best friend had barely got started making it her own.

"Every time I come here, it's that much more perfect."

Daisy beamed. "I love it, I can't wait to move in."

"When's the big day?"

"We need bedroom furniture and for broadband to be installed. Maybe a week?"

I bounced up to hug her. "Seriously, if there's anything I can do, just give the job to me."

"Want to help paint? I've got an afternoon off in a couple of days and a plan to take on the spare bedroom."

"Deal! I am so happy for you."

Hearts danced in her eyes. "It's hard to believe how fast this has come around. I keep wanting to reality check myself, but when I said to Ben a few nights ago that we still needed to get to know each other, he sat down and instructed me to ask him anything. He said I'd met his family, been on a road trip with him, and knew what he was like under pressure— that he gets stubborn and action-focused but eventually becomes reasonable. If that's his worst trait, damn, sign me up to be Mrs Graham."

"You'd marry him?"

She took a deep breath. "God. Yes?"

Another happy sound came from me, and Daisy laughed, the image of a contented woman.

We'd missed years of seeing each other after I'd relocated away. Having my best friend follow me was a dream come true.

She led me into the kitchen, and I forced back my grin to give her my news.

"So, guess who Jackson was caught kissing earlier?"

Daisy spun around, brandishing a coffee pot. "No! He did not. Just a day after kissing you?"

I faked astonishment, widening my eyes. "Well, technically I kissed him, but isn't it shocking? He was right there, inviting this girl onto his lap. Demanding kisses."

A laugh fought to bubble up. My lips crinkled.

Daisy squinted at me, then the penny dropped. "You? Ohmigod. What...how? I'll make the coffee while you brew that tea."

Quickly, and with utter glee, I relayed the story.

My friend fanned her face. "Where did that version of him come from? He's always so reserved. Who knew that underneath he was just dying to get another taste? Do I need to make myself scarce later so you can kiss a little more? Then I can fake a reason why I can't take you home so he has to."

"No, you devious mastermind. It won't happen again. But on the topic, there's something else spillable. Raphael's exam week is coming up. He asked Jackson to move back to the tower so I have someone there overnight." I pulled my list from my pocket and wafted it. "What if he'd agreed to help me with this? That would've been awkward."

The expression of shock on her face was a delight. "Or very nice. Live-in boyfriend."

"God, no. It would've just been for sex."

Which I could barely think about without overheating.

"Sex can be hard to keep in a box, unless you're dealing with a dildo, and honey, he's a real-life man. Getting that close would create a bond."

I considered that. "Not if we were friends, right?"

She went to answer, but an engine purred outside.

Daisy hurried to the window to peek out. "This has to be Mia. I'm so nervous. Are you ready?"

"I've got you," I promised.

I finished the coffee prep while Daisy let her potential new employee in. Mia followed her into the kitchen and gave me a shy smile at Daisy's introduction.

I shook her hand.

She was pretty, with huge boobs I envied, her fair hair tied in a neat ponytail, and her clothes old leggings paired with a warm sweater with a couple of bleach marks on the sleeve. In her hand, she carried a cleaning products caddy. She'd come ready to work. Nailed that first impression.

"Your home is beautiful," she said with an American accent, gazing around.

Daisy thanked her and held up a mug in offer, earning a nod from our visitor.

"You're from the US?" I asked.

"I was born in New York, state, I mean, not the city, but my mom was English, and we moved here when I was young. Never really shook off the twang."

I pointed at myself. "Same. Came here at fourteen and never changed."

Daisy handed over a cup and gestured to the milk and sugar. We all settled around the kitchen table, and my friend gathered her nerves and started.

"Good to see you found the place okay. We're kind of remote here, and all the work is local."

Mia nodded. "My daughter's dad was from Scotland, so I'm right at home. I've only done cleaning work in the city, though. Shoot. What I mean to say is I can vacuum, dust, and polish with the best of them. I love a challenge. You mentioned in your advert that your business specialises in jobs that other cleaners turn away, right? That sets me on fire. I want to know more."

Daisy took a deep breath. "You're talking my language. Day to day, it's mostly maintenance jobs—working families or single parents who need the extra help, a few businesses— but the big jobs when they come in give me life."

Mia grinned, sitting up taller. "My work history is cleaning offices, but give me a filthy kitchen, headphones, and my cleaning products, and I'm a woman possessed."

"Same! I listen to audiobooks," Daisy replied.

Smutty ones. She played dirty books as she cleaned. I kept that nugget to myself.

Daisy continued, giving an outline of the work that would be on a rota and how it got allocated. "I have full-time hours available, if you want them. There are more work requests than I can book in."

Mia nodded enthusiastically. "That's fine with me. I'll take anything you throw at me and I promise to do a great job. My only constraint is my daughter. It's just me and her. No dad anymore."

"How old is she?" I asked.

"Four. She's attending preschool, which is awesome, but I'd need to organise wraparound care if I had a job early or late."

"I can make that work," Daisy said. "I want babies, too, in time. This is going to be a family-friendly business."

"Plus there's plenty of babysitters around here, if you'd prefer that to the school clubs," I added.

Daisy shot me a happy look.

She liked Mia, I could tell. Taking on a member of staff was a huge deal, and her excitement was palpable.

"There's just one small issue," Mia said, her smile fading. "Oh my, this is going to sound bad. If you did make me an offer, and I don't want to be presumptuous, is there any way I could go on the books under a different name than my own? I don't mean to avoid tax. Any official forms can have my real details. I… I just need to work under a pseudonym for clients in case anyone calls, asking for me. I need to be upfront about that."

She'd said no father was on the scene, but I gave her a once-over, seeking bruises on her wrists or throat. Nothing was visible, but my senses were jangling.

Daisy leaned forward. "Are you in trouble?"

"Not with the law or anything bad. Just some people I'm trying to avoid."

"Are they dangerous?" I pressed.

"Oh no. Not to anyone else. I'm sorry to be cagey. I don't mean to be. I also need somewhere new to live, if you've heard of a place." She winced as if she'd said too much.

A phone trilled, and Mia jumped then stooped to search in her bag. "So sorry. I have it on do-not-disturb for all but one person."

I swapped a glance with my friend. I knew she'd want to help, but I really wanted to know more about the trouble Mia was in.

The interviewee answered her call with another

whispered apology to us. She listened and cringed again. "Of course. I'm on my way. I'll be as quick as I can."

She hung up and stood.

I didn't miss how her fingers trembled as she slid her phone back into her bag.

"I'm so sorry, but the woman watching my daughter has to bail. I need to run."

We both stood, too.

"Don't worry. We were about done anyway," Daisy said.

Mia's face fell. "We weren't, though. I wanted to give you a demonstration. I make my own cleaning products, and they smell amazing. Here, have this one. But then this place is so clean, maybe I wouldn't be able to show anything at all."

Crestfallen, she retreated to the door, leaving on the table a spray bottle with a handwritten label.

"You did great," Daisy promised.

"We'll be in touch," I added, squeezing Daisy's hand so she didn't immediately blurt out an offer.

Mia left, her car zooming off at speed.

Another came in the opposite direction.

Jackson. Early.

I had to ready myself for a second kind of interview while stopping all thoughts of his body on mine.

# 11

## *Jackson*

Ariel held back in the shadows beyond Daisy's front door. I parked up, watching her. She wasn't that visible, but she needed to hide better. We had no trace on Larson and no clues either. Since the crash, I'd driven around at night on patrol. Ben had, too. Raphael had pulled daytime shifts. The staff at the snowboarding centre were on alert for any stranger with Larson's description.

Still nothing.

He had to be hiding and waiting for her to make a move. But how did he plan to find her without sitting in plain sight? I had no answer to that, and it was driving me fucking nuts.

Killing the engine, I grabbed my phone, ready to get out.

At the cottage, Ariel leaned in and whispered something to Daisy. The second lass giggled and shot me a knowing glance.

She'd told her about the kiss, then. Fuck.

Some unknown sensation had me slowing my moves to leave the safety of my car. A sudden rush of concern, like I'd arrived for a date and had to walk the line of judgement from her friends first.

Excitement coloured that, as well.

I hadn't been able to stop thinking about Ariel. Professionally, personally, in my bed, on her sofa, against a wall. Endless images warred for dominance.

She'd categorically told me there was no second chance. Exactly as I wanted.

Yet despite that, I didn't know how to get out of the car and walk in there.

Sweat broke out on my brow.

In my hand, my phone rang. I answered it.

Ben spoke over the sound of his engine. "My meeting finished early, so I'm coming out to join this phone call. I texted Daisy to tell her to wait."

I peered back at the door. The women had gone inside, presumably not wanting to stand in the cold while I wasn't budging.

"No problem. Just arrived myself," I replied.

Ben grunted, "I'll be there in a few," and hung up.

Perhaps it should've made things more awkward for me, but my boss showing up was having the opposite effect. I waited for him to park alongside me, and we approached the house together.

Strength in numbers with my unaware wingman.

"Ready for tomorrow?" Ben asked.

He opened the cottage door and gestured for me to go inside. Tomorrow was Leo's TV show appearance. We'd carried out the risk assessment and were going to get our first taste of crowd work, including escorting the rock star past fans outside the studio and monitoring him inside the building.

"Can't wait to get out there," I said honestly.

"Good man."

The hard, focused work was exactly what I needed.

At least on the job, I wouldn't have the idle time to dream of how many ways I wanted to fuck Ariel Gordonson.

Daisy leapt from the sofa and danced into Ben's arms. He bent to press a kiss to her forehead then unashamedly walked her backwards into the kitchen for a more private greeting, murmuring something that made her giggle.

Still seated, Ariel cocked her head at me. "Hey, stranger."

I rolled my shoulders. "Thought I was the babysitter."

Delaying coming in had given me a chance to install the cool veneer I liked to wear. It kept me safe. Made me seem less approachable to others. Usually.

For a long minute, Ariel didn't reply. Instead, she just stared at me.

My veneer cracked. "What?"

She shrugged. "You're nice to stare at. I'm having a moment."

I spluttered, unable to answer.

Ben reappeared. "Don't tease my bodyguards," he ordered Ariel.

She smiled prettily and swapped a look with Daisy who took her seat once more.

"Game plan," Daisy said. "We need one. Justin, my old housemate, is probably asleep but hopefully not yet too wasted to give information. What am I asking?"

"Larson was sleeping on the sofa in your Los Angeles house-share while taking small and probably illegal jobs for your family," Ben summarised. "We know he came after ye but what we need is a better understanding of the man. Is he motivated, capable, or just a stoner like Justin? It's unlikely he'll share details of the jobs he's given with his friends, but Justin might be able to paint a picture to help us assess him better."

"As I see it," I added, staring directly at Ariel. "The most important thing we need is to establish a motive. This man wants ye. Any insight will help us establish why."

I wanted her. That was beside the point.

"Got it," Daisy said. "Calling now. Everyone ready? Gotta hope he's in a gossip-boy mood." She set the recording function on her phone and dialled a number.

After several rings, a woman answered. "Hello?"

"Zara, it's Daisy. Put Justin on the line," Daisy demanded.

"You woke me for that? It's my day off. Call him yourself."

"I don't have his number. Please just do it," Daisy said.

There was grumbling followed by shuffling and eventually a knock. A male voice answered groggily. He swore and came on the line.

"It's the middle of the fucking night," he griped.

"Hello, Justin. You know, if you had a real job, you'd be in work by now."

"Daisy? What do you want?"

"Remember we spoke about Landon recently?"

"I don't remember yesterday, babe."

"I need to find him. Can you help me?"

"What's it worth?"

Daisy gritted her teeth. "Me not reporting you and Zara for subletting?"

There was a pause. "Bitch. Whatever. What do you want to know?"

"Have you seen him recently?"

"Not since you cut out on us. What's the deal between you guys anyway? Are you chasing his dick?"

Daisy ignored his line of questioning. "Do you know what he does for a job?"

"We smoke together, never asked his life story." Justin clicked a lighter and took a drag of something. "Except, couple months ago, we were coming out of Chick-fil-A's when this black car pulled up. Windows too dark to see in the back. The door opened, and a meathead guy got out, and Landon just climbed on in without a word. Next time I saw him, it was days later, and he wouldn't talk about it. Said it was just business."

I swapped a glance with Ben. Landon had found himself in deep shit by the sound of things.

Daisy pursed her lips. "Do you remember anything else about the car?"

"Nah, babe."

"Okay, what about a girlfriend?"

Justin gave a wheezing laugh. "I fucking knew it. Sorry to be the one to tell you, but I'm pretty sure he only gets it up for AI porn."

I liked the sound of this guy less and less.

"There was no one special he ever mentioned? No girl's name?"

"Jealousy looks bad on you. What the hell do you care about that skinny fuck anyway? You'd break him if you sat on his face."

Ben scowled, his fists bunching.

"Can you answer the question?" Daisy said.

Justin gave a dramatic groan. "No… Oh, wait. Yeah,

maybe. He has some chick's name tattooed on him. April? No. Adriene? Something like that."

"Do you remember exactly?" Daisy asked, her voice shaky.

My blood froze. It had to be Ariel.

"One of those. She your rival? You've got me picturing a little girl-on-girl. Now my dick's thick and you've got thirty seconds till I'm beating it."

Ariel held her elbows, her arms across her body in a defensive pose. I'd been trying not to stare at her. Now I just wanted to enclose her in my arms.

Daisy opened and closed her mouth, then forced out her words. "Justin, this is important. I need to speak to Landon. Please give me his phone number."

"Not doing that."

"Can you send him mine, at least?"

"Could do. Say something else to get me hot."

Ben's already bleak expression darkened to thunder, but Daisy stilled him with a small touch to his arm.

She clenched her jaw. "If you hear from him or see him again, you have to let me know. I'll pay you for the information."

"For real? You got it. Still don't get your interest. That jerk-off is a loser and a loner. If it's dick you're chasing, I've got more—"

Ariel jabbed at the phone, ending the call and cutting off the ex-housemate's offer.

"He's wearing my name on his skin," she gritted out. "The audacity. When I find him, I'm going to carve it off him."

Ben grimaced and gestured to me. "Tell me what ye got from that."

"We already knew he did low-level mob work. This could be another paid job for him. The tattoo says different."

"Agreed. If true, it's a warning sign."

Ben turned to Ariel.

My phone rang, Valentine calling. I walked away and answered, listening to the information he'd just received. My heart sank. Hanging up, I came back to the group.

Three faces regarded me. I spoke to Ariel.

"The passport trace confirms Larson returned to the UK two days after your video was posted. Whatever else this guy is, he's motivated and has money to travel."

"If he doesn't have a real job, he's being funded by my dad," she surmised. "Who else wants me? No one."

Heat broke in me. I did. Badly.

As much as I didn't.

The lass threw her hands out. "So what do I do now? Sit and wait for him to find me?"

"He'll have a game plan," I replied. "My guess is he's relying on ye assuming the crash was a random accident and not hiding away."

"So he's haunting the neighbourhood, waiting on me to wander out alone again."

"Then ye won't be alone," I vowed.

I turned to Ben. "Raphael asked if I could stay overnight at the tower while he's away for his exams. Ariel accepted, and I agreed."

My boss inclined his head. "Ariel, how do ye feel about my bodyguards providing your protection? Aside from tomorrow, where the whole team is away all day, and a couple of training sessions we've got planned, I can work out a rota to allow them to be there. Probably more Jackson than

Valentine or me."

I held my breath.

I didn't want her to ask for someone else. I'd keep her safe.

Her gaze travelled to me, her expression dubious. "Is that okay with you?"

I nodded once.

"I have one or two conditions, but we can talk about them later," she added.

Ben tapped the table. "Done."

Daisy pressed his arm. "There's something I wanted to ask you about. Come with me."

She led him out of the room and upstairs, their footsteps diminishing.

I watched Ariel. "Name your conditions."

She flushed pink. Slid a piece of paper from her pocket.

I recognised it instantly, and my blood rushed south.

"If you're officially working as my bodyguard, we don't talk about this."

My throat tightened. If she'd offered again, I couldn't refuse. Didn't want to.

But instead, she was holding the line of no.

"Your choice," I said slowly.

"Is it? Wouldn't you be under some kind of no-fraternising rule?"

My words flew out before I knew what I was saying. "Did ye plan to ask Valentine instead?"

Ariel stalled, just staring at me, astonishment bright in her expression. Then she finally managed, "No."

Ben and Daisy returned downstairs, my boss furrowing

his brow in question.

"I think we reached an agreement," Ariel said with a glance at me.

Had we? But what?

My boss grinned. "Welcome to your new assignment."

ack at the hangar, I entered the bunkhouse, calling a greeting to Valentine.

"I'm going for a run. Want in?" he yelled from his room.

"Sure. Give me a minute."

I sat on the sofa, the log burner warming the living room and casting an orange glow, and searched my emails for ones from Ben. I found what I wanted. My contract.

Then I opened it and scanned the text.

Searched on 'fraternising' and 'relationships', not seeing anything about sleeping with clients. Ben had started seeing Daisy while he was officially protecting her. I'd guessed he'd taken that rule out.

I didn't find it, either way.

# *Ariel*

I slept badly, weird dreams punctuating my sleep. Of creepy, skinny boys, haunting my footsteps. More than once I woke with a gasp, shooting up to dislodge a phantom hand from my mouth.

But I was alone.

The day passed slowly. Raphael crammed in hours of final study then slept. Tonight, he was leaving, and I wasn't about to let anything disrupt his plans, no matter what was happening to me.

Callum McRae, the owner of the castle we lived in, showed up with Brodie, his son-in-law, and two of his young grandsons to install a camera outside the tower's entrance and another in the downstairs hall. The men sat with me and got it linked to my phone, working through the security features.

It was always live, always recording. It notified me when something moved in the frame and tracked any figures. We had the boys test it, running across the snow-covered gravel and sneaking up the steps to test the boundary.

In equal measures, it unnerved and reassured me.

"When your brother wakes, show him how to add this to his phone," Callum instructed me. "No one else can access it, unless ye allow them. It's naw much, but on top of all the other measures we're taking, it'll help."

"Other measures?"

"Jackson's patrol and search," Callum stated.

"His what?"

The older man squinted at his son-in-law. Brodie gave the explanation.

"Since the evening your car was hit, we've had people out patrolling the estate, plus we installed a number plate tracker on the gateposts that alerts us if a stranger drives in. Just to be on the safe side, we also did a sweep of known empty buildings and lodges in the surrounding hills, anywhere someone might hide."

My mouth had dropped open in surprise, so I closed it. "I had no idea. Jackson organised this?"

Callum gave a fond smile. With his salt-and-pepper beard and lined face, he was the picture of a kindly grandfather. The two little boys followed him around like he was their commander-in-chief. "Aye, that he did. He's a good addition to the bodyguard team. His instincts are sound, even if we didnae find anything."

Callum and Brodie left, and I sat in the lounge and just watched the cameras.

I didn't want to be scared, but the sense overwhelmed me, the idea of someone lying in wait in a nearby cabin vivid. I was strong, but no match for a man, even with the self-defence classes Daisy and I'd had.

Jackson had given us those. He'd got grumpy while

delivering them, maybe because of me.

I wished I'd known all he was doing so I could've thanked him.

Of all the dangers I was facing, he made me the most nervous of all. Which was wild because we'd be living together. I needed to put him in a box and keep him there, metaphorically speaking. Not like Daisy's sex toy analogy.

Friends with benefits needed to be friends first.

Taking out my phone, I sent him a message.

*Ariel: What time will you get here this evening? We're going to call my dad at seven.*

*Jackson: Before then.*

*Ariel: Don't forget to bring your toothbrush.*

I waited for his response. He was working in Edinburgh today, I knew. If he was writing back then presumably he wasn't the one doing the driving.

*Jackson: I haven't forgotten a single thing.*

A thrill hit me. He could've replied with a thumbs-up or an okay, but his text felt like it had a double meaning.

*Ariel: Something particular stick in your mind?*

*Jackson: A lot of things.*

*Ariel: Be more specific.*

*Jackson: In a car with a colleague? Not happening.*

*Ariel: How about in code?*

*Jackson: ??*

*Ariel: DYLMK = did you like my kiss?*

No reply came. I paced the room.

Then my phone rang. I jumped a mile.

But not with his name on my screen—it was Bridgette's mother. I had all my students' contact details recorded in case of emergency. If I was going to get a second demand for money from that family for deleting the video that had got me into this mess, I probably wouldn't be polite about it.

I left the call to ring out. The moment it did, it rang once more, her again. This time, I walked away and made a drink.

When I returned, I had a voicemail from the woman lurking.

But also a reply from Jackson.

I greedily grabbed up my phone.

*Jackson: Y,ILYK. NIWYOYKFM.*

God, he was playing the game. Fresh excitement shot through me. I scrambled to work out his coded meaning.

Y,ILYK.

*Yes, I liked your kiss*? I fist pumped the air. That first part had been easy. Onto the second. Handily, he'd given me the sentence divide.

NIW … *Now I want*, or *next I want*?

Y had to be *you*.

OY *off your*? Ooh, *on your*?

I summarised, trying to work out the ending.

*Yes, I liked your kiss. Next I want you on your...*

KFM.

What the hell was the K? FM had to be *for me*. Surely.

The answer came to me in a rush of heat. It was part of the list I'd sent him. One of the two top items I'd left unblurred. *Knees.*

*Yes, I liked your kiss. Next I want you on your knees for me.*

The quiet room spun. My mind summoned the picture of his hard dick ready for my mouth. Of his hiss of breath when I took him in, working out how to lick or suck him until he groaned. *God.* I was getting hooked on these tiny exchanges. It was like balancing at the peak of a snowy slope, the fresh powder pristine, untouched by anyone else.

I stifled a laugh at my comparison. I was the untouched snow, and he was waiting to take me on. Carve his mark.

My blood warmed all the more. We weren't going to do anything together, beyond flirting, but it was the most fun I'd had in forever. I sent him a quick answer, *If only you hadn't turned me down*, my heart racing. Palms sweaty.

Then a thought popped into my head.

A memory from when Viola had been on the phone at my party.

She'd searched for Jackson's name and found out something about him.

My phone was in my hand, the browser one click away.

Fuck it.

A whole raft of heartbreaking headlines filled my screen, and my plan to be friends took a new angle again.

# 13

## Jackson

My phone buzzed in my pocket, but I couldn't answer. We were here, and it was game time.

I needed to get my head out of steamy scenes with Ariel and onto the crowd ahead.

The Edinburgh studio had flaws in its planning. First, the PR team leaked who they were recording ahead of the show being aired the same evening, meaning fans knew to show up that day to haunt the steps. Second, even at the rear entrance, the celebrity had to climb out of the car and walk down a path and up two flights of steps to access the nineteen twenties building, only metal barriers holding back the crowd.

And Leo's fans were legion.

I'd read up on his career in preparing for the role. Leo had gone from being a jobbing musician, playing festivals and building a following, to selling out stadiums. He'd released five albums in the past decade and each broke more records, especially after he'd revealed how his love story with his wife had been the inspiration for a lot of his songs.

Gordain, his father-in-law, had talked me and Valentine through how dangerous those fans could be, how people hated his daughter for marrying Leo and wished her harm. How some made death threats and even doxed him—publicly posting his address, which at the time was in London—because they didn't like the way his musical style had evolved. Typically the threats were empty, but not always.

Celebrities had been hurt or killed by fans in the past.

It drew parallels in my mind to a boy obsessed with my sister. How people had underestimated him and laughed off concerns. Until it was too late.

I took my job seriously because I'd lived through the outcome of such an event.

The car slowed, and my focus sharpened.

Back at Castle Braithar, Leo's home, the family had any number of security features set up, so risk only came when he left the mountains.

Like today. Running the gauntlet of getting in and out of the studio.

Valentine drove us through the gates, and I scanned the crowd of faces. Both of us had spent hours memorising the features of Leo's most concerning fans, a hit list that had been refined and added to over the years.

The car behind kept close to our tail, driven by Ben and with Leo and Gordain in the back behind tinted glass.

The TV appearance was to announce an upcoming album and tour, but the press had gotten wind of Leo and Viola's new arrival, so he was pre-empting that by revealing it himself.

The crowd knew something was up. Numbers were

a lot higher than the studio had estimated for our risk assessment.

"Into position, boys. We've got this," Ben said into our earpieces.

We had to. A lot rode on this, more than Leo's safety. If I couldn't do my job effectively, I'd lose it. The pressure honed my senses. My fingers shook.

We climbed from the car to a wall of noise and energy.

The second car stopped, and Valentine and I crossed on foot to meet it, keeping our focus on the throng of bodies behind the barriers to the left of the entranceway. Most screamed or cried out, their excitement obvious.

Those weren't the faces we homed in on. It was the quiet ones. The loners. Not necessarily male, but the comparisons between Leo's threats and Ariel's stuck at the forefront of my mind.

"Exiting now," Ben advised.

A roar went up, everyone with a phone in their hand.

Leo was out of the car. We flanked him, Gordain going on ahead and Ben at his back. If he smiled or waved, I didn't see it, only keeping the rock star in my peripheral vision while I moved apace with him.

Faces passed, some weeping, others breathless and beaming.

We kept going, swift and purposeful.

At the end of the row of people, in the corner nearest the door, a man stared on. He didn't call out but instead watched Leo as he jogged up the steps and went inside.

A spike of intuition pulled me up short.

I peeled away from the group the second everyone was inside.

"Sticking with the crowd a minute," I informed the boss.

"Roger that," he replied, giving me his trust.

I could only hope I'd earn it.

The four of them plus the studio's team made their way down a corridor, safer now. I took up a sentinel post, keeping a close eye on the individual who'd caught my attention. The forty-something man stared at the doors, muttering something to himself. Plain black T-shirt. No bag. No phone in his hands.

He looked like someone's boyfriend, not a fan, but no one turned to him. Yet he had the prime spot. Must've got there hours early to claim it.

A shout came from further to the left. I glanced at the fuss. A man and a woman tussled for the front spot, another guy grabbing the first dude by the shoulder. Not my problem.

But the distraction cost me. In the seconds it took me to turn back, the muttering man had gone.

I couldn't see him anywhere.

I searched for a while longer then swore and gave it up, heading in to join my crew in the studio. Leo was in makeup, readying to go in front of the studio audience and the interviewer. I found Ben. He raised a quizzical eyebrow, and I gave a brief overview of what I'd seen.

"Not a face from our list?" he asked.

I shook my head, already certain of that.

"Tell me what raised your suspicions," he asked.

That was harder. "He didn't have a role there," I settled on. "Fanatical fans wear merch, often homemade, and take pictures or video. They're often with a friend or partner. They want to be seen by Leo. This man didn't act like that. He wasn't accepting the same freely available experience everyone else was."

My sentence made more sense as I stumbled over it. "I could be wildly wrong, but if the only time you expect to see your idol is in those few seconds, you're capturing that. Excited about it or overwhelmed. Why was he there?"

Ben's eyes darkened. "Because he had another plan."

My blood chilled.

I'd half expected him to tell me to drop it, but instead, my boss shifted tack.

"Valentine," he called. On the appearance of my hulking colleague, Ben briefed him on what I'd seen and issued new instructions. "Val, once they admit the audience, you'll be positioned at the back of the crowd. Jackson, you'll be hard left, in plain sight and searching for that face. Act as we trained if anything arises."

He clapped us both on our shoulders, Valentine abruptly turning away. An assistant scuttled down the hall, and people started hustling.

It was showtime.

To rapturous applause, Leo sauntered on stage, styled to within an inch of his life and a world apart from the frazzled new dad I'd attended at the hospital. I hadn't known him long but I'd known *of* him for years. He'd sold out stadiums around the world and had multi-platinum-selling albums. His online followers adored him and defended him rigorously, including when he stopped meet and greets after his wife received threats.

He waved to the audience and shook the host's hand, an ex-comedian who made a quip that earned an uproar of laughter. The interview commenced.

I spared only enough attention to know Leo was in place, but my focus was on the hundreds of people watching him. Five sections of fifteen rows, all filled.

As part of our risk assessment, we'd talked through the audience selection process. This was no walk-up. People had to apply and give photo ID. Bags and coats were left in lockers. That didn't mean rogue fans couldn't slip in or hide a weapon. One flaw that had caused an argument in the bodyguard office was the studio's refusal to give us the audience list so we could cross-reference it.

Instead, they said they'd do that for us and be sure to cross off anyone we'd flagged. But their version of rigorous checking and ours likely looked very different.

Onstage, Leo confided to the talk show host and the audience of what would be millions when this was aired about the birth of his new son. The crowd cooed and shouted congratulations, some demanding a name which I knew he wouldn't give. Neither Leo nor Viola were willing to give baby Torran's identity out completely.

Two camera operators worked large devices on tracks between the stage and the rows of staggered seating. One moved into my eyeline. I shifted to see past, continuing my person-by-person search. Every face. Every member of crew, the audience, and any hanger-on.

On the far side of the studio's seats, in the sixth row, a figure shuffled back. As if hiding or keeping a low profile.

My pulse spiked.

From all I'd been doing with Ariel, both in reality and all the other things I'd thought and worried about, my senses were ready. Instincts poised to highlight danger.

Making eye contact with Valentine, I tapped my earpiece and slunk off into the wings, circling the stage around the back by quiet corridors. Once I was out of sight, I spoke into the comms system.

"Think I see him. Stage right, sixth row, third in, sitting low in his seat. Checking in on him now."

If I took the same position I had on the other side, I'd be able to see the man clearly without compromising the camera view we'd been instructed to stay outside of. But, if he clocked me watching him, I'd potentially activate the man.

I tapped my earpiece again, my worry increasing. "What's the play?"

Ben acknowledged me. "Talking to the studio now to get a name."

While recording, we had strict rules to follow. The studio had its own security team who managed the audience and waited at the edge of the stage, closer than we were allowed. Ben had to defer to them to manage any troublemakers—part of the insurance and the rules around Leo's appearance.

But a handoff to them via Ben meant a delay. Another risk we'd identified but couldn't mitigate.

I jogged the final distance, slipping carefully back into the wings across from where I'd just been. Counted the rows and heads.

An empty seat met my gaze.

My pulse spiked. I breathed through my nose, scouring the surroundings and all the happy faces watching the show.

"He's gone," I reported on the line, my concern morphing into panic. "I do not have eyes on him."

"Valentine, flank Jackson," Ben ordered. "Keep it calm."

Leo chattered on, detailing his tour. The name of a song on his new album.

Behind him, beyond the backdrop, a shadow moved.

"Think he's behind the set," I snapped.

"Visual?" Ben asked.

"Negative."

But the picture took shape in my mind, and I couldn't see anything else. The loner obsessed with Leo who'd come all the way here with zero smile or plans to make good memories. He meant him harm. Had been biding his time.

He was going to hurt him.

Just like Ariel's stalker planned to hurt her.

Just like my sister's killer had exacted his plan.

"Pull Leo," I gritted out, then I was running.

Several things happened at once.

Gordain strode into the strictly forbidden filming zone towards Leo, Ben with him.

The producer swore and yelled cut.

Our mark erupted from behind the set with his hand raised above his head.

Already, I was running, dodging cameras and wires to vault the stage. Valentine did the same, calling out his warning. The audience gasped, someone screaming.

The item in the rogue fan's hand flashed in the bright light. A knife.

Launching at him, I rugby tackled the guy. I landed hard, mostly on the murderous stranger, pinning him down, the weapon still in his hand.

He bucked at me. Freed his arm.

The blade curved at me.

Valentine scrambled down with us, landing on the man's arm. "Don't fucking move," he snarled.

The knife clattered harmlessly to the floor.

I stared down at the man under my grip, his eyes wild and a strange keening sound coming from him.

He'd got within metres of stabbing Leo but failed.

Holy hell.

The next hour passed quickly.

Police attended and took the attacker away. The audience was ushered out, the interview over. We escorted Leo away under cover of both us and the full studio security team, and drove him to a waiting helicopter. Gabe was behind the controls, and we swapped a grim look.

He flew Leo and Gordain home while we retreated to the cars.

Ben sent Valentine away in the first, opting to have me as a passenger in his.

He got us on the road for the three-hour drive north and uttered my name after minutes of silence.

"Are ye okay?"

I shrugged. "I'm fine. Didn't get hurt."

Perhaps I was okay right now, but when the adrenaline wore off, I wasn't so sure.

"I didn't just mean physical injuries. It's my responsibility to care about your mental and emotional health. What ye did was incredible, but I'm also aware of the parallels with your past. If ye need to talk about it—"

"I'll find someone to do that with," I finished for him.

"Raphael, perhaps."

I shrugged again.

He gave it up, letting me keep my thoughts to myself.

My mind conjured Ariel. More specifically, all the things I'd imagined doing with her. A far better form of therapy than talking about the past would be losing myself in her body, in her list. I had energy to burn and a fuck ton of angst from memories I didn't want creeping around the back of my mind.

My resolve not to touch her shook.

"What did I say about your instincts?" my boss asked, drawing me out of my thoughts.

"What?"

"They're superpowers. That's shite I can't teach. Don't ever doubt yourself again."

# 14

## Ariel

Gabe and Effie arrived at the house, announced by a chime from the new cameras. I peeked at the screen then ran downstairs to let them in.

We climbed the spiral stone stairs.

"Has Raph spoken to Jackson this afternoon?" my older brother asked.

"Not that I heard, why?"

"There was a knifeman at Leo's appearance today. Jackson intervened."

I stopped dead.

"What happened? Was he hurt?" Raphael demanded from the stairwell above.

Gabe squeezed past me and finished the journey. "Gordain said not. He caught the arsehole before he got close. No one was injured."

My shoulders slumped.

My brothers jogged on up, talking.

Still on the stairs, Effie tilted her head at me. "Ye okay there?"

"Yes, sorry. Go on up. I'll just be a minute." Without making eye contact, which would give away the effects of my racing heart, I disappeared back down and sat on a stair, taking out my phone.

*Ariel: Are you all right?*

If he'd been messed up by it, he wouldn't come tonight. I wouldn't get to see him. Raph wouldn't leave.

It was only concerns for his safety that bothered me. Practical stuff on behalf of my brother who cared about him. Nothing more.

His reply didn't keep me waiting long, though it felt like an eternity.

*Jackson: I'm outside. Let me in?*

My heart leapt, and I flew down the remaining steps, throwing open the door, though I kept well back from being seen.

There he was, pink-cheeked from the cold, a sports bag on his back and his gaze fixed on me. Jackson entered, kicking the door closed behind him.

Neither of us spoke.

Hunger. The sense overtook me. That and relief.

He advanced on me, muscles locked, his gaze on my lips.

I took an instinctive step backwards. "Camera."

Jackson stopped short, and his gaze darted to the new installation over our heads.

*God.* If he'd been about to kiss me, I would burn up in flames.

Footsteps drummed above us.

"Jax," my brother yelled.

In a heartbeat, he was there and drawing his friend into a backslapping hug.

Raphael peered at Jackson's face. "Gabe was just telling me what ye did, diving on stage to tackle a knife-wielding fan. Holy shite, ye fucking madman."

He guided Jackson upstairs, taking all his attention with him. But as he passed, my brother's best friend caught my hand in his. Brushed over my fingers.

Then he was gone.

More slowly, I followed them up the two flights to the living room. A seemingly reluctant Jackson had all eyes on him while he recounted the story, describing what he'd done to a dozen questions from my brothers. I settled on the sofa beside Effie. She nudged me with her shoulder and gave me a curious and subtle chin lift.

Effie was the big sister I'd always wanted. My role model and guide. There wasn't much I kept from her, but right now, I didn't have anything to share beyond stolen kisses and flirtatious text messages.

I'd gone from an open conversation at my birthday party to something narrower and more meaningful.

It wasn't a bit of fun anymore. I didn't know how to explain it.

I wrinkled my nose, conveying that there was no news. She shrugged easily, and her attention returned to the wider conversation.

"How does it feel being a hero?" she asked Jackson.

He pulled a face. "None of that. I only followed my job description. How are things on the slopes?"

Effie grinned. "Normal. No heroics there. Trying to change the subject?"

A sheepish smile spread across his stupidly handsome face. "Busted. But according to my watch, we've only got an hour until Raph needs to leave, and there's business to get down to."

Raphael heaved a sigh, raising both eyebrows at me. "True."

We had the call with our father planned.

It was the very last thing I wanted to do.

After we'd settled in Scotland, I'd blocked out memories of my previous life. At least with my parents, I'd mostly been successful. I didn't want to think about that time. Didn't want the reminders of their horrible relationship and how Dad behaved.

The man was a snake, but a controlling, effective businessman, too. For several years, we'd had semi-regular phone calls with him, starting with the one which negotiated him leaving us alone.

The only reason we'd kept contact was for the sake of Azrael, our little brother. None of us could stomach the idea of him growing up not knowing who we were. Yet in every conversation, our father bemoaned the fact that none of his adult children were part of his business, though he meant his sons. He'd complain about how family was everything and outright ignore my challenge that girls were just as valuable as boys.

He'd never once apologised for what he did to me.

Not only for the marriage contract but for the neglect, the way he just didn't care about me. Mostly ignored my presence.

He was a difficult and mercurial character, and I needed to extract information from him to save my neck.

My siblings shared the same expression of distaste.

I curled in on myself. "I know this was my idea, but I've been dreading it. Does anyone have an idea of how we approach Dad?"

"We need intelligence," Gabe started. "If we ask him for it directly, he'll demand something in exchange. So either we try an indirect approach, or we're prepared to give up something."

"What will he ask for?" Jackson asked.

I gave him the answer. "A visit."

Jackson's eyes flashed a warning. "Ye can't go to him."

"Not from me. He's only interested in my brothers. Gabe first, then Raphael. It's a matter of pride for him that he doesn't have control of his sons and isn't able to show them off. Gabe used to work for him. He's never been quiet about wanting him back."

Gabe swapped a look with Effie. "On the subject of families, and before we continue, there's something we need to share."

At last. My heart lifted.

He gestured for his wife to proceed.

"I'm pregnant," Effie announced, rubbing her hands together. "Three months gone. Baby Gordonson is due in August."

I gave a happy laugh and squished her lightly. "We wondered when you'd say."

Gabe squinted. "Ye knew? How?"

Raphael grinned broadly. "Maybe we're just perceptive. Or maybe you've wrapped Effie in cotton wool for weeks and have been entirely distracted."

Gabe's usual serious expression lifted, and joy shone out. "Guilty as charged. All I can imagine is our wee lad or lass."

"I'm going to buy them their first snowboard," I claimed.

"God, can ye imagine a tiny Gabe on a slope?" Raphael laughed.

It was a source of great amusement to us that Gabe had taken forever to learn how to board, and even now was pretty shaky.

Jackson gave his own quiet congratulations. Raphael moved to wrap Effie in a careful hug while I did the same, though less carefully with my older brother.

"About time you joined the dad gang and expanded this branch of the family," I quipped.

He smiled back, pride and a deep sense of satisfaction in the way he watched his wife. "The timing was right. Or so we thought."

I nudged him. "It's still right. Dad won't ever get to play grandfather. Nobody will tell him."

Raphael took my place and diverted both prospective parents' attention with a question. I sat next to Jackson.

"Congratulations, auntie," he whispered to me, shifting closer.

I warmed. The guy had me too mixed up.

Earlier, when I'd searched on his name, I'd stopped at the list of results, the sense of intrusion too big for me to handle.

The headlines had floored me.

His sister had been murdered by an ex-boyfriend when they were teenagers. There had been a manhunt. Jackson had been part of it, including posting video appeals to her kidnapper.

A still from the video had been a thumbnail on my screen. A much younger version of the man by my side, his expression stricken, bleak.

I couldn't imagine what he'd been through, or why he'd been the face of the appeal, and I didn't want to read on when it was his story to tell.

I wondered if he was now an only child. If he'd never get to be an uncle.

I was almost certain if I asked he wouldn't talk about it.

Too much crowded my mind, and I wasn't able to summon an answer. Jackson dragged his gaze off me, smiling at some joke Raphael made.

All too quickly, we calmed, the less happy subject of Dad hanging over us.

I got up, directing my family.

"Gabe and Raph, you'll need to be there in the background otherwise he won't bother talking to me, but don't speak, if you can avoid it. I'll handle him. I'm going to ask if he remembers my problem then take it from there."

Jackson pressed a fingertip to my arm. His touch burned.

"Feed the questions slowly. Don't give him any more information than we know Larson's gathered. If he has sent him to hunt ye, then they have gaps in their knowledge. They knew enough for Larson to be hunting in the right area but no more."

"Noted. I just want to establish if he's in on it," I said. "He raised me for fourteen years. I'll be able to tell something from his reaction."

We arranged ourselves in the room to keep Effie and Jackson out of shot, then set up a phone we used only for this purpose. It only had one number stored.

I pressed it, and the video commenced.

The screen blipped, revealing a smiling, older man with

a boy of seven beside him. The family resemblance between us and the duo on the screen was undeniable. Dark eyes and hair, the same defined features.

But in Dad's face, there was none of the warmth or kindness I knew from my brothers. I couldn't have said what ruthlessness or cruelty appeared like in a facial expression, but what hid under his smacked of it.

"Hello, Dad," I said. "Hey, Azrael. Look at you! You're so tall."

Our father smiled, crocodile-like. "Gabriel, what a surprise. Raphael, well, well. Both my older sons together. I was just giving your brother a lesson. The only child of mine who wants to spend time with his old dad. Give me a moment and we can speak in private."

I sighed, pursing my lips as Dad hustled Azrael out of his office, calling out for Willow, his wife.

The image of the family man. All apart from the gun in pieces on his desk. There was nothing normal about the weaponry lesson he'd apparently been giving our brother.

He returned and settled. "To what do I owe the pleasure?"

"I have a problem," I said.

Dad's focus shifted on the screen. Of course he hadn't been looking at me. "Ah, my Ariel. Always the difficult one."

That was so far from the truth it was astounding. Under his roof, I'd been a model daughter. Snarky, sure, but I'd never rebelled.

I gritted my teeth. "Do you remember at school I had an issue with a boy?"

"What girl doesn't? All those short skirts and the man-trap makeup." He chuffed a laugh. "Gabriel, catch me up, how's business these days?"

"I told you about him," I continued, louder. "It was the

only time I'd troubled you with concerns over school."

Dad's smile shortened. "It's been years since you lived here, Ariel. Why would I remember something like that? Should've kept your legs closed if you didn't want male attention."

My breath caught. One of my brothers growled.

Across the room, Jackson stiffened, his jaw tight.

Summoning words was hard. "Can you tell me if you're familiar with the name?" I ground out.

"What name?"

I watched him like a hawk. "Landon Larson."

Everyone in the room seemed to hold their breath.

Dad cocked his head. "I'm not sure. Gabriel, why sit there in silence? Did this Larson person offend you in some way?"

Gabe didn't reply.

Dad swapped his prong of attack. "Raphael, my second born. Cat got your tongue, too?"

"It was my question, Dad," I interjected.

He gave a testy huff. "Sounds like a conversation for your mother, not your father. Why do you bring this question to me?"

"He's a man of interest to me."

"In what way?"

"I have something to talk to him about."

It was a game, conversing with him. He was evading answers like a pro. But he wasn't denying anything, merely sidestepping.

I waited him out.

"Gabriel, please, let your old man be of use to you," he ordered. "I'm no detective but I have contacts who could help."

My knee jumped. "You can help by telling me what dealings you've had with him."

Dad spread his arms. "Without details, I really can't do anything."

"You're useless to us if you don't know him," I pushed.

His lip curled. A tell that I'd pissed him off. Not only was I being rude to him but I'd taken ownership of my brothers.

When he spoke again, it was precise and measured. Without switching his gaze off the screen, he slotted the pieces of the gun on his desk together. "What are you now, Raphael, twenty-one, twenty-two? Still into guns? At ten years old, you were as good a shot as me. You'd be an asset to the family business if you returned."

I sensed Raphael's flinch. The same horror sank through me.

I gave it one final and desperate attempt. "Can you just give me the contact details for Larson? A phone number? A handler?"

"You already stated I don't know him. Ariel, don't make me repeat your words." He smiled, and this time, at last, it was for me.

I knew this was coming.

He'd sensed an opportunity and he wasn't about to give anything up for free.

But I didn't anticipate the cost.

That ask was Raphael. Our father had laid out his terms.

I had to get off the call. "Then I guess you won't help. Got to go."

Dad didn't hasten to stop me. Instead, he simply raised a hand. "Speak soon, boys."

The line disconnected. He'd hung up on us.

# 15

## Jackson

Ariel turned to her brother, her face pale. "I'm sorry that happened. I should've just called him by myself and not let him see you."

My friend wrinkled his nose. "He wouldn't have even spoken to ye. I'm not worried. Don't assume he's rattled me."

I sat forward. "For the sake of me being an outsider, did he just offer information on Larson in exchange for ye working for him?"

Raphael nodded. "Basically. My sister's safety for me returning to the fold."

Hatred and frustration bloomed in me. In university, he'd confided that his father's world scared the shite out of him. Raphael was strong and fucking smart, so for this to shake him told me just how bad things had been when he'd lived there.

"That's never going to happen," Ariel breathed.

"Agreed," I said. "What was your take on whether he knows anything or not?"

She sighed, her gaze searching the middle distance. "He knows the name. He said 'I'm not sure' rather than no. It's harder to tell if he owns the guy or not. If he makes contact claiming to have discovered something, that'll be the answer."

She looked to her brothers for their views. Both gave glum agreement.

But I didn't imagine she was about to sit around and wait. I held my question about what next, because if she'd wanted her brothers in on a plan, she would've said.

Raphael checked the time. "I need to hit the road. The last fucking thing I want to do now is leave for a week."

Ariel set her jaw in a stubborn slant. "Don't. You have to. You'll be qualified, and your hard work will be behind you. I'll be perfectly fine here, and we'll keep you updated. Don't worry about me."

She was holding in emotion. They all were.

Silently, Raphael gathered together his things.

Gabe and Effie gave their goodbyes then left.

My friend lifted his chin at me. "See me out?"

I descended the steps, carrying one of his bags to his car while he carried the other. Outside, lightly falling snow settled on his beanie hat.

"I didn't want to say this upstairs because I know how my sister will react, but I have the worst feeling about what Dad's up to. My money is on him employing Larson to try to take Ariel."

"For what reason?" I already suspected the worst.

"He could've had another marriage offer, and he'd happily punish her by selling her off. Or it's because of me. I'd do anything for my family. Anything. I don't have his ruthlessness and I can't cut off my emotions."

"If he has her, he can control ye," I replied slowly.

My friend's expression turned bleak. "Exactly. If I'm right, he's given up on Gabe and is biding his time coveting his next in line. It fits, too, because he's making this attempt right at the point where I am going to be of most use to him as a qualified pilot. I'm the risk to her safety." He tore off the hat and tossed it into the car, his dark hair askew. "What if I don't go today? If I'm not qualified, I'm less valuable."

I stood taller, my sense of outrage in full flow. I didn't like where his thoughts had gone. Didn't like the implications he was stretching towards. Raphael dreamt of flying. It was part of his identity, the subject of his university career where he took aviation while I laboured over computer science. His degree was a calling. To not fly for a living would cut him off from a core part of himself, and that wasn't happening to my best friend.

I shook him to get his gaze back on me. "Now listen, for the next week, you're going to do exactly what Ariel said: Think only of your exams and impressing the fuck out of the people testing ye. You'll ace it because you're a fucking amazing pilot, and you'll do it for yourself, aye? Ariel and I will live safely here, and no fucker will come anywhere near her. I promise no bodily harm will come to her. Understand? I've got her, and you've got this. The rest we'll work out when you're done."

Raphael took an unsteady breath.

"I swear nothing will happen to your sister," I repeated. Whatever she was planning, whatever steps she'd take to move the situation on, I'd be there.

"Fuck. Okay. Love ye, man."

He punched my shoulder and climbed into his car.

"Raph?" I said, pausing him in shutting the door. "What's the difference between God and a pilot?"

He heaved a sigh, the corner of his mouth tipping up, though he fought it. "I don't know. What's the difference?"

"God doesn't think he's a pilot."

Raphael concealed a laugh, flipped me off, and sped away. Hastily and without another glance, as if hesitation would change his mind.

In the tower, with the door locked and the world kept at bay, I stole back upstairs. My phone rang again with my mother calling. Entering the living room, I glowered at my screen and let the call go to voicemail, tossing the phone to the couch.

Ariel was nowhere to be seen.

I poked my head into the kitchen, not finding her there.

A noise suspiciously like a sob came from downstairs. I must've walked straight past her in her room. Jogging back down, I called her name.

She answered me, her voice thick. "I'll be up in a minute. Raph said something about leaving us some food in the fridge. Help yourself."

Like I'd walk away.

I tapped on her bedroom door. "Are ye decent?"

For a week, I'd be sleeping in the room next to hers. This was going to be torture.

"Yes," she replied.

I pushed the door open to find her approaching. She kept her head down even as she dashed away a tear with the side of her hand.

My heart ached.

"Ye did good," I reassured. "Handled him like a pro."

"I exposed my brother to a threat. I can't believe I was so stupid."

"No. You're in danger. Your father exploited that. Raphael's status hasn't changed in any way."

She sniffed, still not looking at me. "I don't know why I'm upset."

"Your dad just treated ye horribly. You've every right."

She inclined her head. "He was always like that. Gabe and Raphael were his golden boys. He invested time in them. Spoke to them and sought their opinions and respect. I was nothing to him and I'm still not."

Emotion rocked me. I breathed out through my nose. "You're important."

"Or just a pawn, only useful for men to move around a board. Just...ignore me. The feeling will pass, and I'll be myself tomorrow."

"No," I said softly.

Ariel lifted her focus. Our gazes linked.

"No?" she repeated.

"No, I won't ignore ye. That's impossible. I'm here to do the exact opposite of that."

I couldn't bear it, seeing her upset. I'd never once witnessed Ariel cry in the past so couldn't start to imagine the childhood trauma this had raised. I'd just promised her brother I'd protect her, and right now, she was spiralling.

Reaching out, I caught the loop of her black jeans and tugged her towards me. Ariel stumbled onto my body, both hands flat on my chest. She stared at me, as amazed as I was by my move.

I hadn't intended to touch her. Had no business getting this close.

"What are you doing?" she asked.

"I have no idea."

"You know, it's too bad you turned me down." Then she swore gently and pushed up to meet my lips.

Instantly, my eyes closed, and every other sense went on high alert. Ariel kissed me. Her tentative and slow action drove a wave of need through me, and she angled to better connect our touch.

Fuck it.

Fuck every ounce of resistance I'd held on to.

She needed the distraction, and I'd made a promise. The tight hold I had on my control was lost.

A deeper press sent me crazy, and I tugged her closer, letting our kiss ramp up. Ariel endangered my reason. Her soft lips on mine were my new favourite thing, and I just wanted...

No, it was too intimate. Couldn't allow it.

I gripped her arms and tore my mouth away, needing to draw a line between the fucking yearning in me and the comfort she so badly deserved.

"Ye have a choice," I forced out. "We've been messing with each other, and I'm here for ye in whatever way ye choose, but it's been one fucking nightmare of a day for ye, so I know exactly where I want to bury my face to get your mind off it. If you'd rather I walked away then that's fine, too."

Her wide eyes took on a stunned look.

"Send me away, or let me give ye what I think will help. Just once. Right now."

She took a short breath. "Okay."

"Here?"

"Here."

In utter relief and need, I sank to my knees, pushing her

against the hallway wall. Ariel took a soft inhale, her fingers lightly touching my hair. Her hands shook.

I plucked at the button to her jeans. "These are in the way."

She undid them. Shimmied out and kicked them away. "What do I do?"

"Let me make ye feel good."

"That's what you need from me?"

I grazed my hands over her hips, lost in lust for the beautiful woman in front of me. Nothing we were doing was in order or following a natural flow. We weren't dating. We'd barely stopped sparking off each other. All I knew was that suddenly, this was right.

I kissed her belly. Another to the line of her lacy underwear. I hooked a finger underneath so the material pulled tight, cupping her pussy. I pressed a kiss directly over the material covering her clit.

Ariel took another short inhale, closing her eyes.

If she couldn't watch, I'd make her feel.

Impatiently, I yanked her underwear down and drew her leg over my shoulder. "If anything I'm doing isn't working for ye," I said, "let me know. Your instruction list said to work out what feels good, aye? Listen to that."

I licked her directly between the legs, at long last face on with and tasting her pretty pussy. Instant addiction claimed me.

Also, I was hard as nails from the first touch of her lips, but she had me that way all too often.

Again, I licked her, circling her clit but not touching that little bundle of nerves. I drove in lower. She was already wet for me, as turned on as I was.

With one hand, I held her hip, keeping her where I wanted her. The other I used to open her for me, allowing my tongue access to every part of her that counted.

I slid inside, nearly fucking coming with the sound she gave up.

"Jackson," she moaned.

"I know, baby. I've got ye."

Moving back, I sucked her clit, easing a finger inside her at the same time. She bucked against me, penetrating herself further on my hand. I added a second finger to her tight channel.

All the while, I built up a rhythmic pull on her clit.

There was so much at stake in how I related to this woman. In keeping her safe, in my friendship with her brother. None of it mattered as much as reaching the finish line right now.

My fingers made an indecent noise, thrusting in and out of her. My mouth flooded with her flavour. She tightened around me, and my fucking dick pulsed in sympathy.

I wanted a bed beneath us, time to worship her properly, the ability to explore every inch of her. Memorise the lass. But all of that was out of the question. We had a week together—more than I'd ever spent in the close company of a woman I wanted.

Safety meant limits. If I followed my instincts, this would go too far, and I needed to layer up a defence for my heart. Ariel didn't want more, and neither did I.

But I could fucking make her come for me.

Every other thought fled my brain but getting her off.

On cue, against the stone wall of her hallway and out of sight of the camera view, Ariel splintered, moaning softly and cursing me at the same time. She went silent, panting. I licked her until she stopped me with a grip of my hair.

God, I wanted to continue.

But this was all we needed. I jumped up.

Pressed a kiss to her cheek.

"I'm going to hunt out the food Raphael made us. Come on up when you're ready."

She hid her eyes with her palm. "Take my brother's name from out of your mouth after what you just did to me."

I couldn't help my laugh but I stopped myself from kissing her again.

Then I jogged upstairs, rinsed off at the sink, and got on with prepping her dinner.

# 16

## Ariel

I couldn't get the flush of pink from my cheeks. Stunned, confused, *relaxed*, I cleaned up, found new underwear and my jeans, and returned upstairs.

Facing Jackson after he'd so easily blown my mind was a hurdle I'd not anticipated.

In the kitchen, he had his back to me, plating up two steaming bowls of a winter stew Raphael had made, fresh-cut bread already buttered on a sharing plate.

As great as the food looked, I got caught on my bodyguard's form, watching him in a way I'd never allowed myself to in the past. The stretch of his dark T-shirt across broad shoulders. How it showcased a muscular, strong upper body. How his hair had been cut to a neat line across the back while left a little wilder and messier on top.

I'd dug my fingers into his hair while he'd been on his knees for me. His tongue had been inside me. What would his dick be like? How would he feel bearing down on me, my legs around his waist, pressure building

"Hungry?" He interrupted my thoughts.

"Yes," I breathed. I cleared my throat, making a second attempt that didn't sound so needy. "I mean, that looks good."

He glanced at me, and his lips tweaked in a smile. "It does." He gestured for me to sit and set down my bowl. "We have things to discuss."

"What kind of things?"

"Living together, what we'll do when I'm working. The plans you're brooding over to catch your stalker."

I choked on my first bite of chicken.

Jackson smirked, waiting me out while I took a drink of water he'd helpfully poured.

"Why do you assume I've made plans?"

"Call it a hunch."

I speared a hunk of carrot and ate it. He wasn't wrong. My mind hadn't rested since I'd accepted I was in danger, realised after Daisy's ex-housemate had given me the stalkerish information, then from my own father's machinations. But I hadn't concluded much. Nor did I want to involve my brothers anymore. Both had their own concerns.

I swallowed and focused on Jackson. Talking about this was far easier than addressing other things we'd done.

"All right. I don't have any real plans but I am going to do something." I gestured at the kitchen and the living room beyond. "I can't stay stuck inside all day, every day, sitting idle until a stranger takes action. Tomorrow, I'm going to help Daisy paint her spare bedroom, but that's the sole thing on my agenda. How long can I hide for? A week? Three? If my father or someone like him wants me, they'll wait me out. In the meantime, I'll go insane."

His gaze darkened. "I'm not here as your keeper but I'm

begging ye to talk to me before doing anything. I promised your brother I'd keep ye safe, and that wasn't just for his sake."

I didn't get the last point he made, but I shrugged it off. "I'd be stupid to ignore my bodyguard's help."

Jackson abandoned his food and reclined in his seat. "Is that all I am? Your personal security?"

"What else do you want to be?"

He didn't answer, only glowered.

I tried again. "I'm not looking for a boyfriend, and you refused my offer."

"The sex deal? What, too embarrassed to say it after grinding on my face?"

I pressed my lips together, irritated by his little smirk. So much about this man set me off. He frustrated my senses and drove me crazy. Even the arrogant slant of his jaw while he waited me out had me wanting to leap on his lap to kiss the expression off his face.

Like he'd read my mind, his eyes shone.

His phone rang on the table.

At the same second, mine did, too.

Jackson checked his screen and flipped it over without answering.

Mine was Bridgette's mother calling again. I did the same.

"We need to be friends," I finally said after the phones had quietened. "Without benefits, which was your call, but if we're going to live together and share this space, we need to find a way to coexist."

Slowly, he commenced eating again. "Okay, friend. Who's ringing ye?"

"The mother of the student whose video gave Larson my location."

"Why?"

I took up my bread and dipped it in the rich stew. It tasted divine. My brother got an A-plus for seasoning. "She says I owe her money because the instructor spotlight video was earning big for them. I'm choosing to ignore them both for now. Who's calling you?"

Jackson curled his lip.

"Your mom again?" I guessed.

He inhaled a deep breath, and for a moment, I assumed he wasn't going to reply. But he surprised me.

"She wants me to visit this weekend. Last time I saw her was two years ago."

"Two years?"

He inclined his head. "I didn't answer her calls then either. She came to my dorm building."

"She doorstepped you?" I shuddered at the idea of someone turning up unannounced.

"The horror, I know. Luckily Raphael was there, and he stayed with me through the whole duration, so..."

"It wasn't so bad?" I concluded. I had no idea what a family looked like after the violent death of one of its members, but my instinct said it should've brought them closer, like I was with my brothers since our parents threw us under a bus.

"It was still fucking painful," he confessed. "I just had company to get drunk with after so I could forget."

My phone rang once more.

I checked the caller—the mother again—and groaned.

Jackson gestured to it. "Give that here, friend."

I handed it over. "Why?"

"Can I answer for ye?"

I stared for a beat, my lips parted. Then I gave a single nod.

Jackson accepted the call. "Ariel's phone. No, she's not available, and I don't think she'll care you're interrupting your holiday to blow up her phone again. Since one of her students took illicit videos of her and endangered her life to an internet predator, she's not taking calls."

Silence met his words. Then babbling, the mother scrambling over her reply.

"You're sorry, great. I'll pass that on," Jackson replied. "What? No. I'm not asking her that. Got to go."

He hung up, trying to hold back a smile.

"What did she want?" I asked.

"A favour. Something to do with checking in on their house. Want the details?"

I clucked my tongue. Bridgette and her mother were new to town so probably didn't have many friends to ask. Or maybe they just lost them easily. I wasn't about to bend over backwards for them.

"Not right now."

Jackson watched me. "Was that friendly of me?"

I burst out laughing. "Maybe on a par with the thing you did downstairs."

"Damn. Then my skills aren't what I thought they were."

His eyes twinkled, and my breath caught.

"What was the thing you're not going to ask me?" I said in a rush.

"Something to do with her house. I'm not repeating it. She's wasting her breath making more demands of ye."

I got on with eating my dinner, unwilling to give him anything more than had already passed. There was nothing wrong with his skills, but I wasn't confessing it. Something about Jackson had pulled me towards him from the very first time I'd seen him. That had just been a crush, unavoidable as he was so pretty, but it had only gotten worse with him giving me the cold shoulder.

Now we were on new ground altogether. He'd had his face between my thighs. He'd made me come. First guy to ever do that. My cheeks heated at the thought.

Across the table, with a clean bowl in front of him, Jackson groaned in what sounded like dismay. "Don't blush like that. Stop remembering things."

"You're the one who did those things. I can't unmake the memory."

"It was a moment of madness."

"Not to be repeated. I get that. I'll just have to recall every little detail when I'm alone later."

I jumped up and took my plate to the sink, smiling to myself while running the tap.

Jackson joined me, and we moved into a quiet but efficient clean-up of the kitchen. It was strange having someone else by my side as I worked, as my brother and I split the jobs by days, never getting in each other's space. Jackson even mopped the floor, swiping at my feet to make me smile.

It was cosy.

Warm and safe.

I didn't hate having him around.

In the living room, with the lamps on around us, I dropped onto the sofa and checked my messages. "The garage sent an update on my car. They've already fixed the damage and said I can go pick it up tomorrow."

His eyebrows dove together. "It's better if it stays there. Though I have the urge to check it over again."

"The mechanics would've been all over it, and the police found nothing."

"Doesn't mean there's nothing to find. We'll go together and talk to the mechanic, so long as you're happy to hide."

The lightness that had settled over him during dinner faded, and a warning played out in my mind.

Jackson and I were going to be around each other every day. Our spectacular blurring of the lines had left me more confused over him than before.

He rose and crossed the room to pick up his bag, carrying it back to me. He brought out an item from inside. A phone like his.

"Yours. You'll need to give the number to whoever needs it, but it's secure and untraceable, apart from with my team. It'll also work everywhere."

I turned it over in my hands. "Can I log in to my group chats on here?"

"Who are they with?"

I exhaled breezily. "Dozens of boys I'm flirting with."

Jackson gave me a dark look.

I laughed and gave up the truth. "Work. My family and friends. My girls."

I'd be lost without them. Earlier, there had been a long debate between Casey and Viola over the best ways to get pregnant, the other women chiming in with ideas and suggestions.

As the day went on, the ideas got smuttier.

I was learning so much.

Jackson nodded. "It's fine. Even if you're on social media,

the phone won't let anyone track ye."

"Apart from you."

He held my gaze for a moment then reached into the bag again. Next, he extracted a small box. "Your birthday jewellery."

My pulse rate had picked up from his proximity, and I set my hand to my chest. "So sweet of you."

Jackson snorted. "Sweet? I'm really not. If ye knew the thoughts I was having, you'd think anything but."

I smirked, picking up the box and examining the metal bracelet inside. It was a fine chain with a tiny charm on it.

I picked it up and stared, my mouth open.

The silver charm was a fox. A tiny, curled-up version of the foxy jewellery holder I had on my bedside table.

"Did you pick this?" I asked.

Jackson inclined his head.

"Why that animal in particular?"

The faintest smudge of red appeared on his cheeks. "I had to pick something for the tracking device, and I once saw a fox figurine in your bedroom. From the doorway, I mean. I haven't been snooping in there. It stuck in my mind. It suits ye."

For some reason, my heart raced. I sat back, splaying the fine bracelet over my fingers, the curled-up fox held tight on the wire.

"I love it. I don't think anyone has ever noticed that about me before."

"That foxes are your thing? Bold, curious, pretty creatures?"

I hopped up and collected my notepad from the table. The pad I'd written my list in, but that page had been torn out and was safe in my bedroom. I showed Jackson the fox print cover.

It was an odd connection, but it had stayed with me regardless.

I couldn't stop a fresh rush of feeling that he'd noticed.

"The figurine in my bedroom was from my mom," I explained. "It had been her mother's, and after she left, I asked my father if there was anything of hers I could keep, like jewellery. He said no, but I found this. I don't know why I wanted it or kept it. I don't want memories of her."

I trailed off, still staring at the sleeping fox.

I loved it. It meant something, and I wasn't sure what.

"Did ye ever see her?" Jackson asked softly. "Raphael never said."

"She's alive. She married a Mafia man who was a rival to the people Dad worked for. She upped and left, turning her back on us completely and never called after. It was no big loss. We were only ever accessories to her."

The picture in my head was vivid as it was stark. Mom in a pretty dress, her dark hair tied up, her eyes dry, and suitcases around her. She'd fled without saying goodbye, so it was a made-up image, but one my childish mind had created to mark the separation.

A newer memory struck me.

I frowned.

At the same moment, Jackson tilted his head. "Your da mentioned her on the call."

"I just remembered that. He said what I'd asked him was a question for my mother, not my father."

"Do ye think that was meaningful?"

"Everything he says is. At the point Larson assaulted me,

she was gone and we were not in contact. There's no reason for him to suggest asking her."

"Would he have told her what happened to ye?"

"Dad never mentioned her apart from being disparaging. He used to talk about our stepmother's body and say how sexy she was compared to his saggy ex-wife. That kind of thing."

"Unlikely they were chatting regularly about family matters, then." Jackson exhaled, his intelligent gaze still fixed on me. "Ye said ye didn't talk to her. Was it not allowed?"

"She never tried."

"Did ye?"

I wrinkled my nose. "Why would I? She left me. Not the other way around. I doubt she even cared that we left the US, if she even knew."

"I'm not saying ye owe her anything. I thought ye might have needed closure. That kind of thing."

"Is that why you haven't blocked your mom?" I pushed back.

Jackson shrugged. "I'm naw challenging ye. I'm curious over whether there's any path of contact and why your da mentioned her."

He'd sidestepped the question about his family and left me pondering my own. Just like I didn't want that connection, I hadn't meant to turn into a mournful little soul and spill my heart out either.

"I guess we'll never know." I shook my head, tossed the pad to the coffee table, and replaced the bracelet in its box.

"I can swap out the fox for something else," Jackson said.

"No need. I'll wear it. Can you fit it to me now?"

"We'll do it at the hangar tomorrow. Need a welding kit."

I set it aside, shrugging off the weight that had come with talking about family history. I didn't dwell on the past. There was no point.

"Sorry, I didnae mean to bring ye down," he said.

"If I'm sad, will you make me feel better like you did earlier?"

Fire blazed in his eyes, but he looked away, hiding a smile. "No, Ariel."

"So what do we do all evening?"

Jackson sighed, reclining. "I brought my laptop to do some work. I still have some avenues to explore in building up a profile of Larson and I want to check in on that stolen car. Why don't ye get familiar with that phone and find your group chats?"

He fetched the laptop and dragged the coffee table closer, setting up to work. He could've taken it to the kitchen table and been more comfortable, but he stayed near me.

I liked having him close.

Really liked being able to steal peeks at him.

Enjoyed the half-smiles when he noticed.

After a while of chatting with my girls once again, learning all about the SMEP method of getting pregnant that Casey was trying, I brought my attention back to him.

"I meant to thank you for all you're doing," I said. "The patrols. Searching buildings. I didn't know half of it."

Jackson's gaze flicked over me, the laptop screen lighting him up.

I jumped up and trotted downstairs to my bedroom. Fetched the list from my bedside table and returned upstairs. Placing it on the sofa between us, I carefully added Jackson's number to the new phone.

He glanced at what I was doing. Noticed the page.

I tapped out a message, and it buzzed on his phone.

"What are ye doing?" he asked.

Taking my phone and the sheet of paper, I pushed to my feet and went to the door.

Jackson had awakened something inside me that I couldn't contain.

I wanted him. Needed to explore him like he'd done with me.

All this polite hedging around each other was driving me mad, and there was zero chance I'd be able to do it for the next week.

"Guess my code and you'll find out."

# 17

## Ariel

I watched the *message read* notification on my phone.

Jackson had taken the bait.

It wasn't a difficult one, but that didn't mean he'd obey it.

IYWM, CTMR.

Silence from upstairs. I held my breath.

In my room, I'd turned on my lamp, the space cast in an orange glow. I always kept it tidy, and my bed was big and comfortable, with a patchwork quilt at the bottom I pulled over my duvet on the colder nights. But right now, I was anything but cold.

Fever streaked through me.

I'd been the lucky recipient of Jackson's mouth earlier. But according to my list, I needed to reciprocate. We needed to do it together. Drive each other crazy until we were desperate.

Perched on my bed, I shook.

There was so much to try, and the week ahead was the perfect opportunity to do it. I'd offered, he'd refused, I'd told him we weren't going to talk about it, then he'd gone down on me. The push and pull was unending. If he didn't appear now, I would be done with asking. I'd put away the raging hormones and save them for someone else at a time when I wasn't in danger.

*If you want me, come to my room,* I'd asked.

A sound came. A footstep. More.

Oh God.

Then a figure appeared in my doorway.

Jackson stood in the frame, that same energy coiling around him that I was rapidly growing addicted to.

"Cracked the code," I whispered.

Nerves caught me.

He noticed. His shoulders sank an inch, a more hesitant expression blooming.

No, I wasn't doing that. Not putting him off because I was scared. Aside from my fear, my body was buzzing, heat lighting me up. I was alive with total lust, my breasts heavy and a growing ache at the juncture of my legs.

I jumped up and marched over. Took his hand and yanked him inside, closing us in. Then I guided him back to the bed. Knelt in front of him on the rug.

Jackson sat on my quilt, his gaze locked on me.

Neither of us spoke.

No sounds but the rush of blood in my ears.

If I said another word, I'd give away my utter panic and he'd run a mile. Instead, I picked up the sex list sheet and held it up, tapping a finger to the second part of the top line.

I was going to blow him.

Jackson focused on the words then took a shuddering inhale. But he didn't budge.

This was on me to own.

Like he did to me earlier, I took hold of the waistband of his jeans and popped the button, relief instant that I didn't fumble it or the zipper. Gesturing for him to lift, I pulled his jeans down his long legs, leaving him in just his black boxer shorts.

I stripped those, too. His dick sprang free, already hard. Ready for me to do what I wanted to it. Wide-eyed and intimidated, I wrapped my hand around him. He was velvet-soft over a steel shaft. But so big. Obviously this would work. Everyone had sex. Except the size of him... Fitting him inside me...

Jackson's hand slid around mine, our fingers interlacing. Guiding me, he pumped his shaft using my palm. I watched and learned, squeezing him gently, loving each little sound he made.

"How does that feel?" I asked.

"Fucking magic. I don't want to do anything that scares ye."

"You won't."

I copied the action, gripping him with the same pressure he'd shown me. Jackson released me and reclined on his elbows, his gaze half-lidded and on me.

Leaning in, I licked the end of his dick, still moving my hand.

"Fuck," he drawled.

I did it again, encasing him in my mouth. He tasted divine, and I wondered if that flavour was unique to him. Reaching for his hip, I shifted in until I was between his spread legs, positioning myself better to go deeper.

A virgin I might've been, but I'd watched porn. I knew the theory well ahead of anything practical.

Flattening my tongue, I glided him into my mouth, grazing him with my teeth before I worked out how not to.

Jackson panted and jacked his hips.

Holy shit. I liked every reaction. They took my blooming lust and sent spirals of pleasure through me, chasing pathways to every inch of skin I needed him to touch. This was why a blowjob had made the list. Not because it was a basic opening act, but because it felt so good. And not just for him.

I repeated the act, sucking him down. In the back of my mind, I knew there was no chance I'd be any good at this, not at the start. But he wasn't telling me to stop.

Then his ultra-hard dick pulsed. The taste of him spread over my tongue.

Jackson withdrew from my grip and grabbed both my arms, lifting me from the floor and onto him like I weighed nothing. He kissed me, harder than before, drifting his hands down my arms to constrain my wrists behind my back. Lightly, so I could break away if I wanted, but showing me his intent. That he was owning this.

"I can't watch ye suck my dick without wanting to come in thirty fucking seconds," he said, pressing his lips to my cheek. My throat.

I bared my neck to him, fresh pleasure driving out from the touch of his mouth to my pulse point.

Braced over him, I lost myself for a long moment with his kisses hot on my neck.

"I want to make you come," I whispered.

"There's no chance ye couldnae," he said in return, close to my skin. His words quiet but carrying weight. "What I don't get is why ye picked me."

Surprise caught me. Surely he knew how drop-dead gorgeous he was. There was no way women didn't tell him.

I freed my wrist and palmed his face. His stubble scratched my fingers. Earlier, it had grazed my inner thighs. I waited for a beat until his gaze rose to mine, then kissed him.

Each time we'd kissed had been different from the last. This one carried new emotion. Passionate. Hot. Open-mouthed and wet.

Trapped between us, his dick fitted between my thighs. I took hold of it and jerked him. Jackson broke the kiss and dropped his head back.

All the encouragement I needed.

I slid off him and knelt between his thighs again, getting my tongue back on him and discovering a new, salty taste. In small degrees, this man was revealing himself to me. Not just the competent, smart bodyguard, and the loyal friend, but someone with sensitivities and worries of his own.

Jackson had depths.

I was going to blow him to discover them.

Gripping him, I encased him in my mouth once more, instantly moving. I curled my tongue around him and sucked, building up the pressure. Jackson gasped then urged me on, his hand taking hold of my loose hair.

He was so swollen and hot. His dick stretched my lips the further down I got.

I peered up to find him staring, the fiercest expression on his face. God, that was erotic. It branded an image in my head I'd use when in alone time with just my hands and a vibrator.

It spurred me on. I picked up the pace, adding pressure.

His dick pulsed again. He bucked his hips.

"Fuck. Ariel. I'm going to come. Pull away if ye don't want it in your throat."

No chance I was getting off him.

I'd started this thing and would see it to the end.

Jackson came with a broken cry. A rush of cum coated my tongue, and I swallowed, losing my rhythm. He gripped my head to hold me still, jerking through the last of his orgasm.

Holy hell.

Warmth pooled between my legs.

I'd never experienced anything so *significant*. So huge as giving pleasure this way. It felt like such a gift to be shared with another person.

In a matter of hours, I'd advanced my sexual knowledge massively. I'd gone from thinking about it to doing it, or having it done to me. I wanted more. Needed to burn through my list and have the time of my life doing it.

Happily, I sat back and wiped my mouth with the back of my hand.

But Jackson's expression when he centred his gaze on me was anything but relieved. Some emotion held him that I didn't quite understand. Confusion? Regret? I shuffled back, and he reached for his clothes with hurried movements.

He was still hard when he buttoned his jeans.

Then he stormed from the room without a backwards glance.

What the hell had just happened?

A new flush of heat decorated my cheeks, but it was made of embarrassment, because somehow, what had felt so good had gone bad.

I climbed into my bed and drew the covers over me. It

wasn't that late, but tiredness followed my confusion.

I fell asleep with a knot in my gut from getting something so wrong.

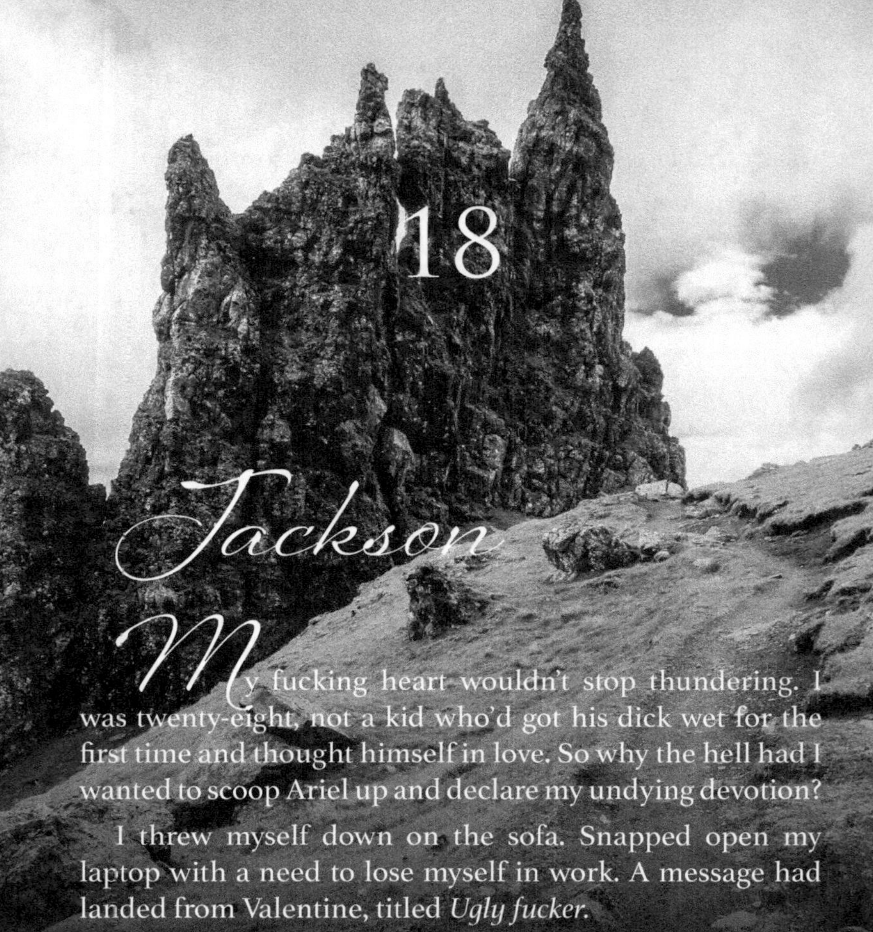

# 18

# Jackson

My fucking heart wouldn't stop thundering. I was twenty-eight, not a kid who'd got his dick wet for the first time and thought himself in love. So why the hell had I wanted to scoop Ariel up and declare my undying devotion?

I threw myself down on the sofa. Snapped open my laptop with a need to lose myself in work. A message had landed from Valentine, titled *Ugly fucker.*

I opened it to find three colour photos, taken from a good-quality CCTV camera. They showed two guys from different angles. One in a loose basketball kit and with shaggy hair, the second taller and in a T-shirt and trousers.

Larson.

Holy ugly fucker.

I dialled him. "Got your intel. That's our guy?"

"Daisy confirmed. The one in the shorts is her pothead roommate, Justin. Larson's the other."

"When was this taken?"

"A few months ago when Daisy was still living there and

he was sleeping on the couch."

We'd asked Daisy to try to recall dates she remembered Larson staying over while hanging out with her roommate. After that, it was a simple call to the building's maintenance office to find someone who'd get hold of the camera footage. For a small fee, of course.

Ben had talked me through the process for when we needed to get intel on people who'd repeatedly threatened Leo. If they had a relevant criminal record or history of doing this with other celebrities, they were fair game. There was always someone who'd give over information or pictures so we could make a file.

It was the first time Valentine and I had worked it through, but it had been a success.

I studied the face of the man who had scrubbed himself from the internet. Memorised him. Small eyes. A long chin with patchy facial hair. Now, we had him from three angles.

"Exactly as I pictured him," I said. "He screams creep."

"A face women should run from and men need to punch," Valentine agreed. "Can ye show it to Ariel? If she last saw him when she was a kid, he'll have changed."

"She's asleep, so in the morning."

There was a pause, then Valentine returned, not so cocky. "All okay over there?"

"Why, is the bunkhouse lonely without me?"

"Naw. I can scratch my balls without ye throwing a cushion at me. I just mean ye sound tense."

I was tense. Stressed to fuck over emotions that were far bigger than they should be and wouldn't stay in their fucking corner. Saying that out loud would make me sound insane. "It's fine. I'll bring Ariel over to the hangar tomorrow so we can fit her bracelet. Then we're going to see her car."

"She's not taking it back, is she?"

"No, it's been repaired, and I just want to see it again."

He paused. "Bug sweep?"

Shite. That's exactly where my mind had gone, though I hadn't fixed on the idea. I sat forward. "Through a mix of luck and judgement, Larson ran into her car, assumed she was in it but found it empty, then took off again without lying in wait for her. We searched for him, but he was gone, ditching his ride to avoid detection. Why leave when he had no other leads? Of course he meant to track her," I said, cold sliding through my veins.

Her car would lead him right to her.

"Thinking like a good little stalker there," my colleague said.

We hung up, and I sat back, awash with better feelings.

My job was to protect Ariel. Now the fog had cleared of the fucking incredible orgasm she'd given me, I could see again. She needed my help, not my fucked-up headspace and panic over whatever set me off in her room.

Even if I had to break part of myself, I'd be what she needed.

# 19

## Ariel

A hand gripped my throat, fingers clawing, nails digging in. I sat bolt upright in the dark, flailing out an arm.

Into empty space.

I snapped on my lamp and swept my gaze over my room, my palm to my racing heart.

I was alone, of course, but the sense didn't leave me like it had done the past few times I'd woken in a panic.

Despite the silence of my apartment, something was wrong. It could've just been a bad dream, again, but I wasn't able to relax. Instead, a spiral of panic gripped me.

On my phone, I pulled up the camera feed for the exterior of the tower and then the hall. Both were normal. No one creeping around in the shot. Nothing appeared out of place. Jackson's car with a fresh coating of snow and ice sat to one side of the outside view, and I watched it, then alternated with staring at the curving stone steps.

I was losing my mind. Utterly spooked by nothing at all.

My bottom lip trembled, and emotion threatened. I hated this.

This was my home. I wasn't going to be afraid. On trembling legs, I climbed out of bed, the cold air wrapping around me. Then I padded to the door.

Opened it.

The low-level proximity light sprang on in the hallway, activated by my door opening.

At least that told me no one had just passed by.

From my phone, I knew it was after three in the morning. If I was trying to kidnap someone, I'd leave it until then. Late enough that everyone else was asleep but before the early risers got up. The perfect time to make an attempt.

A creak came from beside me.

I jumped.

Raphael's door opened, and a messy-haired Jackson appeared, the room behind him dark.

God, I wanted to burst into tears. I clutched a hand to my mouth, holding it in.

"What's wrong?" he asked, the tiredness leaving his features instantly.

"I don't know," I squeaked quietly. "I'm probably imagining things."

"But something woke ye?"

I gave a shaky nod. "It was probably just a bad dream."

"Go in your room. Lock the door," he commanded.

I did, then heard him doing something next door. His footsteps returned to the hall then up the stairs. After a few moments, they drummed back down.

A text came from him.

*Jackson: Upstairs clear.*

I sank into my cushions and nest of blankets, bringing up the camera footage once more. Now, his shape moved on my screen. Jackson descended the spiral stairs, slowly but confidently. In his hand, he carried some kind of bar, I guessed as a weapon.

At the bottom of the steps, he opened the door. Then he exited, locking it behind him.

I sat up, swiping from one camera to the next.

In the exterior view, in just his T-shirt and boxers plus his boots, Jackson looked left and right then set out, prowling beyond his car and out of sight.

Oh shit.

I didn't like this. I hadn't expected him to go out on his own. What if he got jumped?

Minutes passed, and my fear rose. I twisted the sheets in my grasp.

How long did I wait for him to come back into shot before I...what, went out after him? Called Callum or one of the other men who lived in the castle building?

Waking up others meant a delay in getting help. Jackson was out there alone.

I leapt from the bed and snatched my jeans from my chair.

If it was just him versus one other man, there was no way he would lose.

Unless he was taken by surprise.

There were a whole lot of shadowy places to hide out there. I had a good kick to me. If he needed backup, I'd be able to help.

Snow-covered gravel crunched on my phone, the camera

feed still running.

I grabbed it up again to see Jackson return into the shot. He stopped in the tower's doorway and waited, scanning the direction he'd come and around to the other direction.

Then he came back inside, locking up once more.

*Jackson: All clear downstairs and outside.*

I exhaled and sat down hard, discarding the jeans I hadn't yet put on.

I'd sent him out in the cold on a wild goose chase. What a scared little mouse I'd become. All over nothing.

Ashamed, I moved to my door.

A tap came, followed by his voice. "It's me. Open up."

I did, embarrassed. "I'm really sorry about that."

"I'd rather check than not."

Cold emanated from his skin. I reached out and touched his arm.

"You're half frozen. All because of my overactive imagination."

Jackson shivered and set his hand over mine. "Don't apologise for me doing the thing I'm here to do. If ye wake, I'm there. If you're afraid, my job is to make ye feel safe again."

Other emotions warred inside me. Thoughts I'd had after he'd practically run from my room earlier. I didn't want to voice them.

Jackson continued. "Are ye okay now?"

"No," I confessed.

He paused, his fingers curling around mine, still on his arm. "Want me to stay with ye?"

My soul leapt, but at the same time, I knew it wasn't what

he wanted. "Yes, but also no. Not after…" I gestured between us and dropped my hand.

He sighed. "Would it help if I apologised for earlier?"

"Maybe. What happened?"

He pointed inside my room. I returned to my blanket nest, and he followed, locking the door.

Jackson stood over my bed. "Can I get in?"

I shuffled to the side. My bed was made up for two, though I'd only ever shared it with Daisy on a couple of occasions.

Jackson claimed his side, leaving space between us. "Light off?"

I leaned for the lamp switch, plunging us into darkness.

Silence held for a long minute.

His voice pierced the dark. "I haven't slept with anyone in a long time. I got freaked out. I was scared I'd say or do something wrong."

"Like what?"

"Not sure. It overwhelmed me, though."

I turned in his direction, curled on my side. Finally, my heart had stopped thumping. "I looked you up online."

He stiffened. "Yeah, I figured ye would. Or someone else would and tell ye what they found."

"I didn't read past the headlines. It wasn't my business to find that out without your knowledge, so I butted the hell out. But if you ever want to talk, I'll listen."

Jackson sank back into quiet.

He went for so long without replying, I thought he'd fallen asleep.

Then his low voice returned. "No one wants to hear that

degree of shite."

My stomach tightened. The air in the pitch-black room seemed to warm. "I offered, didn't I?"

"I dislike secrets, and I hate people talking about me. That makes me want to close up."

"You don't owe me anything."

Jackson leaned in and kissed my hair, finding the right place easily. "I disagree. Right now, I'm sorry for fucking up. Let's get some sleep."

I thought him wrong. That I'd never sleep with him there.

But I did. Darkness embraced me, and this time, I didn't dream at all.

# 20

## Ariel

Warm arms held me, and a firm, big body curved around mine from behind. In my half sleep, and with faint light in the room telling me it was morning, I gently arched my spine, pressing more into Jackson's embrace.

He was still out cold, yet so wonderfully hot.

Somehow, in our sleep, we'd moved together, connecting up and fitting perfectly. It should've been weird to wake up to, but instead, I only felt protected and safe.

Turned on, too. His forearm tucked under my breast. If he drew his hand back, he could caress me. Feel my hard nipple through the shirt I slept in.

Then there was the matter of his dick. The rigid length of it rested against my ass. I'd already got up close and personal once, and it had me wanting so much more, particularly in this heavy, sleepy state where all of our antagonism and angst was absent.

I flexed again, grazing him.

He exhaled, burying his face deeper into my hair, his lips on the back of my neck. His hot breath sent a spiral of lust through me, the wave of it delicious. My body craved release. I ached to turn around and fit my mouth to his. Or have him reach between my legs and feel me up.

Pull my shorts to the side and just fuck me.

Like he'd heard me, Jackson tightened his hold, grinding into me from behind. His hand moved to my hip, giving me a squeeze that I felt all through me.

"God," I muttered.

The word came out loud in the quiet room.

It broke the spell.

Jackson froze. He released me and rolled away, climbing out of bed with a muttered curse.

I sat up, my hair tumbling over my shoulder, my mind still half in a daze made of hormones and want.

Jackson stared at me, then followed my gaze down to where his dick tented his boxers, swore again and went to the door, opening it to half hide his body.

"Morning," I said breathlessly.

"Morning, beautiful. We need to get up."

"Think you already are."

He barked a laugh of surprise. "Not commenting on that. Get your arse dressed, and we'll head over to the hangar."

He stepped out and closed me in, the click of the bathroom light following.

I dropped back onto my mattress and snuggled in the space he'd left, loving the scent of him on my sheets. Dipping my hand between my legs and chasing the good feeling he'd given me would've been bliss. But time was not on my side.

Jackson didn't let me lounge for long, commanding me up and out of bed. I needed longer than him to get ready so gave up my lie-in and got into prep mode.

Considering how infrequent my trips from the tower had become, I was excited to go out. A peek from the narrow windows showed me fresh snowfall but a sunny day. I picked out a warm, close-fitting cream sweater dress that stopped just under my ass and had a matching belt, plum-coloured leggings, and mid-calf grey leather boots that had decent grip in the snow.

To the sound of Jackson upstairs in the kitchen, I applied light, daytime makeup with a lip stain that matched the plum leggings. With my tumble of dark hair, it looked pretty.

At least I hoped it did.

On any usual day, I'd assess myself in the mirror and decide if I was people-ready. Today, I only wanted to be Jackson-ready. For him to give the smallest sign of appreciation.

With a few old clothes thrown in a bag for use when painting with Daisy later, I took my locket from my fox figurine, giving the little creature a pat for luck, then climbed the stairs. Entering the living room, I slid the locket around my neck. But I fumbled the clasp.

The necklace fell from my hand to the rug.

Jackson leapt from the sofa and crouched in front of me. On one knee, he picked up my lost item of jewellery and held it up.

"Weird way to propose," I quipped.

He smirked at me and stood, the necklace in his fingers. "Not sure *marry me* would cut it without a ring."

I turned, and he lifted my hair, brushing his fingers over my neck to clip the locket into place. Then he took my shoulders and rotated me back, checking it was in place.

"Pretty. Is it special? I know ye said your ma didn't leave ye jewellery."

"Daisy sent it to me for my birthday a couple of years ago. It's empty, though. I never put a picture in there."

Again, we stood close together. Enough for me to catch the fresh aftershave he'd applied.

I wondered if he'd taken care in dressing, like I had. Would a guy wear aftershave to work normally? It didn't seem likely, but what did I know?

"Hungry?" he asked softly.

"Actually, no. Not at all."

"Then let's get out into the snow, little fox."

My jaw dropped, but Jackson was already walking away. He'd nicknamed me. I...liked it.

Bundled in coats and thick hats, we left Castle McRae through the back exit. Callum and his wife, Mathilda, were in the great hall with their daughter, Skye. She lived on an island out in the Western Highlands so she wasn't here that much, but her husband, Artair, was Effie's other brother, Brodie being the younger, so I'd been to stay with them a few times. Her son, a tall almost-teenager named Mathe was at her side, and he jogged over to say hi.

I got a hug and lingered for a minute to chat, introducing Jackson.

Instantly, Mathe's eyes lit. "You're a bodyguard? Do ye really get to smash people out of the way for Leo?"

Jackson grinned. "Smashing is frowned upon, but we do have a special rugby tackle for the worst offenders."

"Can ye show me?"

He obliged, demonstrating to the boy.

Skye sidled over to me. She cast a meaningful look at Jackson and raised her eyebrows at me.

"Effie has a big mouth," I griped in a whisper.

"What? I didn't say anything," Skye replied. "But it's true, then."

"No comment. Are ye going to see my brother and Mrs Gossip today?"

This earned me a smile from the beautiful blonde woman. "We are, after we've visited with Viola and baby Torran. Effie said they had news. I can't wait for there to be another new bairn in the family."

I giggled, amused by how bad secret-keeping was in the close-knit family I'd happily found myself in.

A few minutes on and we got away, with me huddled down in the back of Jackson's car. For most of the journey, both of us were quiet.

"It must be nice, having so many people looking out for ye," Jackson said out of the blue.

"We crash-landed in this place, and it was the best thing that ever happened to us."

"Same for me with meeting your brother," he mused. "By the way, I have something to show ye. Finally got a shot of Larson. Do ye want to see?"

"God. No, except also yes, I guess so."

He passed back his phone, open on a photo.

I gazed at the face of the man I hadn't seen since he was a boy.

His face had thinned and hardened, losing its youthfulness. The image had come from an overhead camera, but the angle was good.

I'd never have mistaken him, but seeing him was

something else.

It brought a memory of fear. Of someone overstepping the line so badly it broke my bubble of childhood safety. That had been pretty weak anyway. My father moved in circles where people were killed and women routinely misused. But I'd been more or less safe until the point Larson had decided otherwise.

My happy start to the day dissolved.

We arrived at the hangar, Jackson driving into the structure itself so I could climb out unseen. While he took his car back out, I journeyed through from the open front where the helicopters came and went to the offices built as a block under the domed roof.

As at the castle, familiar faces were everywhere.

Voices called out greetings. Besides those I'd become related to, there were people who flew with my brother or had kids who trained with me on the slopes.

Valentine jogged over, his dark hair tied up in a man bun and grease on his face. "Where's the almighty hero?"

I tilted my head. "You mean Jackson?"

"That's the man. I'd forgotten his name since people started only talking about him with God-like reverence."

From my other side, Jackson appeared, his mouth twisted in wry amusement and his expression patient. "Go on. Get it out of your system."

I produced a smile. No act like his at the TV studio could go down without a healthy amount of piss-taking afterwards.

Valentine smirked. "The king called. You've been urgently reassigned to protect his crown jewels."

Jackson sighed. "Any more?"

"Wait, Jamieson had one."

I leaned into Jackson and whispered, "Who's Jamieson?"

"He's part of Leo's pyrotechnics team. Professional fire starter."

Valentine grinned bigger. "By all means shoot for the stars. Just aim at bodyguard Jackson first."

We both groaned. Valentine led us around the back of the office to a mechanic's desk.

He gestured to the setup on the table. "Am I doing this or are ye?"

Jackson regarded me.

"You do it," I asked him.

Valentine nodded. "Wise woman. I've never tried this before. Probably would weld your arm to the bench or something."

Jackson guided me to sit, readying the equipment on the table. "To be honest, neither have I. I only had the training demonstration to go on. It's low risk, though. I wouldnae do it if I thought it could harm ye."

"I trust you."

He flashed me a small, somehow personal smile.

"Huh," said Valentine in an interesting tone, stepping back. He leaned on the wall, ankles crossed, and his expression curious.

Jackson collected the bracelet box from his jacket, revealing the tracking jewellery. "First I need to measure it around your wrist. It's too long, see. So I'll cut it here and it'll be loose enough so it doesn't dig into your skin but also won't be able to slip over your hand. Next, I'll weld it shut."

He put a pad against my wrist and, using tweezers, held the bracelet together, bringing a framed and tinted screen over my arm. Then he fired up a pen-like device.

"A pulse arc welder," he explained. "Shut your eyes when I say as it'll produce a burst of light."

Jackson set the tip to the broken links and gave the word. I closed my eyes. The arc welder clicked, producing a bolt of light bright enough to see through my eyelids.

"All done," he said.

I gazed down at my new permanent decoration. It was delicate enough to be pretty but reassuring as it couldn't be taken off.

"Now no one can misplace me."

"Exactly what we need," Jackson said.

"Will your team have trackers on your bodies, too?"

His lips curved. "There's no one chasing after us, fox."

Valentine leaned over. "Fox? Ye have nicknames? Revolting."

I rolled my eyes at him. "He means because of the charm. Here."

I held up my arm, and the big man peered at it.

"Okay then, foxy," he drawled.

Jackson stilled, his gaze lowered at his colleague.

Valentine didn't even try to hide a smile. "Yeah, just as I thought."

Jackson ignored the tease and asked Valentine to find something for him while he directed me into the hangar's kitchen for breakfast. My appetite had woken up, so I made use of the coffee, toast, and cereal available.

As I ate, he suggested a change of plan for the morning.

"I have a hunch about your car which makes me think Larson will be watching it."

"It's been in a garage for days."

"True, but also it would take little effort to swing past and see what the mechanics were working on or if the damage has been repaired. I'll go by myself, if you're happy for me to, and I'll wear a camera so ye can see what I'm doing. Ye can hang here with our resident mischief-maker."

Valentine reappeared with a device shaped like an old handheld radio.

I agreed to the plan, and Jackson left us, heading out on his mission. A sense of worry descended over me.

In the bodyguards' office, Valentine set up a laptop. "That's Jackson right now." He showed me a map. "We might not wear trackers like your shiny silver handcuff, but our phones give out a live signal that we can each see."

"I have one of those phones. Am I on there?"

"Naw. Same with Daisy, you're only trackable to a single person. Jackson, in your case, though Ben can switch that out."

His phone buzzed, and he checked it then changed the view on the laptop to a live feed. "Jackson's arrived."

Side by side, we watched the picture change from black to a car park and the reception of a repair workshop. Valentine relaxed in the office chair that was too small for his overly tall body, but I couldn't do the same.

I'd got used to Jackson being nearby. I didn't like him being out somewhere else. If it had been too dangerous for me to go, that meant he was putting himself at risk, too.

Onscreen, he explained himself to the mechanic who I'd already spoken to, and then moved through a line of cars until he came to my Mini.

Jackson produced the device Valentine had found for him and activated it.

"It's a bug hunter," the other bodyguard explained to me. "It picks up the signal from tracking devices. Most phones have a similar feature—under the safety settings, there's an option to scan for unknown trackers—but this one is better."

I shivered. "It's bothering me that you guys even need to have that. How often do people try to track Leo?"

"A lot. Ben told me they routinely discover trackers in gifts, luggage, and even food deliveries."

We both went quiet, watching as Jackson opened the car. He hadn't even got inside when the device gave up a bleeping sound.

I wrapped my arms around myself.

Jackson drew the bug hunter over the front seat then reached under it, extracting a small shiny disk from beneath.

"Holy shit," I whispered.

It was real. Oh God.

But he kept going, circling around the other side to repeat the process. The bleep sounded once more.

Two. My would-be kidnapper had hidden two trackers in my car. Without Jackson, I would've been driving that around without any clue my location was being broadcast.

My stomach cramped.

Still, he searched. In the back of the car, another matte-black tracker had been pushed between the seats. A fourth laid in wait in a shopping bag I'd left in the boot.

That one was shaped like a tiny toy elephant, something a kid might drop. Innocuous but deadly.

Moving away from the car, a grim-faced Jackson appeared on the screen. "I'm going to put them all back where they were and ask that the car remains here."

"Can we use them to draw him out?" I said. "If I get in that car and drive it away, he'll follow, right?"

"No way in hell is that going to happen. It's too dangerous."

I bristled, freaked out by what he'd found and upset by how deep this was going. "It's my life and my choice. I want this over with, and we have a method to bring him in."

"It isn't a bad idea," Valentine said.

Jackson swore. "It's the worst idea. The opposite of keeping her safe."

"I'm right here," I snapped. "Don't talk about me like I don't have a say in this."

The office door opened, and Ben came in. His gaze flicked over me, clocking my no doubt red face, then to the laptop. His eyebrows dove together. "Catch me up."

Valentine gave him a short overview.

The boss of the team nodded. "Ariel has a point."

"Hang on—" Jackson said.

"Ariel has a point, but at the same time, we can do this without endangering her," Ben said. "We'll work out a plan with your input and consent, Ariel, but probably without your direct involvement. But we'll need to do it tomorrow. Valentine and I have an assignment this afternoon. We'll discuss it in the morning. That suit everyone?"

I exhaled, giving him my agreement.

Jackson did, too, then hung up his call.

Ben and Valentine left the room, talking about the work they had on, leaving me alone with just the blipping movement of Jackson's personal tracker making its way back.

And to hell with me if I didn't stare at it the whole way home.

# 21

## Jackson

An accusation I'd had thrown at me in the past by my mother was stubbornness. Once I got an idea into my head, she'd say, it stuck, and no one could talk me out of it.

She meant she couldn't get me to see her twisted point of view when it came to my sister's murderer. That wasn't stubbornness. It was decent morality.

I approached the bodyguard office with Ma's number blowing up my phone. Again. I left it to ring, entering the room.

Curled on the sofa, Ariel watched the view of people busying around the hangar. Ben's office had an exterior window that looked out on the mountains, but this space didn't share that.

The lass locked on to my phone. "Your mom again?"

I lifted my chin.

"Want me to answer it for you?"

It was a challenge, based on the fact I'd taken a call for her last night where I'd aimed to solve a problem. But her facing off with Ma was anything but a good idea.

I shook my head in the negative and crossed the room.

"Sorry I yelled," I said.

"You didn't yell. You just decided exactly how to move me around."

She mimicked plucking up a piece on a chessboard and setting it down on a new square.

I closed my eyes for a second. "You're right. I did."

Ariel's gaze jumped to mine. She waited me out.

"The more of those fucking trackers I found, the more scared I got," I confessed. "The thought of ye being in that car was an immediate 'no' in my brain. I can't explain it any better than that, but I need ye to know I'm not trying to be controlling."

"So you're good with me driving it tomorrow?"

That same instant reaction was on the tip of my tongue, but I needed to rein it in or I'd lose her trust. "No, but I won't get in the way of a plan we've all thought through and agreed on."

Ariel watched me for a beat longer and sighed. "I have no intention of throwing myself Larson's way. I just want this to be over."

"I do, too."

"I know. I'm finding it hard to be rational about any of this."

"Same, little fox."

Her lips curved, just a tiny bit. "I'll try to keep that in mind. Like I said, you get under my skin."

I sat next to her and took her arm, exposing the bracelet I'd welded on. "A tracking device under your skin would suit me, but this will have to do."

She laughed, and it was like the fucking sun had come out.

Ariel got up and walked to the door.

I followed. "Don't know why ye think I'm joking."

"Weirdly, I don't. Now are you driving me to Daisy's so I can get painting, or do I have to hitchhike?"

We got into my car. I'd taken one of the hangar's 4X4s on a circuitous route to and from the mechanic's garage to avoid any risk of detection, but still, I drove to Daisy's with one eye on the hills around.

"Are ye still grumpy with me?" I asked on the way.

"No. Forgiven," Ariel replied from the back seat.

"How long do ye think you'll be at Daisy's?"

"A few hours. Will you pick me up?"

"Whenever you're ready." Then I made an offer, my breath catching in my throat. "I'll cook dinner tonight."

It took a moment for her to reply. "I'd like that."

I dropped her off and retreated to park at a lay-by further down the track. There, I waited, unsure for what but not wanting to leave Ariel's orbit. Imagining I heard an engine. Picturing someone creeping across the slopes of the glen.

She was safe, locked in Daisy's house. I had work to do with Ben and Valentine.

Still, I lingered.

I couldn't shake the feeling Ariel was in constant danger, despite the fact I had no reason to worry about Daisy's place. It was set alone in a quiet glen, a few other houses down the road but far enough away to give a sense of isolation.

Nothing had happened there.

My phone buzzed. Another dragon model picture from my best friend.

*Raphael: This one has armour. That do it for you?*

I laughed, needing the distraction like never before.

*Jackson: Eyes on the skies, my man.*

*Raphael: You think I'd text and fly?*

*Jackson: What's the number one biggest problem for aviators?*

*Raphael: This is a joke, right? For fuck's sake. Hit me.*

*Jackson: Bad altitude.*

I put the Toyota in gear and hit the road, unstuck from my paranoia even if I couldn't stop thinking about Raphael's sister.

She'd be fine.

If she wasn't, I'd be able to find her.

Back at the hangar, I joined a meeting with Ben and Valentine plus some guy who ran tour security in the US. When Leo next played over there, we'd be his personal team but we'd buy in the extra bodyguards we'd need to ensure his safety.

But try as I might, my focus kept slipping. I had my phone on vibrate so I couldn't miss her call, but still, the what-ifs hit me. What if she wasn't able to text me? What if she and Daisy were both in danger?

In the seat next to me, under the cover of the table, Valentine tapped out a message to someone.

My phone buzzed.

*Valentine: Just pull up her fucking tracker, dude.*

I breathed out and did as he suggested. The dot on my phone's map pulsed, showing me she was still in the glen.

Thank fuck for that.

Another message came in from my housemate.

*Valentine: Has she seen you nakey yet? How did the tattoo go down?*

He'd laughed up the tattoo across my ribs after seeing me emerge from the shower a few days earlier. From what we knew about Larson having Ariel's name on him, I knew this question would be coming.

But I wasn't about to answer now.

Ben glanced my way, his brow furrowing at what was on my screen. How I was tracking her. He'd recognise the view for sure. In my interview, he'd made the point of asking me how I'd handle a man threatening a woman under my protection. Implying I had the potential to become unhinged.

He wasn't wrong. No matter what I'd assured him, when it came to Ariel, I couldn't keep my reason.

Still, I stowed my phone and tried to chill.

I was losing my mind, but so long as she was safe, it didn't matter.

# 22

## Ariel

Daisy blew a strand of hair from her eyes, white paint across her nose from a previous attempt. "You're sleeping together, then?"

"Not exactly, though technically he stayed in my bed. And there were...shenanigans prior to that."

She grinned. "My favourite thing in the whole world."

I chewed my lip. Around us, paint dried on the walls. It had taken me a hot minute to bring myself to talk about Jackson. Daisy had been patient, waiting me out, though it was obvious I had more to say than just about the trackers he found this morning.

For some reason, now I'd started, my words about him dried up again, just like the paint.

"Any further news on Mia?" I asked instead.

"I offered her the job. She was thrilled but needs to find somewhere to live for her and her daughter and that's a problem. There aren't many options around here, and she has to leave her current home."

"Right. Because of the trouble she's in. Did she explain any more about that?"

"Nope. I liked her enough to trust that she isn't a bad person and I didn't want to pry."

I'd got that sense, too. "So they need a little house. Maybe there's someplace in the village?"

"Ben's talking to Gordain about it. Apparently there are some old cottages out the other way from the hangar. He started repairs but needs a concentrated effort to make them liveable. He'll ask for volunteers," she explained. "Okay. Back to your news. Did you like what you and Jackson did together?"

"God, yes."

"Do you want to do it again but you're worried about asking?"

I pointed at her with my paintbrush. "Yes! Exactly that. How did you know?"

"Because it's hard giving yourself over to someone like that. It takes either trust or a complete surrendering to the moment. You don't fall into that last category, at least not when it comes to people, so it's nice to know you trust him."

"That part's easy. He's been vetted already by my brother and Ben. They both like him."

There was also the fact Jackson was slowly opening up to me. I was dying to know what had happened with his family, but at the same time, receiving that amount of information felt almost dangerous, though I had no idea why.

"Is there any point where trusting someone too much becomes a bad thing?" I asked.

"Only if they're a bad person who turns that around and uses it against you. Like you know all their secrets, therefore you're now also responsible for fixing them."

Jackson didn't fall into that category. He didn't rely on anyone as far as I could see.

"I like him as your sexploration buddy," my friend said.

"Say that word again?"

"Sexploration. Sexplore him until you're both exhausted."

I laughed and dipped my brush in the paint, continuing on down the line of masking tape. We'd made good progress, and the paint had gone on nicely, only the edges left to finish. When we were done, there were cookies waiting, cooling on a tray downstairs.

A knock echoed through the house.

Both Daisy and I went still.

"Was that the front door?" I asked.

Daisy furrowed her brow. "I think so. No one's ever used the knocker before, so I've never heard it."

She trotted to the hall and peered out of the window.

Her gaze slid back to me. "No one's there."

"Any car?"

"No."

"Could the breeze have done that?"

Her doubtful expression gave me the answer.

My heart rate picked up.

I checked my phone for a message from Jackson in case he'd returned early. There was nothing.

The same fear I'd had a dose of during the night returned.

Daisy jogged to another window and stared out into the bright afternoon. "I can't see anyone, but that was definitely a knock." She stepped back to me, her fingers twisting together. "You stay here. I'll go downstairs and have a look around."

"No, don't do that," I said fast.

Panic coiled in my belly.

I could picture it all in my head—Daisy leaving to check, her vanishing and not responding to my shouts, me following and scared out of my wits for her but also for myself. Picking people off one by one had to be a tactic, and we were not going to fall for it.

Daisy focused in on me then quick-stepped back and closed the door of the bedroom we were in, her movements jerky. "Shit. You're right. We heard a knock, but no one's there. In a horror movie, that's a lure."

"Isn't it? We can't separate. Don't leave me."

"Never. We're smarter than that."

Taking up my phone, I sent a quick message to Jackson.

*Ariel: Can you come to Daisy's? I think someone's here.*

Typing the words felt ridiculous, alarmist, but the choice was us investigating ourselves or getting him to come out and do it. I knew the decision he'd want me to make. My stance on being independent and not a pawn came with responsibility for my safety. I wasn't taking any risks.

A thud sounded downstairs.

Daisy and I grasped each other in fright.

"Does this door lock?" I asked.

"No. Get in the closet," she whispered.

At the back of the room was a wide built-in wardrobe with a heavy old door. We hadn't gotten to painting in there yet, and we crept inside, closing the doors.

Daisy sent a message, too, the screen casting her face white.

Not all that long ago, we'd been worried about someone

taking her. Now I was certain it had been because of me. My family, my fault.

She gripped my fingers.

We both held our breath and listened.

One of the very best things about her home was the perfect calm of the surroundings. There was no people noise, only birdsong and nature sounds. Different from my tower at Castle McRae with a general sense of being near others.

It made the creak downstairs all the louder.

Daisy sent a second message and held up the screen to show me what she'd written to Ben.

*Daisy: We're hiding upstairs. There's someone in the house.*

The one above it, asking if he was able to take a break and stop by, hadn't been read.

I checked my messages. Jackson hadn't replied either.

I wrote in my phone's notepad for Daisy to read.

*If they're in a meeting, they might not see for ages.*

She took my phone and wrote back.

*What do we do? Someone's downstairs, right? Do we rush him and try to get outside?*

I couldn't deny I was spooked. We'd both heard the sound, and it had been purposeful. A knock for attention. A lure, as Daisy had called it.

Horror movies weren't my thing, but I got a flash of the kind of mind who'd want to terrorise someone else. Larson had been beneath my notice as a teenager, or I'd pretended so. Now, I couldn't make the same choice. If the man had been so obsessed with me to not only track me down but to do so in a manner designed to scare me, that was something else.

As I read it, a message pinged up on my The Girls chat group. Casey, not working my shifts today, had shared pictures of her and Cait plus a couple other moms with their kids, hanging out at her house.

She lived in the glen, too.

An idea came to mind. I wrote it out for Daisy.

*What if we get the moms to come here? Make a lot of fuss and noise outside. It'll scare him off.*

She nodded quickly, and I jumped to the chat, tapping out my request.

Instantly, Casey was writing back.

*Casey: OMG! On our way. Don't move.*

We didn't plan on it.

Huddled together in the wardrobe, both of us listened for any sound from outside.

The minutes stretched on. In the strappy top I'd stripped down to paint in, I shivered, the cold day and the unheated house only half of what gave me the chills.

I hated this. It wasn't my personality to hide away. I wanted to fight, but equally, I didn't want to come face to face with Larson.

Admitting it wasn't easy, but I was scared of him.

Seeing his photograph this morning had made him all the more real. Coupled with what else I knew—the tattoo, the trackers, the crashing into my car—it pointed to a dangerous man.

If he found me here, what would stop him from grabbing me and taking me with him? Not Daisy. She was no match for him, same as I wasn't. Maybe together we'd be able to keep him at bay.

A creak sounded nearby.

My heart raced, panic overspilling.

That had been in the hallway outside the bedroom. He was here. Inside the house and up the stairs.

It was too late for anyone to get here to help.

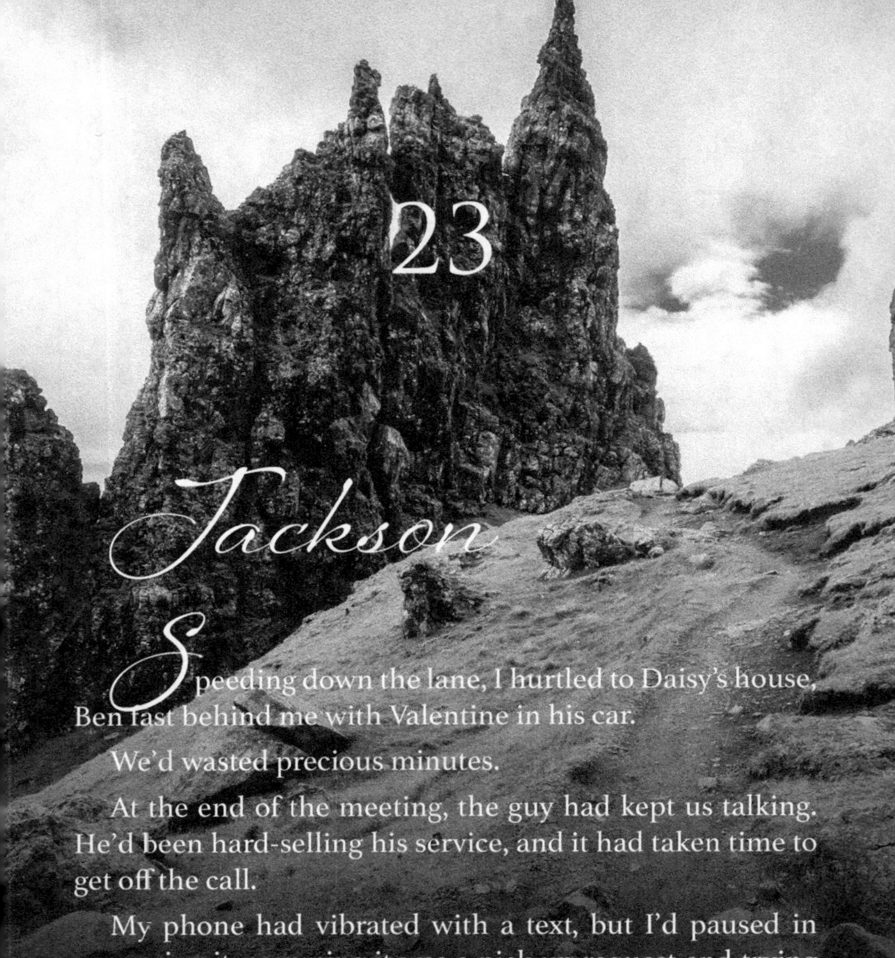

# 23

## Jackson

Speeding down the lane, I hurtled to Daisy's house, Ben fast behind me with Valentine in his car.

We'd wasted precious minutes.

At the end of the meeting, the guy had kept us talking. He'd been hard-selling his service, and it had taken time to get off the call.

My phone had vibrated with a text, but I'd paused in answering it, assuming it was a pick-up request and trying to be professional in front of my boss.

But seconds had passed, and the guy hadn't shut up. I'd snuck a look at Ariel's text.

Then I'd taken off, running.

Ben must've got a similar one from Daisy as he'd sworn and been right behind me.

I couldn't think about that. Couldn't think about the reaction I was showing and how bad that looked for my career here. All I knew was I needed to get to her.

I pushed my car to the limit, taking the corners fast.

At last, the cottage came into view.

Two vehicles were parked outside. The front door was open, and a figure stood in the frame.

I identified Casey, one of the lasses who lived nearby.

Another woman rounded the corner of the house.

I flung myself from my car to the tune of them yelling.

"The moms are still outside," Casey shouted.

"And the cavalry's arrived, too," the other lass howled, banging something against the wall. I was pretty sure she was named Cait, but my brain was empty of all but action.

I sprinted up the path.

"Where are they?" I demanded.

Casey hopped off the step, clearing the way. "Upstairs. She called us in because there's an intruder, but she said in her message not to go inside, just to make a fuss. The front door was open, so he's still here. Hurry!"

I half fell in the door, Ben and Valentine right with me.

"Ariel," I bellowed, pounding up the wooden stairs.

If I found him, I'd tear him apart. Savage his fucking throat.

The landing was empty. The main bedroom, too. I spun around with my fists clenched, panicked. Furious.

"Here," Valentine hollered.

He and Ben had gone the other way. I ran back along the hall and into a freshly painted room.

At the back, Ben was pulling Daisy into his arms. I pushed past, seeking Ariel.

She stood from a crouch in the wardrobe, her expression wild. *Afraid.*

Fuck it.

Fuck appearing professional and pretending I didn't care.

I marched to her and wrapped her in a hug, banding my arms tight around her, pressing her body to mine. Carrying her a few steps away, I brushed my hand over her head.

Speaking took effort.

"Are ye okay?"

For a long moment, she didn't answer. Instead, she just clamped me to her, her heartbeat pounding.

Mine raced, too. It only slowed from holding her.

She was here. Not hurt. Not taken.

A small nod was my reply, but neither of us let go.

Slowly, reality poured in. Behind us, Daisy explained to Ben and Valentine what had happened. Ariel shifted in my arms.

We disengaged.

I gazed at her beautiful face. "Talk to me."

Her gaze sought something in mine. "Someone was here. We're sure of it."

"Ye didn't see him?"

"No, but he knocked, then we heard him walk through the house. Casey and Cait arrived and started their intimidation routine, then you showed up."

I twisted around. "Ben, are there any cameras here?"

His dark glower deepened. "Not yet because we havenae moved in. If it was Larson, why the fuck would he knock?"

There was only one answer.

"A fear tactic," Valentine said. He backed out of the room. "I'll see if the lasses downstairs saw anything. Them being here before us could've saved ye both."

Ariel shuddered.

This time, I resisted pulling her against me. Already, my boss was watching me with concern.

I'd raised his suspicions.

By force, I made myself stand taller. Step back from Ariel.

Ben took up his phone. "I'm calling a search," he announced. "The mountain rescue team had a training evening and were just starting to arrive at the hangar. Daisy, don't leave my sight for a second. Jackson?"

I waited on his command. If he did anything but send me away with Ariel, I wouldn't be able to do it.

Others could search. As far as I was concerned, she was only safe with me.

"Stay with Ariel." He switched his gaze to her. "Happy to go home and lock the doors?"

"Give me a blanket fort and an armed guard and I'll be happy," she replied.

In relief, with my blood rushing and heat burning me up, I tucked her under my arm and didn't look back.

At her tower, we threw off our coats and snowy boots by the door and climbed the stairs.

Around the first corner, Ariel stopped me with an abrupt turn.

On a step higher than me, we were face to face. She reached out, palmed my cheek, and kissed me.

Something broke inside me.

A stop removed.

A dam bursting.

I drove a hand into her hair and the other around her back to hold her still. Then I attacked her mouth. We kissed with a fever, a clash. She stumbled back, and I went with her, dropping us to the stone steps, keeping our connection. Ariel curled her legs around my waist and I knelt over her, the press of our bodies taking this from passionate to desperate.

Her soft lips met mine over and again, nothing sweet in the demands she made. I tongue-fucked her mouth, earning a moan of pleasure.

Dimly, I was aware that she'd brought me down just out of sight of the camera watching her stairs, and I was glad for it. I had lost all reason and control. Her brother getting an eyeful was the least of my concerns.

But something else was. I still needed to be sure of her safety.

"Going to move us, aye?" I told her.

She nodded, matched urgency in how she clutched me.

Picking her up, I carried her up the steps, unable to stop kissing her. Feeling my way with one hand so I didn't fall.

I checked the bedrooms and bathrooms, letting her draw her mouth over my neck so I could see. Then onwards upstairs to the living room and kitchen.

There was just enough light to show me we were alone.

We had the all-clear.

I sank onto the sofa in the cradle of her hips, grinding into her and hating the existence of clothes.

Ariel tore her mouth from mine and pushed me back. I sat on my haunches, my brain engaging just enough to say words I should've already.

"I'm so fucking sorry I didn't get there faster."

She reached to click on the lamp, the warm glow enveloping us.

"You came."

I held in a laugh. "Not yet."

Ariel's pink cheeks flushed more.

Then she took the hem of her top and stripped it. My breath caught. I stared at her tits.

"Tell me what I can and can't do."

"You can do everything."

"Will I scare ye if I kiss your body?"

She answered by reaching back and releasing her bra clasp. The offending item of clothing fell away, revealing heaven. High, round tits, the outline of which I'd glanced at too many times. Fucking jerked off to memories of.

With a hungry groan, I swooped in and kissed the swell of her breast, cupping the other and brushing her nipple with my thumb. Ariel shuddered, holding me closer while I got acquainted, showing my passion for her while keeping it gentle.

The fucking arsehole chasing her had assaulted her like this. I wanted to replace that with my touch.

With my tongue, I circled her nipple then sucked, nearly dying at the feel of her in my mouth. She arched into my warmth. I licked her, switching to the other side to do the same. She cupped her tits for me, squirming under my attention.

"Is this good?" I asked her.

"So good."

"Tell me what feels best."

Watching her, I lapped at her nipple, then sucked. With my thumb, I brushed along the tight little bud, lengthening it.

Ariel's eyes shuttered. "The combination of sucking and using your tongue. God, it's incredible."

I repeated it, working her in steady repetition, loving her squirm. The flush of red across her chest and up her neck to her cheeks.

I'd never done this. Spent time worshipping a lass. I didn't want to stop.

"Take your shirt off," Ariel demanded.

I paused and sat back, shedding the T-shirt and nearly tearing it in my haste. Exposing my bare chest.

My heart hammered from more than just being turned on.

I'd worried about this.

Valentine had laughed about it.

As expected, her gaze set on the black script across my ribs. Like the drunken moron I'd been at the time, I'd got a woman's name inscribed in my skin. My sister's. A memorial to her, done when I was eighteen and so deep in grief and loss with my family imploding that I wanted the pain and the permanent scar to match what I felt inside.

I tensed, waiting for her judgement.

Ariel traced a finger over the letters. Then she kept going to reach for the waistband of my jeans.

"These, too," she ordered.

"Are ye sure?"

"If you don't get inside me in the next thirty seconds, I'm going to die."

My soul leapt out of my body. I stood and stripped my jeans and underwear, my dick fully hard and doing all the thinking for me.

In turn, Ariel stripped her lower half, baring her fucking knockout body to me as she reclined on the cushions. Long legs, gleaming skin, a soft belly. I wanted to devour her.

Spend hours on every inch.

But, under her spell, I waited on her word.

"Now, Jackson," she ordered.

"Ye want me to fuck ye? I can make ye feel good without that."

"Don't make me ask again."

I crawled back over her, dropping a kiss to her knee then another to her belly. She took hold of my arm and pulled me up to bring my lips to hers. When she kissed me, she reached for my dick. Fitted it to her entrance.

All thoughts of taking this slow went south.

I jacked my hips and slid inside her.

Oh fuck. God. She felt phenomenal. Hot and tight, gripping me.

Ariel whimpered, clinging on. I enclosed her in my arms, fucking into her until my groin hit hers.

"Tell me to stop if I hurt ye."

"Don't you dare."

Easing out, I glided home again, her body taking me like a dream.

"More," she demanded.

I sat back, needing to see. Needing to witness her virginity lost on my dick. I put space between our bodies and drove into her again, lost on the sight of her body taking mine.

Obsessed. Hopelessly turned on.

"Look," I commanded. "Look what you're doing."

Ariel lifted her head, her lips parted, then her eyes flared and she fell back.

Working her in repeated, slow glides, I dropped kisses on her shoulders, stooping lower to her tits. "You're so fucking beautiful."

She moaned again, curling her legs around me to bring me closer.

I kissed her lips. Her cheek when she twisted to gasp.

It was all too dangerous. Fear of losing her had heightened every sense. Being inside her felt too good, and I wasn't about to embarrass myself by reaching the finish line first.

I travelled my hand down our bodies to the place where we were joined, grazing over the connection. Loving the feel of my hard dick entering her body. Then I came up higher to her clit, circling it with the pads of my fingers.

"God," she uttered.

"No, just your bodyguard."

Ariel gave a laugh that turned into a cry as I drove circles into her sensitive flesh. Yesterday, I'd learned the pace and pressure she liked. Now, I doubled down on that, fucking her with the same even strokes. Caressing her body and deeply in love with the small sounds and reactions she gave.

I'd be of service to her however she wanted. Learn how to protect her without her feeling controlled. Learn how to fuck her and get her screaming fast.

Ariel bucked, her nails digging into my back.

"Tell me how it feels," I asked.

"Strange. Perfect."

Around my dick, she pulsed.

Both of us quietened, the only sounds the hit of my body against hers. Our mouths fused. Our bodies worked together, seeking release. Comfort. Connection.

Then Ariel broke her mouth away, her breathing shuddering.

She was coming.

My dick spasmed too, swelling all the more, but I wasn't ready yet. I willed my control to last out and focused only on her, keeping up that pace. Delivering what her body needed.

"That feeling… What you just did…" She tried and failed to make a sentence.

Ariel arched against me, her control failing. Then she splintered, moaning my name into the tower room's air. Her orgasm gripped me, and I saw her through it, utterly enchanted with the flush across her cheeks, the relief on her face. Then abruptly, I rose, bringing her with me as I sat back with her on my lap.

I hugged her hard.

Never stopping. Riding the high of how tight she'd become from coming on my dick.

In several more thrusts, I spilled into her. My climax had chased hers, and nothing but this mattered. Holding her to me. Her arms and legs banded around me. My dick buried inside her.

I should've pulled out, but that was a distant thought because this had to happen and neither of us had any chance of stopping it.

I'd taken her virginity and come inside her. It was my last defence from a precipice I'd tried to stay away from.

I'd tried to save her from me and the obsession that I feared.

And I didn't regret a thing.

# Ariel

Cooling, I drew shapes on Jackson's shoulder, his strong muscles firm under my touch. Getting to explore him like this was something else.

He had his face turned away from me, his head tucked down.

"You okay?" I asked.

Jackson gave a low chuckle. "I just attacked ye on the stairs and ruined your sofa. Should be me asking that question."

"I attacked you first."

He lifted his head and brought his gaze to me. His blue eyes were hazy. "Hold on to me."

Still buried inside me, my bodyguard stood and carried me downstairs. In the bathroom, he turned on the shower and set me down.

I scooted against the wall, suddenly embarrassed at being naked. Now we'd started this thing, I didn't want to stop, but I also didn't know what to do.

Also there was the matter of his cum dripping from me, a brand-new and unexpected sensation. I'd broken all the theoretical rules I ever set for myself but I couldn't bring myself to care.

I dipped my fingers between my legs.

Jackson tested the water and turned back.

He gave a low growl and crowded me, pressing a kiss to my lips. To the patter of the water falling and the rising steam, he kissed me until I didn't need to breathe anymore. All I needed was him in my veins. His mouth on mine. His heat surrounding me.

Then he dropped a hand to join mine, sliding his fingers over my soaking core. "Love feeling that."

I reached for his dick. Since we'd had sex, he hadn't fully softened and was already rock-hard again now. He groaned, jerking in my fist.

"Want to fuck ye again," he gritted out.

"Do it."

"You're not too sore?"

I shook my head, uncaring about the ache from the rough use. I loved it. Wanted more.

Taking my hips, Jackson turned me so I was braced over the sink. Then he guided my stance wider and fitted his dick between my thighs again. He rubbed his hard length through the mess we'd made.

I curved my spine, ready when he pressed inside me.

Jackson placed his hand on my lower back, taking a position behind me, and began a second onslaught.

Like last time, instant lust bloomed. This was a pleasure I'd never felt before. I'd used vibrators in the past, penetrating myself and eventually liking the feeling. But this was new. My whole body was alive. The act of doing this with an experienced man was unbeatable.

I only needed him more.

Without his mouth on mine, I was solely focused on the feel of him inside me, and I pushed back, needing it harder from this angle. Jackson gave a low laugh and palmed the base of my throat, guiding me to stand upright.

In the bathroom mirror, his big body outlined mine. He took a greedy squeeze of my breasts, and we both gazed at the sight of his hands on my flesh. I looped my hands back and around his neck, twisting to kiss him.

He used both hands on my tits, twin delivery of caresses and pulls at my nipples. Sparks danced along my nervous system. Every part of me on fire for him.

All along, he kept up the persistent action of his hips. A perfect fit of his dick inside me, filling me.

In the steaming-up glass, Jackson's reflection kissed the side of my face, nudging me to watch his hand move down my body to my thighs.

I gasped and reached to wipe the glass clear.

He smiled. Palmed me between the legs, holding me there for a moment then continuing that same action on my clit that had me seeing stars upstairs.

It was one thing feeling it but another entirely seeing it.

I couldn't stop staring.

His dick moving into me. His fingers in a constant caress. I shivered. He paused, then yanked open the shower door. Losing our connection, he guided me inside and under the spray. In the hot shower, Jackson dropped to his knees and fitted his mouth to my pussy, unashamedly loving me with his tongue. The heat added something new to the mix. I put my head back and closed my eyes, focusing on that feeling alone.

He traced his fingers over my thighs then to my entrance, sliding inside me easily.

In minutes, he brought me to the edge and over.

I crumpled, overcome with good feeling. I hadn't even finished when Jackson stood and hoisted me. Automatically, I wound my legs around his waist, and he sank into me again, bottoming out with ease.

He pressed my back against the cool tiles, angling to support us both.

Then he touched the tip of his nose to mine. "Hello."

I giggled, springing my eyes open, dizzy from coming hard and fast.

The whole talking during sex thing had sounded so weird, but I got it. If I could catch my breath, I had a hundred different things I wanted to try. I'd barely touched him other than holding on.

Instinctively, I knew he'd do anything I wanted.

"Need to come again," he said with a kiss to my cheek.

"Like this?" I asked.

He groaned as an answer and set up a fierce pace, sliding in and out of me and getting faster and harder. I held on, unable to do more. I loved this. How close we'd become, and the trust in sharing our bodies. I loved that he knew what to do and could lead the way while I still fumbled.

I was crazy about how easily my body responded to him.

This time, he wasn't touching my clit. Only hammering into me and chasing his pleasure. Yet fresh heat wound in a tight circle inside me. I tucked my face into his neck and concentrated on that, squeezing my thighs and strangling his waist.

"God, love," he muttered.

He slowed from his frantic rhythm to a series of steady hits, shifting back to watch my expression. If I'd wanted to, I couldn't have asked for this. But he read my mind, or my body, and somehow knew what I needed.

I drove my fingers into his hair, tugging him in to kiss me again, a surge of desire guiding me to put all that emotion into the kiss.

Jackson stuttered in his actions. His dick pulsed, and he slammed home.

God, I'd triggered his orgasm.

Mine hit immediately after. A powerful bolt that came from deeper inside me. Open-mouthed against each other, we breathed it out, our chests rising and falling. Bodies alive with the perfect unity while the hot water rained down on us.

I came down from the delicious high with the sense I'd run a marathon or skied for hours. Muscles aching. Exhaustion settling over me in a wave.

"You're perfect," Jackson whispered against my temple, his voice raw.

But I was pretty sure the perfect one was him.

We washed off and dried up with shared smiles and small touches. I was an addict. Now I could touch him, I didn't want to stop.

Still, I had to force myself to back away.

Jackson wasn't mine. He was helping me out in a number of ways, sure, but he'd laid his terms out already. I wasn't looking at a boyfriend. That was fine. I didn't want one. But if we could do more of this? Yes, please.

Upstairs in the kitchen, he poked through the fridge, checking out the limited supplies. Raphael had warned me I needed to arrange a food shop. I just hadn't brought it to mind until now.

Jackson pulled out a broccoli and red pepper, finding chicken in the freezer.

"Sit," he ordered.

I did, with my chin on my hands, content to watch him. The core of my body felt so well used, with a dull ache that made me think of sex every time I moved. My thighs and hips carried the feel of his fingertips.

"I've never done what we just did without a condom," he said.

Yikes. I hadn't thought of any of that beyond just my immediate need.

I raised a shoulder. "My brother had a series of medical tests ordered by Ben ahead of him joining the bodyguard service. Kind of assumed you did, too. Oh, and I've been on the pill forever so I'm covered."

He snuck a look at me. "All my tests were clear. We just acted insane."

I didn't conceal my smile. "I know. But it was worth it."

Jackson abandoned what he was doing and strode over. Dropped his lips to mine. "Good?"

"Amazing. Satisfying."

"Mind-blowing. Life-changing." He punctuated his words with kisses.

I laughed, and he released me, returning to the food. In thirty minutes, he'd cooked a healthy dinner. In ten more, we'd eaten it. I cleared up while he took my place, just watching on, though he kept offering to help.

"I see why my brother likes you," I said. "You're a useful houseguest."

He groaned, palming his face. "Don't mention your brother while I'm sitting here fantasising about ways of fucking ye again."

I stalled in washing the plates, a little lost in the thought.

I'd wanted this—to use the time I had stuck indoors for exploring sex. This was far beyond where my thoughts had taken me.

My mind supplied another image. How scared I'd been hidden in Daisy's wardrobe. I sent her a quick message to check on her, framing a question to Jackson at the same time.

He'd been terrified, too.

I knew from the small information I'd gathered that he'd been part of a desperate search for his sister. He had her name on his skin. This had to be all the more real for him.

I glanced over to find his gaze on me and his expression pensive.

"Did my tattoo weird ye out?"

I tilted my head. "How do you read my mind like that?"

"Like what?"

"Just then, and when we were…"

His lips curved. "Nice to know. Answer the question."

"No, it didn't freak me out. I felt bad because you've been running around after me. Must've sparked memories."

Jackson rose from the seat and crossed the kitchen to stand behind me. He took hold of my damp braided hair and lightly tugged my head back. His lips landed on mine for a brief kiss.

"No, I wasn't thinking about my sister at any point today.

Only ye. There was no other space in my head."

It was dangerous how much I liked that.

He watched me for a moment. "Want to know what happened?"

Holy shit. My heart pounded. I tried to force calm. "If you want to tell me."

He backed off, finding a couple of beers in the fridge, then entered the living room. He settled on the couch in the lamplight and patted the seat next to him.

I curled up, leaving distance between us to give him space.

This was so cosy. An innocuous setup for the pain I knew would come.

"I'll never look at this sofa the same way again," I quipped, tension coiling in my gut, alongside a real need to know what happened to him.

It burned in me.

Jackson smiled, but it didn't reach his eyes. He held up his phone with a picture on the screen. A family beamed back at me. A teenage version of him, a shorter, pretty girl in front of him, and their parents behind.

"Lisa Marie was a year younger than me. My pain-in-the-arse little sister, and my polar opposite. She was bossy, outgoing, and highly social."

"I like the sound of her," I said, examining the still.

She'd *died*. I couldn't imagine how it felt for him to see this photo.

"You'd have gotten along a lot better with her than me." He set the phone down. "Everything was fun to her. She even loved how we'd been named—our parents had been huge music fans. I was named for Michael Jackson, she was named for Elvis Presley's daughter, Lisa Marie. Neither our mother or father considered it weird that Michael and Lisa Marie married in real life. My sister thought it hilarious and used to tell everyone, and I was so embarrassed by her. She used it as a threat to get her way when she wanted a lift somewhere or for me to do her chores or whatever. But she always made up for it, just by being herself. When I was fifteen, I was assigned by my home tutor at school the awkward role of befriending a new boy, TJ."

From the twist in his lips, I immediately knew TJ was the killer. Oh shit, so he'd known him first.

I stayed silent, giving him the floor.

"At first, I liked TJ. Our birthdays were the same week, and we shared the same hobby, so he called himself my brother from another mother. He had a loud personality which was the opposite of mine. He did reckless shite while projecting this wholesome boy image so authority figures loved him. In comparison, I was so buttoned up. We fell away from being friends when I realised he just didn't give a shite about who he hurt in his life. This was after he got fired from the supermarket we both worked at for stealing alcohol and blaming it on a man who couldn't defend himself. When we were a few months shy of seventeen, he asked if he could ask out Lisa Marie. I didn't like it, but I told her, of course. I wasn't her keeper. But I warned her off him. Told her about his petty rebellious acts and his lies. She made a big deal out of my negativity and said if I made a fuss, she'd surface the naming joke again. I pushed her into his arms. They started dating."

He worked his jaw, setting his gaze on something across the room. "She fell in love with him in weeks, but her personality changed. His did, too. He was jealous and possessive, and she stopped seeing her friends because of fear he'd get angry over what she was wearing or who she spoke to. I think he was probably violent towards her, or at least threatening. To all of our relief, she broke up with him the day after his seventeenth birthday when he'd got drunk off his arse and screamed shite at her about talking to his friends at his party. He'd called her a slut. It was her last straw."

He breathed, his focus still not on me.

"A week later, and TJ had been around every night, begging and apologising, but my sister refused to see him. My da had the police come for him, but Ma sent them away. She felt sorry for TJ and blamed Lisa Marie for not handling the breakup well."

I swallowed. "Your mom blamed her?"

He rolled his gaze my way. "It gets worse. After the cops left, Ma told TJ to wait, then sat my sister down and told her that TJ was a good boyfriend, and she'd been wrong in flirting with others. That's why he'd got upset, not that he was in any way fucked up. I couldn't believe what I was hearing. Da yelled that she was blaming the wrong person, and I did, too, but our mother had always had issues with Lisa Marie, picking on what she wore, where she was going, how she spoke. She took TJ's side and backed my sister into a corner, claiming she wanted a peaceful life back and Lisa Marie was holding all of us hostage to her hormones, including her poor ex-boyfriend who only wanted to make things right."

"How could she?" I whispered.

"Easily. She had someone else in her ear, feeding the lines to her. I stood in front of my sister and defended her, and that drew the fire my way. But she stepped up and told everyone that she'd met someone new. A boy she'd been talking to online. Then she walked out, and the next time I saw her was in a coffin."

My heart pounded. I stared at him. "TJ took her?"

"At first, everyone assumed she'd gone to a friend's house to cool off. A message came from her phone saying she needed space and to leave her alone. But the next day, her tutor rang to ask why she hadn't been in class. I'd left that school by that point and was on course to join the military, like my da had before injury retired him. I hadn't any reason to see TJ, who was in the sixth form, and I was glad to not be near him."

I remembered the video on the search results page. He'd put out an appeal for her. "There was a search," I said softly.

He snorted. "It seems so obvious now, but hindsight paints a different picture. Ma rang around her friends, and no one had seen her. By evening, when she didn't return, she got angry, claiming Lisa Marie had gone off with this new boyfriend and was even more to blame for worrying us all. It was my father who again rang the police and got them to start looking. From the moment he made the call, I didn't rest. They took it seriously, forming search parties and going around the houses of all known associates of hers. TJ's da gave him an alibi. He himself acted a victim. He even came to our fucking house and played the aggrieved ex card, saying shite like if only she'd stayed with him, she'd be okay. How dare she scare everyone like this."

He exhaled, his expression so full of pain that it hurt my heart.

"She was already dead. He'd forced her into his car and driven her out to the woods where he took her life by his hands to her throat. He'd done it right after the big argument, then he'd watched on while we hunted, put out appeals, and hoped for her. It was three days until her naked body was found by dog walkers. She'd been out there all that time."

I wanted to hug him, but I didn't know if I could. Jackson's hand shook where he scrubbed it over his face, his gaze lost in the memory. I couldn't even comprehend what he'd been through.

"The speculation online was rife. People blaming me, or my father, without knowing anything about us. The armchair detectives tore our family to pieces," he continued. "It took weeks longer before they had the DNA evidence to charge TJ. Then two years for the trial where he pled not guilty, and every single second of it had to be gone over in excruciating detail."

"All while you were trying to come to terms with it. God, Jackson. I can't imagine how it felt to live through that. Hearing you describe it broke my heart. Please tell me the murderer got life."

"He was found guilty of manslaughter, not murder. His claim that they went to the woods for consensual sex which went wrong was defended well enough that they couldn't prove him a liar. His sentence was laughable because of his age. He's served nine years so far."

Pure anger swirled at how the asshole had forced that court case and got away with a lesser charge. What the family must have suffered hearing it all. And I knew Jackson wouldn't have hidden from the damage. He'd make himself hear every word.

"What happened to you in that time?"

Jackson seemed to come out of his haze, his focus settling on me again. "The military didnae want me, which was a good call because I was a headcase, so I went off on a rampage, getting then losing jobs, drinking too much, sleeping around. My parents split, and Da moved abroad and fell into alcoholism, and there was no home to go back to."

"God. Your mom didn't keep a room for you?"

"She threw out every single one of my possessions, so no, there was no space in her life for me anymore. I ended up in trouble with the police, then by sheer luck, I was given a chance by a young offender's scheme to go to back to education. I was sick of myself so I took the option, and it was exactly what I needed. I studied for a year to get the entrance exams covered for university, then got a free ride on the course I chose, which was a shot in the dark as I had no direction beyond climbing out of the hole I'd fallen in. I worked two jobs, bought my car third-hand so I had somewhere to sleep on the nights I couldnae use the dorm, and found myself again after years of being lost."

"You're amazing," I offered.

He pressed his lips together, looking away. "I've explained more than I meant to. Jesus, ye must be sick of the sound of my voice."

I wasn't at all. It was filling in the mystery block that was the man I'd liked from first sight. Even if he'd driven me crazy after.

"Don't stop. Was Lisa Marie's online boyfriend actually real?"

"There was no evidence of that. She was probably just trying to get away from TJ."

God. My heart panged again, and my thoughts returned to the call he'd avoided. "Did your mom ever show any regret?"

At this, he stopped talking. He chewed over the question for a long minute until producing an answer. "No."

From his tone, I sensed how he was done with the topic. Recounting it all had to be exhausting. "Tell me how you met my brother."

"We shared a couple of lectures. I'd made a vow to steer clear of getting close to anyone. He walked straight through that, adopted me, and took me home for the end-of-term breaks, correctly identifying that I had no one else asking. In the holidays, I used to work catering, serving at hotels or wherever, but finding somewhere to stay was hard, and it was miserable being alone at Christmas. I didn't want to accept every single time, but he always had ways to persuade me. I liked it here a lot. I liked everyone I met and every place I explored. When he first mentioned the word *bodyguard*, it was like the pieces of my life fell into place."

"He's a fixer," I said, proud of Raphael for what he'd done. Jackson had so badly needed a friend, and my brother had been there.

"That's a good word for him."

"Raph took the most damage from our family falling apart. He saw what I didn't when our father was gearing up to sell me off. Dad exposed him to some pretty horrendous stuff, and he had the bravery to stop it and work with Gabe to get us away. I didn't realise it for years but when I did, I thanked him. He's got that gene. He saw you and knew you needed help, too."

Jackson watched me. "He's the best. You're pretty fucking special, too."

There were things we weren't saying. Things that had become increasingly apparent.

Us sleeping together had the potential to mess up their relationship, and from our conversation, it had become all too clear how important that was to Jackson.

He needed the job he had here, the one my brother had talked up and got him excited for. Jackson didn't have a family to fall back on or anywhere else to go. No other group of friends.

A strong sense came over me that I needed to back out of whatever it was we were doing.

I could ruin it all, if things went wrong. It would be my fault, and I just knew he'd walk away rather than make things awkward for me.

Right when I was getting started with him, I had to call it off.

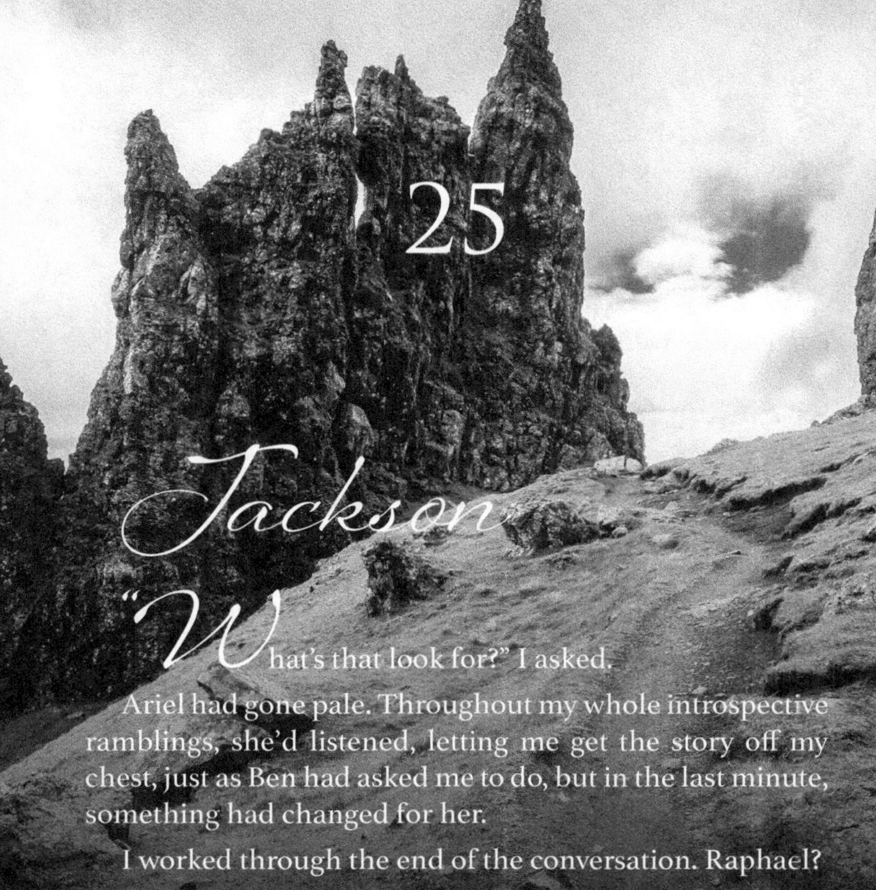

# 25

## Jackson

"**W**hat's that look for?" I asked.

Ariel had gone pale. Throughout my whole introspective ramblings, she'd listened, letting me get the story off my chest, just as Ben had asked me to do, but in the last minute, something had changed for her.

I worked through the end of the conversation. Raphael?

I pinned her with my gaze. "Oh no. Get that out of your head."

She blinked at me. "You don't know what's in my head."

I took her hand and kissed her palm.

"Yes, I do. I can read your mind, remember?"

She flushed. In my imagination, I enclosed her hand in mine and tugged her to my chest. Kissed her again. Spent the rest of the evening doing all the things she wanted to try.

But I was riding a dangerous edge of possessiveness.

During sex, I hadn't cared. I'd taken ownership and claimed her.

A warning played out inside my mind. After everything

I'd just told her, about the dangers of an obsessive man, what the fuck was I doing?

Ariel had given me an out.

For her sake, I should take it.

With difficulty, I forced my lips to move. "Nothing has changed between us. We're better acquainted now, that's all."

"Acquainted," she repeated, her voice strained and her expression unreadable.

"If it complicates things, for the sake of being friends, maybe we shouldn't do that again. But I don't want to feel bad about it either."

She swallowed and glanced away. Nodded. "If that's what you want, I agree."

It was the wrong decision. Everything inside me screamed that I was a fool.

My phone rang with my mother's name on the screen.

I exhaled, frustrated at what I'd done to myself as much as my mother's persistence.

Ariel squinted at the device. "From her position of denial, she's still trying to see you."

"She hasn't stopped."

"Changed your mind about letting me help?"

"No."

I glared at the phone until it went to voicemail.

Ariel wouldn't meet my gaze. Instead, she took up her phone and placed a call.

"Hey, Daisy," she said. She spun away and listened to her friend.

I'd been dismissed.

I hated it.

Even if this was exactly what both of us needed.

I took the opportunity to speak to Ben. My boss relayed the details of the search, ending with nobody found, and advised that he and Valentine were fitting cameras to the cottage while Daisy remained at Castle Braithar.

From Ariel's words, Daisy was telling her the same.

"Do I want to go stay with you?" she repeated.

I shot my gaze to her, hating the thought.

She raised a shoulder. "It's okay. I'm safe here. Sleep well."

I finished my call, and Ariel stood from the sofa, finally bringing her gaze to me.

"I'm going to bed."

"Can I come?" I asked, my mouth getting the better of me.

She balled her hands into fists as if fighting some instinct. "To bed with me? No. Neither of us think it's a good idea, remember? I'll be by myself, reading my list and imagining each act, but working things out solo. Feel free to picture that all you want. Good night, Jackson."

She went to leave but did the same halt and turn.

Ariel quickly stepped back to the couch and wrapped me in a hug. I returned it, shocked but needing it more than anything.

Her knees pressed into the cushions either side of my hips, and despite how reassuring and lifegiving a hug it was, my body woke up in anticipation of more.

I tightened my arms around her, burying my face in her hair.

Her scent filled my nose.

Her warmth brought life back to me where I'd been so fucking cold.

Ariel let me hold her then pulled back. For a beat, she examined my expression, something I didn't recognise in her gaze.

Then she exhaled, climbed off me, and left for real this time. I tipped my head back on the sofa and hated myself for my part in shutting us down.

Taking up my laptop, I attempted some work. Tried to read emails. To piece over the training list Ben had sent through.

But my mind drifted and fixed on Ariel, downstairs in her room.

Without conscious decision, I was messaging her.

*Jackson: What item from your list stuck in your mind most?*

*Ariel: I don't think you want to know.*

*Jackson: You think wrong.*

*Ariel: Okay. You asked for this. One of the girls wrote about waking up with him between your legs. I'm currently enjoying picturing that.*

My groin tightened.

*Jackson: Licking or fucking?*

*Ariel: Based on my limited experience, the second choice, probably. But either works for me.*

I palmed my dick through my jeans. I really had meant to stop from complicating things even more, but it had been a moment of madness. Self-preservation after I poured out my history. I didn't mean it.

I didn't mean a fucking second of it.

Another message came in from her.

*Ariel: I want it to be pitch-black. I want to be toyed with. I want to be a little bit afraid when I come to consciousness, but to be reassured by a kiss to my cheek then fucked to within an inch of my life, all while barely being awake. I want to come again then fall asleep with him still inside me. I want him to use me like that.*

And just in case I was under any illusion of her thoughts, she sent a fast follow-up.

*Ariel: And by him, I mean you. You asked, so deal with the answer. Now you know what I want.*

On my still-open laptop, a message dinged.

I spared it just enough attention to read the words. It was a report on the car Larson had stolen and crashed into Ariel's Mini.

I opened it. Tried to read it. Blinked hard and tried again.

The car had been found burned out far to the south, no fingerprints possible from it, and its smashed-up state not helping to link it to the previous accident, yadda, yadda.

Nothing new to think about.

I shut down the laptop, turned off the lamp, and stole downstairs. Outside Ariel's door, I paused.

A buzzing sound came from within.

Holy fuck. Unless she'd taken an electric toothbrush out of the bathroom, that could only be one thing.

And this time, I hadn't been invited.

In the bedroom next door, I shut myself in, making sure to slam the door loud enough for her to hear. But try as I might, I couldn't pick up any further sounds from her.

I was hard.

Out of my mind with need.

So I sat in the fucking dark and waited.

An hour later, I released the hold on myself, jumping to

my feet and driven by the request she'd made of me.

I left my bedroom and entered hers, snicking the door quietly shut behind me and engaging the lock. Velvety blackness surrounded me, and nothing came from the bed but Ariel's soft, even breaths.

She slept.

It was my job to wake her up in the best possible way while acting in the worst.

Enclosed in my fist was a keyring torch. I clicked it on.

White light chased long shadows to the corners of the room, highlighting the edges of furniture and the still figure under the blanket.

Keeping my gaze on her, I prowled over.

Removed my shirt and tossed it to the floor.

Ariel lay on her side, facing away from me, her tumble of dark curls spread over the white pillow and her face pale under my light. With infinite care not to wake her, I plucked the blanket from her sleeping form and drew it down and off her body.

I thickened in my boxers.

My dick hadn't calmed since her texts and now leaked for her.

My gaze travelled up her legs and to the skimpy sleep shorts she'd chosen. Lacy ones. The edge cut across the curve of her backside, disappearing up to a narrow slice of material that barely concealed the place between her legs.

Her equally scant strappy top had ridden up to expose the dip of her waist, though her tits were hidden by her arm and her position.

She'd chosen her sleepwear with me in mind.

I forced my brain to check that statement. Her text

messages were my instruction, not some insane obsession I was developing with her.

Still, the darker part of me was taking charge.

In her sleep, Ariel grumbled and rolled to her back, perhaps missing the warmth of the blanket in the cool room. No matter, my body would be on hers soon enough.

I was enjoying watching her first.

My breath caught at her new position. At the outline of a nipple under her shirt.

One arm lay on her white sheet and the other over her belly, in the way of my gaze.

Gently, I picked up the offending arm and brought it to mirror the position of the other.

Exposing the shape of her tits completely.

High and tight under her camisole. The curve of them so fucking sexy I wanted to sink my teeth into her.

She didn't wake, so I got bolder.

Her knees were bent and angled to one side, and her cheek pressed to the pillow, so I took an ankle in my hand and eased her leg outwards, setting it down then doing the same with the other.

Then I inched up her top with a fingertip until I'd revealed her tits.

Both her nipples hardened, my torch lighting them up.

I bent over and blew on the nearest. Then I touched my tongue to the rigid bud, nearly fucking coming at the sensation.

Holy fucking shite.

Her fantasy of being played with while she slept had been something I'd never considered, but it spoke to a part of me that needed this separation from the active, enthusiastic version of her I'd fucked on the sofa and in the shower.

She couldn't say no, so neither could I.

Both of us were caught up in her request.

I breathed through my nose and backed up, travelling my torchlight and my hungry gaze down her belly and to her shorts-covered pussy.

Holding the light between my teeth, I used both hands to guide them off her, moving with more care than ever.

My heart raced.

Her pussy gleamed, wet for me even though she didn't even know I was here.

Except her body clearly did. Her body wanted more of the small touches and avid attention. Of how badly I needed her and intended to fuck her into the mattress so she woke screaming. It knew what it needed.

I shed my boxers, and naked, knelt on the bed between her spread legs. Her trust was a fucking turn-on beyond anything else. Her fantasy driving me insane.

Still going slow, and holding the light so I could see every detail, I grazed a knuckle down the crease of her leg, not touching her clit or going inside her. Not yet.

I repeated it, dipping into her arousal.

Ariel shifted, driving her shoulders into the mattress. Her legs stayed spread, her chest on display with the cami across the top of it.

Her nipples stayed hard despite nothing touching them now apart from fresh air and my twisted focus.

I snapped back to staring at her pussy.

Eased my finger in to the first joint.

Held my breath.

Then I pushed further, just feeling her.

Maybe I could make her come like this.

I withdrew and sucked my finger, loving the taste of her. What I intended to do next needed both hands as well as my mouth, so I reached over to set the light down on her bedside table, balancing on her little fox figurine.

Right beside a dildo.

I stared at the slender device then grabbed it, settling back on my haunches and examining the rubber cock. This was what she'd got off with earlier after I'd been a dick and driven her to her room to fuck herself.

Well, if she wanted this, then I did, too.

I closed in on her pussy and dipped to kiss her clit. Then I took a long lick and a light suck, still not alerting her with anything too rough.

She got wetter still, her thighs damp.

I got bolder. Notched the dildo at her entrance.

Slowly, I pushed it inside her, watching each inch vanish into her tight body and pausing whenever I thought she might wake. But Ariel accepted it like a good girl, fast asleep and taking what I needed her to.

Her tits rose and fell where her breathing quickened.

I released my hold on it and stopped, waiting until she'd settled again, no further signs of her becoming conscious.

Holy shit, it was in her. Buried deep while she slept.

I tapped the end of the dildo, jolting her so her tits wobbled.

Christ, this was a fucking joy.

Ariel flexed in her slumber, a heel driving into the mattress. The dildo bobbed. Fuck, she'd pulsed around it? My neglected dick wept, and I palmed it, jerking myself off with slow strokes, my attention locked on the toy impaling her.

I leaned down and enclosed her clit in my mouth, just warming her with my tongue flat and her flavour an explosion on my taste buds.

Ariel Gordonson was an addiction I never wanted to get over.

Nor was I ready for this to be finished.

She gave a little gasp of confusion, and I retreated, waiting her out until she calmed, though two lines on her forehead remained.

When I was sure she'd gone deep under, I positioned myself between her thighs and set my knee to the end of the dildo to keep it inside her, then moved over her body, not touching in any way, but supporting myself with one hand to the sheet. Looming above her, I watched her face, jerking my dick in silent reverence.

Could she come like this? Did I want her to or did I need her awake?

It all felt so good. My dick harder than ever. Long and thick in my hand and dying to be inside her.

When I got close to my limit, I stopped, gripping myself and breathing through it until the feeling subsided.

Edging myself as I edged her unconscious body.

Then I retreated to her tits again, enclosing her nipple in my mouth like I'd done her clit. Slowly sliding my fist up and down my dick, careful not to rock the bed too much but in deep with the feel of her in my mouth.

Though I kept my orgasm at bay, the need in me didn't end. It brimmed over until my whole body was electrified.

Like she could feel me, Ariel squirmed. Her tongue darted out to moisten her lips.

Her eyelids flickered.

My time to play alone was up.

She was waking, which meant I needed to deliver the second part of her fantasy.

I grabbed my light to turn it off, plunging us into darkness once more, then reached between us. By touch, I flicked the button on the handle of the dildo, a muted buzz following.

Ariel gasped, and I pressed an instant, hot kiss to her cheek so she knew it was me, then roamed down her body to return my mouth to her pussy. Holding the vibrator, I eased it in and out of her, sucking her clit in the way I knew she liked, alternating with flicking it with my tongue. She groaned, and her hand landed on my hair, the touch light and unguided as if she hadn't fully come to.

She bucked, my name a whisper on her lips. "J-Jackson, please."

I nearly fucking came on the sheet.

Ariel moaned again, and I knew she was approaching the finish line. This, we'd do together.

Pulling the vibrator out of her, I thrust my hard, leaking dick inside her soaking channel instead, stretching her where I was bigger than the toy and so fucking happy about being in heaven and deep inside her. I held the vibrator to her clit and fucked her like my life depended on it.

Ariel's fingers gripped my hair, and her other hand dragged my face to hers.

I kissed her, instantly tangling our tongues, pouring in gratitude for the experience she'd asked me for and allowed me to share.

Not for a moment did I slow. I slammed into her over and over. She was so close to the edge that she gave an abrupt cry and gripped me, both with her arms around my back and her internal muscles around my dick.

Ariel came with a choked cry and tore her mouth from mine to press her face to my shoulder. I followed instantly, losing my grip on the dildo right as I killed its vibrations, tossing it aside.

With my head into the pillow, I jacked my hips and came a flood.

My dick throbbed, the climax a cliff I'd thrown myself off.

Nothing beat it.

Nothing ever would.

My cum inside her. The feeling of her body taking mine.

I saw stars, each named for her, then I wrapped my arms around her and buried my face in her hair.

Together, we lingered in our high.

Right before I fell asleep, I worked my dick enough to get it hard inside her. Then the heavy darkness sank me under.

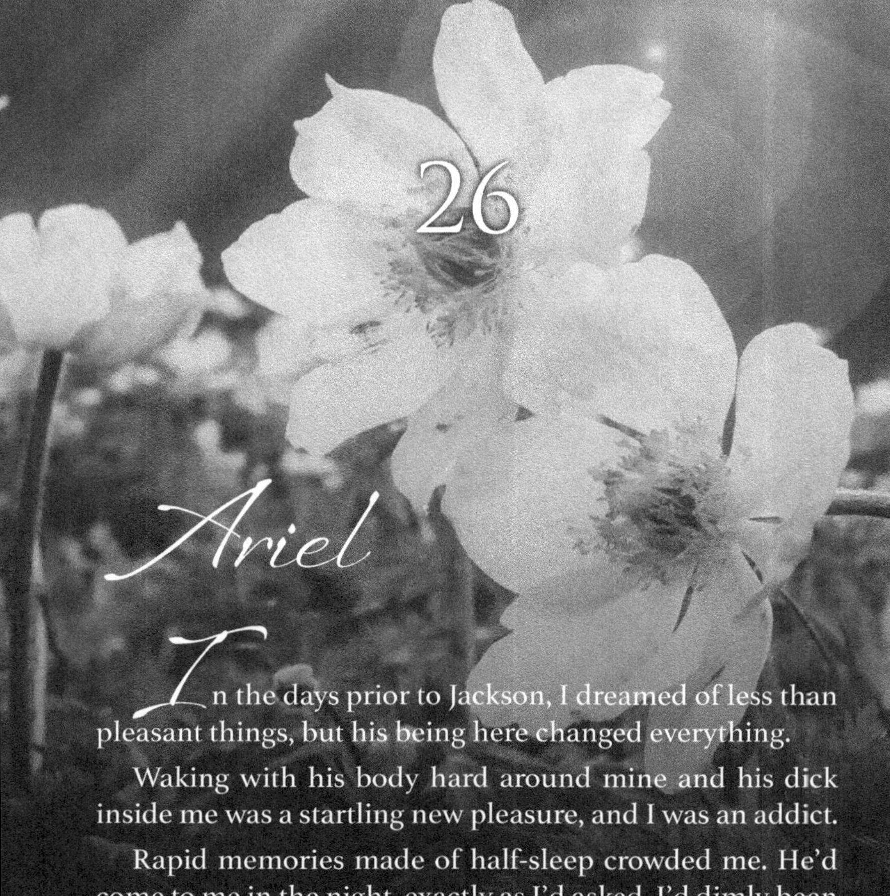

# 26

## Ariel

In the days prior to Jackson, I dreamed of less than pleasant things, but his being here changed everything.

Waking with his body hard around mine and his dick inside me was a startling new pleasure, and I was an addict.

Rapid memories made of half-sleep crowded me. He'd come to me in the night, exactly as I'd asked. I'd dimly been aware of him fucking me...

With my vibrator? God, yes.

That was so far beyond hot it burned through me.

I needed to know what he'd done to my unconscious body. I grazed my nails up his bare shoulders, digging lightly to wake him.

Jackson stirred. Pressed a kiss to my jaw.

"Tell me everything," I asked into the hushed, barely there dawn.

His dick throbbed, thickening further.

I caught my breath, already so turned on.

"Ye were out cold. I took care not to wake ye when I stole away your blanket and arranged ye on your back."

I reached between us and thrummed my clit. "Did you touch me?"

"It was more that I watched, at the start. Your nipples, your pussy."

"So you didn't wake me?"

"Exactly, fox."

Jackson rolled me to my back, lying between my legs. He gave a lazy thrust, his eyes still closed. "I played with ye, and whenever there was any sign of your waking, I stopped."

"To keep it going."

"For as long as I could. I fucking loved it."

A thrill shot through me. He'd enjoyed my fantasy, too.

He kept moving, drawing his hefty dick in and out of me.

"I sucked your clit while ye slept. Then I found your toy. I fucked ye with that, too."

"You put it inside me? How did I not wake up?"

"My dick had opened ye, maybe."

"That, and the fact I'd fucked myself with it after I went to bed. I still had your cum in me, so it felt amazing."

He groaned, getting faster.

Gripping him with my knees, I flipped us so he was on his back. Jackson held my hips, blinking at me in surprise.

"While we're still doing this, I'm striking off another item from my list," I informed him.

"While we're still doing this?" he repeated.

I rose up and descended, working him and working out how to be the cowgirl. Or was that only when I faced the other way and this was just riding? No matter. "Yep. You blow hot and cold, so I'm not relying on you. I'm just taking what I can get."

Jackson gave a low laugh which turned into a jerky inhale when I got the angle right. "Can I say sorry?"

"Again? Don't think so."

"Then I'll find a way to show ye instead."

"Bring it."

Then there was no more time for talk.

I rode him until I lost my rhythm, liking it far too much. Jackson took over, gripping my hips and hammering up into me. I came and triggered him again. We both heaved for breath. Clutched at the other.

Slept again.

When I next woke, Jackson was still hard and deep in me.

As if he was warming his dick inside me. Keeping safe.

Had we stayed close like this since our last round, or gravitated back together? Him to me or me to him?

I squirmed on him. It was undoubtedly late, and I never slept in, but this was new and different. I wanted a week of living in my bed doing exactly this.

Jackson would freak out any minute and call it off again.

That would hurt. I'd learned from him that I didn't like rejection.

Let alone the fact that today, we were going to lay a trap for Larson. Catch him and bring him in.

Jackson lifted his head, fitting his mouth to mine. Fused it.

We moved against each other, smaller actions, a gentler grinding of his dick into me. Our legs twisted together, our fingers flexing, interlaced with the other's. No space between us.

This time, when I came, it was easy and blissful. A relaxed release which sent a warm glow down every limb.

A long minute of silence followed, then the bodyguard in my bed nuzzled me. "Morning, little fox."

I opened my mouth to reply, but my phone blared from my bedside table.

Jackson rolled off me with a quiet comment about letting me take my call in peace, and I grabbed my phone.

"It's Ben." I pointed to the name of his boss on my screen.

Jackson paused at the door, and I answered the call, tugging the blanket up to my neck, not that Ben could see my naked and well-used state.

"Ariel, we've had something come up. Valentine and I need to go with Leo and Gordain down to Glasgow. We'll be out most of the day. Can we take a twenty-four-hour rain check on our sting operation?"

A mixture of emotions bubbled inside me. I wanted to bring an end to my fear of kidnap. At the same time, I was enjoying myself way too much with Jackson and didn't want it to be over.

"You're the worst," I told him. "Just joking. Tomorrow works for me, too. It's not like I've got anything else on."

"Appreciated. Leo sends his apologies. Viola offers baby cuddles if ye need to get out of the house for a while."

"Tell her I'll message her. Do you need Jackson as well?"

Gordain snorted. "Tell him if he answered his phone, he'd know his assignment for the day. He's all yours, so no worries."

The bodyguard boss hung up, and I grinned at the man

hanging on my bedroom doorframe.

"A day to ourselves?" he concluded.

"Whatever will we do?"

I knew what I wanted to do all day, but my body needed a break, even if my mind wouldn't stop conjuring images of Jackson fucking me seven ways from Sunday.

He pressed his lips together, offered me the first shower, then shut himself in his room.

Under the hot water, I rinsed myself clean, tracing a finger between my legs. I was swollen and raw from the night. The problem was, the sensation was providing a constant reminder and only making me want more.

I glanced over my clit and closed my eyes, tipping my head back to the shower wall, chasing the feeling.

Then I stopped.

It was better when Jackson did it.

He seemed to have a magic touch when it came to my body. When he was inside me, it was like nothing I'd ever felt before. An addictive rush that led to a perfect explosion of good feeling. Over and over again.

Was it like this for everyone? I needed to ask my girls.

I finished up and climbed out, still horny.

Jackson took over the bathroom while I dried my hair in my bedroom. He was quicker than me, though, and when I was done, I discovered him upstairs making breakfast.

He peered over his shoulder from the stove. "Poached egg on toast okay? We don't have much else."

"That sounds perfect. We should go shopping for food. Do you think I'd be safe if we went to a supermarket?"

He carried a plate to the table. "If we drove out far enough away from home, I'd think so. But ye wouldn't leave my sight."

I picked up my fork and gestured to him. "No problem there. Pretty sure my body would riot if I wasn't near you."

He plated up his food and sat across from me, his cheeks a little red. After a minute of eating, he framed a question. "What did ye enjoy most last night?"

I tried to contain my smile and listed on my fingers. "Loved the passion of nearly screwing on the stairs, getting down to it on the sofa, then again in the shower. Waking up to you fucking me blew my mind. I also really love the feeling when you come. When you twitch or pulse inside me. That is chef's kisses delicious."

"Hard to deliver that last item more than once a session, but good to know."

"What about you?" I asked, finishing my last bite of toast. Sex really worked up an appetite.

Jackson raised a shoulder. "Everything."

"Name one thing."

His gaze shifted downward, but his lips curved into a satisfied smile.

I held my breath. "You're not about to say we can't do it again, are you?"

His focus darted back to me.

For a long moment, we just watched each other. In the past, his gaze on me had churned me up. I wanted him to look at me, but with lust, not tolerance or whatever he'd felt when he'd seen me as his friend's younger sister.

I was something else to him now. What, I wasn't sure. And I wasn't going to ask either.

He shook his head in the negative.

"Good," I breathed.

Jackson gave a laugh, jumping up to clear the plates. "Good, she says."

"Hey, at least I'm giving information."

"On the subject of information, tell me the next top three things from your list."

I pulled the sheet of paper from my pocket. Shook it out. "More sex toys sounds fun. From behind again but on all fours. Semi-public with the risk of exposure."

On the table, his phone buzzed.

"Your mom again," I told him. "I'll do the dishes. You handle that."

He exhaled in frustration and returned to the table. "I'll need to talk to her eventually. But Christ is she persistent."

"Where does she live?" I asked.

"Inverness."

The phone kept vibrating.

Last night, he'd rejected my help. I had a rush of intuition that things had somehow changed.

"Let me answer."

Jackson put his hands on the table and regarded me. Not pushing back. But waiting.

I stumbled over my words in my haste to get them out. "We can have coffee with her before we buy food. Get this over and done with."

He'd answered my call and handled my problem with my student's mother.

I wanted to repay the favour.

"We have the time," I continued my argument. "I'll pretend to be your girlfriend and act the controlling bitch if that helps. Or I can butter her up. I'll be whatever you want me to be."

I expected an outright refusal. Jackson hadn't swayed on this at all. To my entire surprise, he slowly nodded.

"A neutral venue works," he said. "I could never go to her house and hate the idea of her coming here. She knows where I work. Do it."

I snatched up the phone. "Are you sure?"

He dipped his head.

My breath caught, but I swiped to answer the call before it rang out. "Jackson's phone. How can I help?"

There was a pause. "Who's this?"

"I'm Jackson's girlfriend."

He swore under his breath and turned away, pacing back to the sink.

"Well, I'm his mother. Put him on the line."

"It's so nice to talk to you, Mrs Reid. I'm afraid he's not available right now. I'd be happy to take a message."

She spluttered, clearly annoyed. "Ye can tell him to be home for seven this evening."

Facing away from me, Jackson tightened his grip on the counter, his knuckles standing proud.

"This evening? That won't be possible. We have other plans. But if you desperately need to see him, we'll be in Inverness in an hour or so. We could meet for coffee? I'd love to say hi."

"He's my son. What other plans can he have that come above mine? Ye tell him—"

"I'm sorry," I cut in. "Maybe I wasn't clear. We won't make it this evening. It's on our terms or not at all."

His mother went quiet again. She had a gentle voice, entirely at odds with her words, and not dissimilar to her son's measured tone. But that was where the comparison ended. For all his reserved nature, Jackson had no artifice.

A sound came like she'd muted us and was finishing a separate conversation. "Coffee will have to do, but ye can tell him from me that I'm disappointed."

"Give us an hour, and I'll text you the address."

I hung up, breathing out.

Jackson hung his head, his dark hair falling forward. Abruptly, he turned and came back to me. Stooped to kiss my lips.

"Thank ye."

I could have replied and said something about taking the bull by the horns, but instead I kissed him back. Knelt on the chair. Lost myself in his lips.

It couldn't last. We had to go, and this wasn't going to be easy.

I'd make sure for his sake that coming home would make up for the pain.

In broad daylight, we drove away from Castle McRae, with me hidden on the back seat. Jackson took the A9 north, pulling over after a while so I could move to the front seat. I'd tucked my hair under my beanie hat, tugging it low to my eyes, but even so, I couldn't shake the sense of unease.

Fuck Larson, honestly.

I hated the man for making me feel like this.

Yet we drove unimpeded, and I began to relax. "I want to tell my friends about you. I mean my girls. More than just Daisy."

He turned a wide-eyed gaze on me. "That has consequences. Your brother and Ben being the main ones."

I wrinkled my nose. "Ben doesn't have a leg to stand on. He and Daisy were screwing within hours of meeting each other."

"I did not need to know that."

I gave a happy laugh. "Reassuring, though. As for Raphael, I'll tell him when he calls. Or you can, if it's important for your friendship."

Jackson watched the snowy road. "What am I saying, exactly?"

"Whatever you want. We've been sleeping together and today we're fake dating. Or that I lured you into my bed. Or maybe you accidentally tripped and fell into me, over and over."

This earned me a smirk. "Fine."

I took my phone and tapped a message, delighted with the ability to share. My girl group was a lifeline.

*Ariel: If I'm going to try a sex toy, beyond my slim vibrator, what should I pick at the shops today? Bonus points if it's good for him, too.*

Immediately, three people were typing.

*Isobel: Oh no, you can't write that and not give details.*

*Daisy: Love that he's down to play as well.*

*Isobel: Who are we talking about? Daisy, tell us if she won't.*

*Viola: Got to be Jackson, right? Valentine went out with Leo this morning.*

*Casey: Remote-controlled vibrator. Hands down.*

I giggled, tapping back a confirmation.

*Ariel: We're working through the list. Yes, it's Jackson.*

*Effie: I KNEW it.*

*Viola: I'm THRILLED for you. Second vote from me for the remote-controlled toy. Game changer.*

*Casey: I bet you two are on fire together. So compatible. Still want more details.*

*Isobel: Love him for you! He's super hot.*

I sensed Jackson's gaze on me and peered over.

"It's nice to see ye smiling," he said.

"I asked for sex toys recommendations. It'll be nice to see us both happy."

"What do they think of your choice of partner?"

If I hadn't been paying attention, I could have missed the small note of concern in his voice.

He cared. He needed approval.

"They like you."

Now he grinned.

But our levity couldn't last.

The closer we got to central Inverness, the more Jackson shut down. His expression flattening. His movements becoming more tightly controlled.

I texted his mother the name of a café at the end of Bank Street where it met Ness Bridge, and she replied that they'd see us there.

Jackson found a parking spot, turned the engine off, and exhaled. "I need ye to stay in the car. Which is a real problem because I can't leave ye alone. This was a mistake."

I dropped the seat belt I'd just unclipped. "What? Aren't

I supposed to be your get-out clause?"

He didn't answer, just glowered in frustration out the window.

Something was wrong.

What had changed? I pieced back through the trip. Then my brain homed in on the new information. "Your mom said 'they'. Is that the problem?"

He twisted in his seat. "There are things I haven't told ye, almost as bad as the shite I did share."

"Tell me now?"

"The other person she's referring to is her husband. The man she married after she left my da."

"What kind of man is he?" For Jackson not to like him, he had to be bad.

"He's TJ's father."

I stared, trying to start a sentence and failing.

His mom had married the father of her daughter's murderer.

"Were they united in their grief?" I managed.

"No. Nothing so simple. Remember I said someone was feeding my mother lines when she was yelling at Lisa Marie to take TJ back? That was the father speaking. They'd been having an affair almost as long as I'd known the son."

I pressed my fingers to my mouth. I didn't like the way this was going. A picture started forming, filling in the blanks Jackson had left. His mother was harassing him to see her, but it was more than him hating her choices.

"Please don't tell me they support TJ," I whispered.

Slowly, Jackson inclined his head, his lip curled. "It's insane to say, but throughout the search for Lisa Marie and the subsequent court case against TJ, my mother still blamed my sister. She *blamed* her for getting herself killed, and used words like 'crime of passion' and 'a terrible accident' and 'she drove him to it'. It isn't just the influence of her new boyfriend. She made a choice and stuck to it."

"No wonder you've refused to see her. I'm sorry I encouraged you."

I reached for his hand. He didn't pull away.

"I own my decisions. She has something to say to me, and she won't stop until she's heard. I need to do this."

"Then I'm coming with you." Before he could protest, I finalised the argument. "We've come all this way, and I'm not letting you out of my sight. Let's get this over with."

# 27

## Jackson

In a busy café under the shadow of Inverness Castle, I scanned the crowds, my mind on Ariel's safety despite what we were here to do.

The threat, however, was all mine.

My mother stared through the sea of bodies. She'd cut her hair into a bob and highlighted it blonde, but she was still the image of my sister grown up.

She even had Lisa Marie's cake order on a china plate in front of her. The chocolate fudge cake my sister had loved.

Ma was playing mind games already.

Ariel squeezed her fingers in mine. "I'm with you. We've got this."

*We.* I'd avoided this meeting for so long. I couldn't have done it without her.

Together, we approached the table. My mother didn't rise. Neither did the man at her side.

I refused to even dignify TJ's father with a glance in his direction.

Instead, strung tight with tension, I pulled out a chair for Ariel then sat beside her, capturing her hand in mine again. A lifeline.

Ma gestured with her head to the queue of people at the counter. "There's no table service here. You'll need to stand in line. Or send your girl."

"We won't be staying that long."

She narrowed her eyes at me then at Ariel. On the phone, Ariel had introduced herself as my girlfriend but hadn't given her name. Suddenly, I was determined that my mother didn't hear it. She didn't have the right.

"You've got me here. What do ye want?" I asked.

Ma came back to me. "Other than to see my only child?"

Her only child? Whose every possession she'd destroyed when she'd turned her back on me?

I couldn't answer.

She sniffed. "As you'll be aware, in two weeks, the parole hearing is coming up."

"Why would I know anything about that?"

She scoffed. "Don't be difficult, Jackson. TJ's your brother."

I recoiled, unable to conceal the reaction. In everything I'd told Ariel about my family, I'd tested myself. Whether I'd been acting in grief. If I'd overreacted and lashed out.

My mother neatly put paid to that train of thought.

"The individual who murdered my sister is nothing to me," I retorted. "And ye wonder why I don't want to meet up when ye say shite like that."

Ariel shifted at my side. I twisted to find her gaze on Ma's husband.

The man was full-on staring at her.

My heart pounded, adrenaline eking into my system.

All the control I prided myself on was in danger of being lost.

"Don't fucking look at her," I bit out, keeping my voice low because there were families around.

My mother took an exaggerated gasp, her face red. "You're so hostile and rude. For years, your behaviour has been tearing our family in two."

I couldn't stomach that. "As far as I see it, whatever was left of our family after his murderous bastard of a son tore us apart was then set on fire by your taking up with him. Da's heart was broken. I was left sleeping in my car. Can't ye see what you've done?"

"You're wrong. The fault lies with your slut of a sister. It always has," TJ's father intoned.

My last semblance of restraint fled.

Regardless of his shitty words, I saw TJ.

I launched over the table, grasping him by the lapels.

My mother gave a little shriek and reached for me, but Ariel stood, too, blocking her from interfering.

"Aren't ye going to stop him?" Ma demanded.

"If he didn't do that, I would've," my fake girlfriend replied.

I leaned in to TJ's father, dimly aware of people at nearby tables scattering away. He'd aged since I'd last had the displeasure of seeing him. Deep lines in his skin. His nose bulbous and purpling.

"Talk about my sister like that again and I'll end your miserable existence. No, I won't stand witness for your son. I wouldn't at his trial and I won't now, though I wish I'd stood up for the prosecution and had my say. He deserves to rot in jail."

I released him, shoving him back to the bench while staying on my feet.

This was over. I never should've come.

TJ's father clutched at his throat and wheezed. "You'll go to that meeting and you'll give the character witness ye should've years ago. It's your fault he's locked up. He was your best friend." Then he dropped his voice. "If ye don't, there's a dozen people watching on who'll back my claim of an assault charge that will lose ye your precious job. Welcome to unemployment."

I'd heard enough. With Ariel close behind me, I stormed from the café and out into the freezing February day.

We marched back to the car, my brain a mess.

Inside, I turned on the heat and put my face in my hands. "I'm sorry about that."

The violence. The loss of control.

"They set you up."

I opened and closed my mouth. She was right. "Shite."

With a groan, I banged my head on the seat, the adrenaline simmering and my mind returning.

"You really didn't get to give evidence against him at his trial?"

"I was considered unreliable because of my fucked-up state. I'll never forgive myself for that."

"He was found guilty. You didn't need to be there. Forgive yourself." Ariel kissed the side of my face. "Out."

"Out?"

"Of the car. I want to drive."

We were safe enough, far from home and the greater danger of the man hunting her.

"Fine," I muttered. "For the record, I can drive when stressed but I won't miss the chance of ye in my driving seat."

"Spank bank material?"

"Ye have no idea."

Ariel snickered a laugh, and we traded places.

She drove me out of Inverness, confident and gunning the engine with glee.

"Ever had a fake girlfriend behind the wheel of your car?" she asked.

"It's a first."

"She's a lovely drive," she crooned. "So smooth and responsive."

"Stop. You're turning me on."

That earned me a bigger laugh. I relaxed back, trying to release the stress from the shitty meeting.

"I wish I'd punched him," I confessed.

Ariel waggled her head. "Kinda wish you did, too, but then his threat would hold water."

"It could already."

"No way. Ben would never fire you for that."

"The decision would be out of his hands. I can't have a criminal record. If I do, I can't get a visa to travel to all the places Leo will play gigs. I'd be useless to Ben, and I was already skating on thin ice with the amount of trouble I'd got into when I was younger."

We approached a trading estate with a large supermarket, but Ariel kept going, taking the exit out of the suburbs and into the countryside.

"Food?" I pointed back the way we'd come.

"I'm taking a detour." She slid me a peek. "First, I want to make you feel better by blowing you in a lane somewhere. Tick off outdoors sex from my list at the same time."

I swore, my dick already thickening.

Ariel drove on, taking the coastal road.

We wound our way past white frosted fields, the icy sea far beyond whipped into waves.

In a narrow lane, cute bungalows lined the route, the end of the track turning into a walking path.

Ariel backed into a field entrance and switched off the engine.

"We have an unknown amount of time until someone walks by. If we're lucky, they won't investigate our car. If we're not, we'll have to stop. In other words, you have minutes to come, and as I'm new to this, I need your help getting it right."

I couldn't breathe.

She undid my seat belt and reached for my jeans. I didn't stop her.

Widened my knees.

Then she freed my dick and bent over to enclose it within her lips. A low groan came from me, and I jerked into her hot mouth.

She kissed my shaft. "I said guide me."

"Keep sucking. Grip the base of me with your fist and match the movement."

"Slow or fast?"

"Pretty sure any slight pressure and I'll explode in your mouth."

She laughed and returned her attention to my dick. A wave of need broke over me. I would never not want this woman. Never not be desperate for a single touch or look my way.

Having her on my dick in a race to get me off was a killer blow.

She moved up and down me, keeping her tongue flat and the action repetitive. No showboating.

Only dedicated, consistent pressure.

It felt so fucking good.

I glanced from the hedgerows around us down to her bobbing head. She'd removed her snug hat, so I dug my fingers into her hair, the other hand gripping the headrest at my back.

I rolled my body, chasing the feeling generating in me.

Ariel slid her other hand between my legs, holding my balls.

I gave a growl.

The windows steamed up on my side of the car.

A figure moved ahead.

Bright emotion broke over me.

"Someone's nearby," I gritted out. "Finish me off, fast."

Ariel moaned, the sound going straight to the centre of me. Her grip tightened. Her pace sped up.

The man walking his Labrador strolled away, but thoughts of getting caught had cracked my brain.

In long strokes, Ariel took me right to the edge.

I muttered a warning, but then I was coming, my balls tightening and releasing.

Ariel stayed on me, her throat working.

I saw stars. Fucking galaxies created by her tongue.

Any stress in me evaporated, and I gave a satisfied groan.

She eased off me. "Wow, that didn't take long."

I couldn't speak. I kissed her instead, dazed and fucked up in the best way.

She grinned and drove us away, not waiting for me to come back to earth or even do up my jeans. She'd won me over, and I was hers to do with as she wanted.

An hour later, we'd trawled around a big supermarket, grabbing a trolleyful of food and even finding an interesting adult toy selection in their chemist range. Ariel picked up a box plus lube, sliding me an amused smile.

I followed her around, thinking up meals and snacks to please her.

The problem was, I'd gone beyond the bounds of lust.

I wanted her. Needed her close. She'd been there for me today, and I'd never forget that.

I'd got used to being alone. Then Raphael challenged that and made me his friend. His younger sister had seen his efforts and raised the stakes.

I'd resisted the pull of my obsession, but it had been a losing battle.

I was falling for the perfect soul that was Ariel Gordonson, and I didn't have a fucking clue how she'd react if I told her.

# 28

## Ariel

With the disguise of my beanie hat tugged down low and a face mask on, I drove us back to Castle McRae. Jackson ushered me inside then made two trips to bring up all the shopping bags. Side by side, we put everything away, snacking on premade sandwiches we'd bought.

I cleared the packets away, unable to hide a yawn.

Jackson's arms curved around me from behind, and he hugged me to him. "We need a nap. Considering the lack of sleep last night."

I twisted to face him, stretching my arms around his neck. Then I kissed him.

He allowed it but grinned and inched back. "Sleep, not sex."

I pouted and trotted downstairs, him close behind.

We stripped to our underwear, my bra getting thrown into the chair, leaving me in just my cami, and climbed into my bed, the act so natural neither of us commented on it.

He was supposed to be sleeping next door, but he'd spent more time in my bed than Raphael's. I didn't want him in a different bed.

Too easily, we fitted together. Him on his back. Me on my side, cuddled into him, my head on his biceps, and his arms around me.

I lifted my head to capture his lips in another kiss.

It was cosy, the room dark and my bed warm. I'd meant the kiss to be comforting, but neither of us stopped, losing minutes on each other's mouth. Our hands slid together, fingers interlacing, arms stretching above our heads. Jackson rolled me to my back, his hard dick pressing into me through the layers of our underwear while I tightened my legs around his waist.

Every movement was slow and easy. The buildup of heat delicious.

Still, neither of us took it any further than the close hold and the touch of lips. I didn't remember this kind of closeness being on the sex list. If not, it should have been. A true afternoon delight.

This was so far from my reality of working every day and being out in the hills. It was a break from normal life that I would never get over. An education in sex from a man I cared about and who was far deeper than I could ever have guessed.

I balanced on the edge of sleep and awake, eyes closed, unwilling to bring this to an end by stopping. I needed more, but I wasn't sure what.

Jackson slowed the kiss. Broke away. Pecked my cheek. "I want to be inside ye."

"Thought you said no sex?"

"Just inside ye. Warming my dick. To fall asleep like that."

"Tell me how that feels for you."

"Connected."

Without opening my eyes, I nodded, loving the idea.

Jackson reached between us and stripped our underwear, kicking it out of the bed. Then he guided my legs around him again, fitted his blunt end to my wet core, and thrust inside me.

I gasped, open-mouthed at the solid length of him buried deep inside. My stretched pussy fluttered, and his dick throbbed in response.

He breathed, his hold on me fierce, and his heart pounding. But he didn't fuck me. And I didn't move either. Instead, we relaxed.

Another first. Another deeper connection. My pussy warming his dick so he could sleep. So he didn't feel adrift in the world as he must've done for so long.

My heart rate evened out.

Under my touch, his did, too.

Finally, I lost myself to sleep.

I woke alone.

The bed was still warm beside me, and I listened hard, picking up faint sounds coming from upstairs. Jackson was still here, then. I didn't know why I'd expected him to vanish.

Relaxing back down, I slid my hand between my legs, touching myself. Checking to see if he'd come in me while I'd slept, using me like I'd given him permission to. The thought gave me a thrill, though I needed a blow-by-blow account afterwards to get myself off, too.

My exploration suggested he hadn't. Which meant only good things to come.

I reclined, my mind stuck on all things Jackson. I wanted to hate his mother, but the impression I'd taken away was that she was brainwashed. Lost to a man. She had to miss her daughter, surely.

My thoughts took another direction. My mother had walked out on us. She'd done so without a backward glance and had never made contact since. Her situation was different in that men ruled the roost in that world. Toxic masculinity to the max. It was hard to understand the mindset she must've had, but I tried. If all she knew was the rule of whichever man she'd chained herself to, then was that to block out some other major trauma? Not doing any thinking for herself?

I didn't want to forgive her, like I didn't think Jackson should forgive his. But that didn't mean I couldn't try to understand.

Then there was the odd comment my father had made. That my concerns were questions for my mother, not my father. Was that a clue?

Steeling myself, I grabbed my phone and found my stepmother's social media accounts. Sent her a private message, asking her to get my mom's phone number for me. Once, Willow had offered to do that. I'd refused her. Now felt like a good time.

Other messages decorated my screen. A group chat with my brothers, and Raphael updating us on his progress. Something from The Girls where Casey was hinting at some hella sexy act she was trying with her guys which I'd definitely be reading in detail later, and then one from Jackson.

I read it quickly.

*Jackson: In case you wake, I'm putting dinner in the oven. I'll be down soon.*

I replied with a love heart.

Another message came in from him. A code.

*Jackson: IWTWYCIFOTM, LF.*

Glee filled me. I loved him doing this, and him using punctuation? It sent little bursts of joy through me.

I squinted, trying to get his code.

The last two letters were easy. *Little fox.*

The first three came to me quickly, too. *I want to.*

But what did he want to do to me? I puzzled over it, trying to make a sentence. An action. Then I reached for my list and tried to make it into one of those.

Had he even read the full list? I wasn't sure.

Try as I might, I couldn't determine the middle part of his clue.

After a few minutes more, footsteps descended the spiral stairs, and Jackson stepped into the room, something hidden behind his back. I sat up, letting the blanket fall to my waist.

His gaze sank to the outline of my boobs under my delicate purple top. Typically, I didn't wear pretty underwear every day. I'd taken to doing so for him.

He moistened his lips. "Did ye guess my code?"

I shook my head in the negative, unable to stop my focus from sliding down his body to his tented boxers. He'd put on a plain blue T-shirt to do food prep, and with a smirk, he stripped it off, dropping it to the floor.

"Want a clue?" He prowled closer.

Breathless, I nodded again.

Jackson went to my wardrobe and opened the door. Inside was a tall mirror. He angled it at the bed until I could see my reflection, and raised his eyebrows.

I grabbed my phone.

*I want to...WYCIFOTM, little fox.*

"Watch you come in front of the mirror?" I said slowly.

Jackson smiled, his expression pleased and devilishly turned on. From behind his back, he brought an object.

The sex toy we'd bought earlier.

He handed it to me, keeping the small remote control that came with it. "Cleaned and ready to play."

I examined the little rubber device. It was about three inches long, oval shaped, and completely smooth, with a cord for removal. It buzzed in my hand, a low, rolling vibration, then stopped.

I hitched a breath and lifted my gaze to Jackson.

He retreated to the wall directly in line with the mirror, watching me. "Get on the quilt. Face the mirror," he ordered.

I threw back the covers and climbed on top, the lower half of my body naked from where I'd slept with him inside me.

I wanted to ask him if he'd woken up that way, but more, I wanted to follow his instructions.

I reclined on my elbows, knees up. My reflection in the mirror showed a flushed face and a mostly naked body.

I plucked at the cami. "Keep this on or take it off?"

"Leave it for now. Press the toy to your nipple."

I did, and the buzzing returned with a flick of his remote control.

Pleasure spread, and my nipple hardened in response. I pushed it harder then retreated and swapped to the other side until both nipples pebbled under my cami.

Already, I was wet. I had been since his text, fresh arousal making me ready for him.

Keeping up the action, I tilted my head back to see him behind me.

Jackson smiled and advanced on me to deliver an upside-down kiss. His hand drifted over mine, and he claimed the toy, leaning over me to put his mouth over my nipple, not shifting the material first so he left a wet patch where he sucked. I arched into his touch, gasping where he used the vibrating egg on the opposite side.

Then the vibration stopped, and he returned to kiss my lips. As he slicked his tongue over mine, one hand landed on my knees, guiding them apart.

In the mirror, I'd be bared to plain sight. My core glistening. Dripping for him.

Jackson's knuckles drifted down my inner thigh, his kisses moving down my throat.

Open-mouthed, I took an inhale, loving the sensation of being played with.

Then cool rubber touched the apex of my thighs, sliding into my arousal. Without warning, Jackson pushed the toy inside me, two fingers following it to embed it deep within my body.

My eyes flew open.

Before I could react further, he flicked the switch, and the vibration started.

I let out an ungodly sound.

I'd used a vibrator many times, but this was something else.

Jackson groaned low but pulled away from me. In my mirror view, he parked himself against the wall, gripping himself through his boxers, his fingers wet from where they'd been inside me with the toy.

"Open your legs so I can see. Touch yourself while I

control the speed," he said.

I hadn't realised I'd brought my knees together, so I spread them, lifting again to see myself in the glass. The cord of the toy was all that was visible, but the pulsing didn't stop. Mindlessly, I moved my hips, the mirror image so erotic.

"Fingers on your clit, Ariel."

With an unbidden moan, I obeyed.

The sensation from the pulsing inside me was driving me mad. It wasn't enough on its own to drive me fast to the edge, but it was building me up, gently stimulating my pussy. I lightly touched my clit and I throbbed hard.

He'd ramped up the speed.

Desire spiralled, lighting up every part of me.

I moaned out his name and made another pass over my clit, soaked from everything he was doing to me.

The actions of the toy and my fingers slowly built me to a rush of pleasure. I neared the edge and locked my gaze on Jackson.

His boxers were off, and his dick gleamed in the low light, leaking for me while he jacked it.

"I'm close," I breathed.

All smiles were gone.

Only a deadly serious, utterly devoted man stared back at me. "Say my fucking name," he ordered.

I dropped my head back, mindless.

Vibrations kicked up another notch, a rolling pulse that I matched with how I touched myself.

Then I was coming, his name on my lips, over and over while I splintered.

I dropped back, my hips lifting and falling over

themselves. The vibrations stopped, and I sank down, knees still up. Relief complete.

Jackson broke his tight hold and rounded the bed, his avid gaze on the core of my body, the mirror forgotten.

He knelt over me, gripping his dick and his gaze flitting over me, like he was deciding where to come.

He yanked down my cami to expose my breasts, taking a grab, still fucking his fist.

"I want you to come inside me," I begged.

His gaze flew to mine.

He reached between my legs, finding the cord of the sex toy.

"Leave it," I said.

He paused but angled himself to fit his ultra-hard cock to my entrance. "I don't want to hurt ye. I'll go shallow."

I didn't care about pain. All I needed was him. The buzzing returned, and Jackson tossed the remote control to the bed, collecting me in his arms while he thrust inside.

Both of us groaned. Where his dick touched the toy, he pushed it harder inside me. But there was nowhere for it to go, barely enough room for him. Maybe if he'd been smaller this would have worked.

Not that I wished that for a second.

I opened my mouth to change the plan, needing this to work with him, but then he began a slow rotation of his hips, opening me up.

Jackson swore, moving faster.

With the vibrations, it was all I could do to grab on to him. Let him fuck me with the toy right there.

He slid in and out, stretching me but not going deep.

I loved what he was doing. Protecting me this way. But I

needed everything.

I shoved my hand between our bodies, grasping the cord and tugging. At the same second, Jackson thrust into me. He bottomed out, the toy still inside, my pussy stretched around both.

I cried out in pleasure. He gritted out my name and then pulsed, coming. It triggered a second orgasm in me. I spasmed around him, holding him tight. Utterly lost.

Jackson stilled, reaching for the controller. The vibration stopped, and he withdrew from my body, pulling the toy out after with a wet, indecent sound from my arousal and his cum.

Then he sank back into me, still hard. Seeking the warmth and safety of my body.

He wrapped his arms around me, and I banded mine around him. We breathed together, coming down from the high.

How the heck did we do these things? We worked together so perfectly. Everything we tried only made it better. A more perfect fit.

Reverently, Jackson kissed my temple, his heart still racing. "Fucking hell, little fox. What are ye doing to me?"

I wished I knew.

I had the same thoughts about what he was doing to me.

One other stood out in my mind, new, bold and insistent. What if I wanted more?

# 29

## *Ariel*

Dinner was a feast of the lasagne Jackson made and a salad I threw together. The cheese was burnt to crispy on top. The tomatoes were bursts of flavour.

"This is perfect," I told him, finishing my last bite.

All of it. The meal. The evening. Him.

He shrugged, his gaze down, but a pleased smile spreading. "Raphael taught me."

"What did I say about summoning my brother?"

His amused gaze lifted to me. "I'm not inside ye right now, so it doesn't apply."

His grin was infectious, and the thought of sex with him again utterly delectable. I leapt up to clear the dishes, happiness lightening my step.

As I worked, I shared the thoughts I'd had on contacting my mother.

"It's a good idea. An unexplored path," Jackson mused. "She might have insight into your father. I was thinking about Larson. We still don't know what he wants and aren't any closer to finding out. Something's bugging me about it."

"What's that?"

"His acts aren't volatile. He hasn't done anything since he laid his trap. He got a clue from the video, came here on a hunt, found your car, and set the trackers. Maybe staked out Daisy's place and tried to find ye there. That's it. What felt like escalation calmed. How does that sound to ye?"

I considered it. "Controlled. Not the actions of a desperate man, despite what we first thought."

"Exactly."

I rinsed down the sink and dried my hands. "Maybe he isn't obsessed with me."

Jackson went quiet, lost in his thoughts.

Together, we left the bright kitchen and entered the living room, the lamps warding away the dark evening.

He stopped. "Obsession is still a danger, ye need to know that." He breathed through his nose, energy coiling around him like he had something important to say. "I run that risk. I think all men do, but I've always tried to avoid it."

My pulse skipped a beat. Did he mean with me? Because the thoughts that had sprung up in my bedroom weren't quitting. They were getting stronger. "There's one circumstance when it's okay."

That intensity grew. "What do ye mean?"

"When it's shared."

Something simmered in Jackson's gaze. Good or bad, I couldn't be sure.

On the coffee table, my phone chimed with a message.

I leaned over the armchair to grab it. "Speak of the devil. Or the stepdevil. It's Willow, my father's wife. I asked her for mom's number."

Jackson moved in behind me. Pushed my hair to one side and kissed my neck. I hooked his waistband and pulled his body against mine, trying to focus on tapping out a reply. He ran his hands under my shirt and caressed my belly.

I'd never get enough of his touch. It scared the hell out of me, how strong my need was getting, but all I wanted was more of him.

Jackson dropped to his knees and kissed my leg.

For dinner, we'd thrown on shorts and T-shirts, the apartment cosy from the central heating on high to keep at bay the winter's night.

It made easy access for him to ease his fingers into my clothes and caress my hips.

The phone in my hand rang, the call coming over the social media app I'd used for messaging.

"It's Willow."

"Answer it. She can't track ye," he commanded.

"With you doing that?"

He tugged my shorts off me. Made me widen my stance so I was bent over the arm of the soft chair with my legs apart.

Then he kissed my ass. "Go ahead and talk."

I thumbed to answer the call, putting her on loudspeaker. "H-hello?"

"Ariel, it's Willow. I got your message. I'm driving, so if there's background noise, ignore it."

Jackson glanced his fingertips over my swollen pussy.

My breathing caught. "Thanks for calling."

"I've expected you to ask about your mom for a long time," she continued, giving me a gentle telling-off for my neglect as a daughter.

I couldn't care less about my stepmother's opinion. She wasn't even that much older than me. My focus was squarely on what Jackson was doing between my legs.

"Uh-huh," I managed.

"Her husband is a piece of work," Willow continued. "Did you hear about the deal where he undercut Rosso and nearly brought a war?"

"Tell me," I said, needing a moment, though I didn't give a damn about Mafia battles, and my father had done enough dodgy shit to have no leg to stand on. Rosso was an East Coast mobster he'd once messed with.

In all this time, I'd never forgotten a name.

Try as I might, thoughts of my parents had chipped away at the wall I'd put up between my old life and new. Dad had never concealed his business dealings from me. He didn't like to acknowledge my presence so clearly thought it beneath him to censor his words around his daughter. If Willow was shocked by my mother's husband, she'd blow a gasket at what Dad had done. Betrayal in their circle was a death sentence.

She gave up a string of gossip, the sounds of traffic ebbing and flowing around her words.

Jackson slid two fingers inside me, then brought them out to rub my wet arousal up and down my core. Then he came back to my rear hole. He grazed a finger over it, teasing that untouched place.

I stilled, fascinated.

He penetrated me there, just lightly.

God, that felt strange, but also good. I needed more.

He paused, as if waiting for my go-ahead. I flexed my hips to encourage him.

It impaled me a little more. I clamped down on a whimper, not wanting Willow to clue in to what I was doing.

She didn't hear, chattering on. "Your father said he's lucky he didn't wind up dead."

Jackson sank his finger deeper, gliding the same two that had been in my pussy back to that spot. Pushed them inside, too, then held them still.

A shock of pleasure blazed.

My pussy pulsed. Or somewhere inside me did. I rose on my tiptoes.

He gave a low laugh and moved his hand in and out, teasing and finger-fucking my pussy and ass.

I adjusted to the intrusion, shifting my position to allow him better access.

This was fun. It wasn't so much that I couldn't give the occasional sound of interest to Willow's monologue, but it slowly built me up. A delicious tease.

Jackson moved beneath me, shouldering his way under my legs so he had his back to the chair. He was too big for that. I wobbled to keep my feet. His tongue touched my clit.

A sound burst from me. An abrupt gasp.

"What was that?" my stepmother asked.

"Stubbed my toe," I sputtered the desperate lie.

"Oh, honey. You should be more careful. As I was saying."

She began again. I lost the plot, twisting my fingers into Jackson's hair as he devoured my pussy, his digits still penetrating my two holes.

He closed that hand, bringing his fingers together inside me so they were touching through my walls. Then he rubbed.

Holy fuck.

I spasmed again, so suddenly close to the edge I could see the precipice. Feel the sharp drop-off approaching.

"Are you listening to me?" Willow snapped. "The number."

"Oh. Wait," I almost moaned.

"She needs ye to write it down," Jackson whispered.

"Just looking for a pen," I said louder.

Except all I wanted was for Jackson to continue.

He disengaged from me and stood, collecting my foxy pad and a pen from the coffee table with his unsullied hand. I took it, gazing at his smug grin.

He grabbed my hips and turned me back to the chair, standing behind me.

"Shoot," I said to my caller.

Jackson held my side, positioned his dick at my entrance, and thrust in.

"Fuck," I yelled. "Shit. Sorry, Willow. Dropped the pen."

"What is wrong with you?" she huffed.

I scrambled for mental capacity.

If only she knew.

His dick felt so good. Unbeatable, the slide out and punch home.

He gave that same low chuckle, for my ears only, and returned his finger to my asshole, sinking the tip in with another thrust.

"Go ahead with the number," I said weakly.

Haughtily, she read out a string of digits. I scribbled it down, my orgasm closing in.

"Just be aware of who you're talking to when you call," Willow said. "She didn't make contact for a reason."

But I only knew Jackson's wicked ownership of my body. I hung up on her without a goodbye and draped onto the chair, on tiptoes for him and an addict for his every move.

He jacked into me over and over, keeping his finger still so that extra sensation added up and sent me insane.

Then I was falling. For him. Into climax. Both and hard.

He came in me and swore with my name mixed in.

My heartbeat pounded in my ears.

"Ariel," Jackson said.

But fear struck me. I didn't want him to say anything that would change what we had. Not more and not less. It was perfect exactly how it was, and any change could break it.

So I reached for the coffee table and grabbed my list. Pointed to an item on it.

He groaned. Nodded. "Fuck, yeah. Give me a minute to recover."

An explosion rang out, shaking the furniture.

We both froze.

That had come from outside.

Not from us. Not from our lovemaking. But a blast so loud it shook the tower.

And fear replaced every one of my blissful feelings as fast as they'd come.

# 30

## Jackson

Rapidly, Ariel and I dressed. As I moved, I hit the button on my phone to group call my team.

It rang on loudspeaker, Ben joining the line first, then Valentine.

"Explosion outside of Ariel's tower. We're inside." I thudded downstairs to the bedroom floor, Ariel's hand in mine. Upstairs in the tower, the windows were tiny. Down here, there were a couple of larger ones.

"On my way," Ben snapped. "I'll call Callum."

"I'm in my car," Valentine added.

With shaking fingers, Ariel brought up the camera feed on her phone.

I stalled in my footsteps, my breathing stopping. To the right of the screen on the external view, a vehicle burned.

My car.

The one I'd worked my fingers to the bone to afford. A car I'd slept in when I had nowhere else to stay. Flames shot up from the bonnet, the rear seats already fully ablaze.

"It's my Toyota," I said through a thick throat. "Some fucker set it on fire."

Valentine swore, Ben silent where he was presumably on another line.

All I could see was the flames.

Then reality rushed in. I lifted my gaze to Ariel. "Shoes, and something to cover your mouth from the smoke. We're going to need to run."

Wide-eyed, she nodded, darting into her bedroom.

"Callum's outside," Ben returned. "It's just your car, nothing else around it and no one in sight that he can see. The fire brigade's on its way, but he says to leave the tower by the exit into the great hall. Don't go outside. It could be a trap. Callum'll meet ye in there."

Ariel emerged with her boots on, plus a bag in her hands, my jeans, and two scarves.

I dragged the jeans on, and we jogged down the stairs to the entryway, the scent of burning strong in the cooler air.

Smoke seeped in around the exterior door.

My car had been parked right outside the tower.

Ariel shoved a scarf into my hands, and I held it to my face, not stopping. The acrid fumes stung my eyes until they watered.

Ariel fumbled to open the internal door that led down a corridor to Castle McRae.

The key turned. But it wouldn't unlock.

If a second explosion went off, we were sitting ducks.

She tried again then smacked it with her hand, switching her anxious gaze to me. "I think it's jammed."

She coughed, choking on the fumes, and I nudged her aside.

A whoosh came from outside, then another boom.

It shook the stones around us, and I ducked, crouching over Ariel, protecting her with my body.

The tower around us was ancient. The stone blocks that made up the walls thick and heavy. If it fell, we'd be crushed. No way to survive.

I should be panicked. All I knew was I needed to get Ariel out of there.

But nothing fell. I jumped up.

"Come on!" I yelled at the door, wasting precious oxygen. Then I shoulder barged it.

Again, I put all my weight into it.

A third time, and it gave. I fell through.

Ariel scrambled after me, helping me to my feet.

She booted it closed behind us, and together, we sprinted down the narrow corridor to the great hall.

Callum was approaching from the other side, the huge man's forehead creased in a frown. He wasted no time, guiding us across the echoing space to the staircase that ran up the internal wall. Two others, carrying fire extinguishers, jogged down the stairs, passing us to run out of the huge oak front door.

At the top, we entered a corridor with other apartments that families lived in, then up another set of stairs to the solar—the apartment Callum shared with his wife.

"Go inside. Lock the door. Keep your phone on," he ordered.

"Are we in danger?" Ariel asked. "Will the walls hold?"

He glowered, his lip curling. "Will the walls hold? Are ye kidding? My castle has withstood sieges from armies. These stone walls are impenetrable. No fucker will touch ye under my roof."

Then he was gone, and I twisted the big key in the lock and pulled Ariel into my arms.

We slid to the floor.

Breathed.

It took a long moment for my heart to calm.

"Sorry about your car," she uttered against my chest.

"I don't care about that as long as you're safe," I replied.

"You loved it, though."

I loved her more.

I couldn't say, but neither could I deny it to myself for a second more.

What had started as the need to avoid her had turned into repeated clashes, wanting nothing more than to be near her, to know she was safe. The hunt for her after her car was hit had kickstarted something in me, and now, I was so far over the line it had become invisible.

I fucking loved her, and if it killed me, I'd protect her.

A walk-through of Callum and Mathilda's solar showed me we were alone. From their lounge windows, the red glow of the fire far below filled the night.

Ben and Valentine updated us on the search they'd commenced. On Ariel's camera view, the fire brigade extinguished the blaze with water piped up from the loch.

By the early hours, a smouldering pile of metal was all that was left behind.

The police showed up, and Callum brought them to the solar. We scrolled through the video feed's history but saw nothing. My car was parked right at the edge of the camera's range.

No movement until the blast apart from thirty seconds

before, when a small animal slunk past the edge of the screen.

A fox, perhaps.

Whoever set the fire took care to stay out of view.

A patrol was arranged for the rest of the night, and Callum returned to us again, his lady with him. She held out her arms for Ariel, holding her close, a surrogate grandmother to a lass in need.

Likewise, Callum gave me an unexpected hug.

A wave rushed me, the need for comfort and for someone to say it would all be okay, a sense I hadn't had in a decade after my ability to gain family comfort was lost.

I didn't stop him ruffling my hair.

We moved to their sofas.

"The police agree it's arson," Callum told us. "That was no accident."

Ariel stuffed her hands under her legs, her expression bleak. "This is my fault. It's bad enough that Jackson's car has been destroyed, but what if the castle had caught on fire? Multiple families live here, and they were all in danger because someone's chasing me."

Mathilda hushed her. "This is the fault of the person who set the fire, and them only. Stone can be cleaned and cars can be replaced. You two can't. The most important thing is that no one was hurt."

She was right. I'd clung to that car as it had been my only real possession. I had a decent salary now. A first paycheque I'd barely spent.

My shoulders sank. "Thanks for sheltering us."

The lady of the castle's gaze slipped from me to Ariel, her expression knowing. "It's better if you stay here for the night, just until the smoke dissipates and the scene cools down. You can have Lennox's old bedroom." She summoned a small smile for Ariel. "Together, I mean."

Everyone knew, then.

I'd got so lost in Ariel, and in hating secrets, that I hadn't thought about the implications of being with her. I needed to have that conversation with Ben. With Raphael.

But more, I needed to curl up around the woman I loved and fucking sleep.

The following morning, there were updates but no real news. The overnight patrol had passed undisturbed. No culprit had been discovered.

In a car borrowed from Callum, and with an escort of two, Ariel and I headed over to the hangar.

Today, we were going to catch a stalker.

# 31

## Ariel

An icy blast swept across the front of the aircraft hangar. I huddled in the thick jumper I'd borrowed from Mathilda and hurried, Jackson's hand clamped firmly around mine.

In the depths of the building, Valentine strode from the bunkhouse, pulling a long-sleeved tactical shirt over his head, his hair damp like he'd just got out of the shower.

He lifted his chin at us. "Jax. Foxy. Good to see ye both still breathing."

Jackson grumbled at him, and Valentine grinned.

We entered the bodyguard office, Ben and Daisy already waiting along with a couple of members of the mountain rescue team. My friend leapt up and hugged me, and we curled on the sofa together.

Jackson didn't sit. He'd dropped my hand outside the room and now stood in front of a large screen on the wall, a map of the area displayed.

Ben cleared his throat. "In the room, Jackson, Ariel, Valentine, Daisy, Lochinvar, Cameron, me. On the line, Gordain and Raphael. Gentlemen, can ye hear me?"

"Loud and clear," Gordain announced over the open phone line.

"Roger that," my brother confirmed. "Ariel, are ye okay?"

I shook my head, not that he could see. We'd messaged each other last night, so he was up to speed. "No. I'm furious."

To my horror, my voice broke. I hadn't wanted to get emotional, but I'd reached my limit. It was one thing hiding out, but at least I'd felt safe in my tower and no one else had been in danger apart from me. Larson had upped the stakes.

I forced back rising fear and gritted my teeth. "He exploded Jackson's car. I'm out for blood."

Ben held my gaze. "You'll have it. Or at least a non-lethal version of it. The objective of the day is to lure Larson out of hiding and bring him in. I had a conversation with the police about this last night and told them my intention. They'll either be here, or they won't. They're understaffed, and I'd rather get this over with now. Everyone in agreement?"

We all nodded or voiced accordance, and my heart pounded.

This was happening. We'd catch him. I couldn't wait to get out there.

Ben left his desk and went to the map, pointing out locations as he spoke. "The plan is to use the trackers Larson hid to lead him to a new location. Ariel's Mini will be driven from the mechanic's, through the lanes, and out to a cabin west of here. Prior to that, the rest of us will get into position in the hills surrounding. The cabin is rigged for sound and video. Once in place, we sit and wait."

I wrinkled my nose. "Assuming he can't resist following me."

Ben inclined his head. "Larson isn't likely to set up a tail. He'll wait to see where ye go and bide his time. I'm not expecting this to be over quickly."

Jackson snorted. "And ye won't be going anywhere."

I blinked at him. "What are you talking about?"

"You're staying here, in the middle of the hangar, with people around ye at all times. The mountain rescue team will be operating training from the command centre, and you'll be in plain sight of them and under their care for as long as this takes." Jackson gestured at the mountain rescue crew members present. "Cameron previously worked as a bodyguard, so he knows the protocol better than anyone. Lochinvar saves people on a daily basis. Plus there's a full crew at the pilot school today. There's no way anyone can come for ye here, and Daisy will keep ye company. You're in safe hands."

I opened my mouth, swinging my gaze between the people in the room. I'd woken up determined to get out there and find the man who was threatening not only me but Jackson, too. I didn't want to be managed. Coddled. But equally, I had no intention of becoming a hazard.

I knew from Cait, who'd married Lochinvar, that she'd had a stalker who'd pursued her here, years ago. She'd driven out, and he'd caught her. Lochinvar had turned the world upside down to get her back and nearly died for his efforts.

Horrendous. Ugly and violent.

I couldn't even comprehend the same happening to Jackson if I was the one in the clutches of a maniac.

My rebuttals died on my tongue. "Who will drive my car? If Larson is watching, he'll know it's a trap if someone else gets in it."

Ben answered. "Isobel. She used to race so is probably the best driver on the estate. She'll wear your ski suit and hat, which she is collecting now from the snowboarding centre. You're about the same height and both dark-haired, and if she hides her face well enough, it should work."

Dread sank through me. "I don't like putting her in danger."

"We don't think she will be. Even if Larson pounces quickly, the rest of us will already be there and can respond. The more likely scenario is that he'll wait it out until he can't resist any longer. Isobel will leave the car at the cabin, change clothes, then ski away. Lennox will pick her up soon after. We worked out a route earlier that'll mean she can get away fast on a cross-country ski trail."

"While I stay here and the rest of you lie in wait," I muttered, then turned my gaze on Jackson. "What about you?"

"One option is that I wait in the cabin," he replied.

Instant panic rushed me. "Just sitting in the line of fire until he arrives?"

His expression remained stony. "That's the idea. He blew up my car. He already knows we're...friends."

Pressure steadily built around me. There were too many people watching, or listening, in my brother's case.

My voice came out tight, my stomach sickening. "You plan to go face to face with him?"

"It's the best way to find out what he wants."

"Or to get yourself killed."

He worked his jaw. "Ben, Valentine, and Gordain will be

close by and watching, so we'll know the minute he shows up."

"I hate this idea," I gritted out.

"What else are we going to do? We're not the police. To capture and interrogate him is a police matter, and we already know they aren't prioritising this. Once there's proof he's done something wrong, they will. So it's up to us to talk to him. That's our objective."

I gave a single, adamant shake of my head. "Then I'll be the pawn. I'll sit in the house and wait for him."

Jackson's reaction was immediate. "Not happening."

I stared him down, the rest of the room fading around me until it was just us, locked in this battle. "Then the same applies to you."

There was a moment of balancing.

Stubbornness meeting protectiveness.

A silence seemed to settle into realisation across the whole team.

Ben tapped his desk. "The alternative is no one's in the house after Isobel leaves. Jackson can take a guard position like the rest of us. Watch and wait."

I shot my gaze to him, hope replacing my panic. "I like that a lot better. What happens when Larson appears?"

"Like Jackson says, we have microphones in the house. We can talk to him remotely."

I exhaled. "Okay. I agree."

Too quickly, everyone was moving, positions set and the plan underway. Jackson and his team left, and Isobel turned up at the hangar in my clothes, looking remarkably me-like. She hopped into a taxi someone had rustled up to drive out to the garage, and I got lost in the memory of how I'd huddled around Jackson for as long as I could in Callum and Mathilda's spare bedroom. We'd slept, locked together, but had otherwise just held each other.

What if that had been the last time?

"Come on, nothing's going to happen for hours. Let's get some breakfast into you," Daisy said, curling an arm through mine.

She led me to the hangar's busy rec room, pressing a cup of tea into my hands while she buttered toast.

But fear had curdled my stomach, and I couldn't eat a thing.

A couple of hours passed with the only updates expected ones.

Isobel had left the car at the cabin and skied safely to meet her husband.

The bodyguard crew were in position and waiting.

There was nothing, literally nothing, for me to do but sit and stare at my phone.

It buzzed, and I leapt to answer it.

But it was only my brother.

*Raphael: I had a cryptic message from Willow last night. She sounded fake-worried about you and mentioned our mother. Any clue what that was about?*

I'd forgotten all about that plan.

I sighted Lochinvar lurking outside the door of the rec room. At my gesture, he came in.

"Can I use your ops centre to make a phone call?" I asked.

It was too noisy here.

The man scratched his thick black beard, then nodded. "There's a line of enquiry I need to follow up, but if ye stay in there, I'll take the bodyguard office."

"A line of enquiry?"

His frown deepened, and his gaze leapt to Daisy. "When the two of ye lasses were terrorised out of the cottage, we had the whole crew out on the hunt. This morning, one of the new members let slip that they'd seen a woman walking a wee dog. They hadn't thought to mention it, because obviously she wasn't the person stealing through your house. But I'm pissed off that any assumption was made at all, and also, it's an avenue we didn't explore." He gestured to the room. "Go ahead and do your task while I do mine."

He left us alone, stomping into the room opposite.

With Daisy at my side, I settled at the big table in the ops centre, the door closed.

Before I could chicken out, I sent a quick text identifying myself then dialled the number my stepmother had given me.

It rang. I set it to loudspeaker, my chest tight.

Daisy turned her big eyes on me.

"My mother," I whispered.

The woman who'd walked out on me. Left me to a father who saw me as nothing more than baggage at best or merchandise at worst.

Daisy took my hand in hers, the solid support I relied on.

The longer the phone rang, the more my anxiety rose.

The line clicked. I jerked forward.

But it was the call timing out, no answerphone.

Deflated, I sank back in the seat.

Of course she wouldn't answer a strange number calling at... I peeked up at the ops centre's big clock. Performed some mental maths. It was ten AM for us, which made it two in the morning for her.

Even if she was awake, I had no reason to expect her to want to talk to me.

My single line of attack had failed.

There was nothing for me to do. Nothing but sit here and wait. Panic over someone getting hurt.

Frustrated, I dropped my chin to my chest, wanting to damage something.

For several days, I'd used up my energy on Jackson's body. I hadn't missed work or anything else, because I'd got so wrapped up in him. Now, I was gunning to do something.

And my single thing had failed.

I exhaled and turned to Daisy.

My phone rang.

I jerked back to it. My mother's number was onscreen.

My pulse pounded, and I swiped to answer. "Hello…" I swallowed bile. "Mom."

Empty space filled the line. Then a little reply came. "Ariel?"

That voice… I'd forgotten the sweet baby-doll tone my mother deployed. She hadn't always used it. Normally only when talking to my father. It set my teeth on edge.

"Yes, it's me. Willow gave me your number. Is it safe for you to talk?"

"It's safe. I'm alone in the house. Well, guarded, but no one's listening." There was another pause. "What was it you needed?"

I dropped my head back, stunned into silence.

What did I need? Years of explanation? Of knowing she gave a damn?

I forced myself to calm. "I'll be brief. I spoke to Dad recently, and he made an offhand comment that a problem

I was having with a boy was a subject for my mother, not my father. Considering I haven't seen you in years, have you any idea why he'd say that?"

My mother made an off sound. "Don't mention him to me. Your father hated me."

I bit my tongue, leaving her to explain.

"He hates all women," she added. "He barely respects the men he works with, and that's only through fear. Even that doesn't stop him from his deals. You know he never hid his ambitions."

I squinted, a little bit lost.

She hiccupped, and I wondered if she'd been drinking.

"I suppose you want to know why I left?"

I wanted to bring sarcasm but retained control. "I've wondered."

"I had to leave. Or he'd have killed me," she said in a rush, her doll-voice higher still. "I wasn't young or beautiful as I had been. After birthing his three kids, I didn't have the tight body and I wasn't willing to get surgery. Not for him. I met another man and fell in love."

"You married a murderer," I let slip.

She tutted. "Don't be naïve. They're all the same. That's just the way of men. Ted would never hurt me. In comparison with your father, he worships the ground I walk on, and he's the only man your father fears, the only person who could protect me."

Naïve? My blood boiled. "Meanwhile, you left me with Dad. The man who hates women and who scared you. Why didn't you take me?"

At last, I'd asked the question that had plagued me.

The door swung open. Raphael walked in.

I stared at him, open-mouthed. How many days had passed? Had he finished his exams? When he'd been on the call, I'd assumed it was just for information.

His gaze locked on to the phone.

"Oh, honey, I couldn't," our mom breathed. "Not any of you. Even if he didn't value you, the boys belonged to him, and my husband would never take another man's child. I knew your father would marry you off soon enough. You'd be safe from him."

Safe? This was getting me nowhere.

Only angrier at her selfishness, even if I understood the self-preservation which had led her to leave.

I heaved in a breath, needing to wrap this up. "Then you don't know anything?"

"What was that he said again? That it was a question for me rather than him? He probably wanted you to do this. He always liked me to know what he'd been doing. Quiet torment. He never forgave me for leaving him, even though he didn't want me. But what do I know? You know more than me, you were always watching him and listening. Just be a good girl and do what he wants. You'll be fine," my mother promised.

I was so done.

I hung up on her, shaking my head.

Daisy choked. "Do what he wants? She knows you're not there anymore, surely?"

I stared between her and my brother.

"Yes, she knew," Raphael stated. "Which only confirms a suspicion Jackson had."

"When did you talk to Jackson?" I asked.

"He left me a message, catching me up on a few things."

My brother's expression gentled.

I needed to know everything in that message. Every last word.

But my brother focused on that first damning question.

"She knows you're not there but still expects our father to marry you off. Mother dearest, whose husband loves her and tells her everything, just confirmed exactly why you're being hunted."

I breathed out. "Because Dad means to do it again, and he's bragging about the deal."

# 32

## Jackson

I drummed my fingers on the steering wheel, edging madness. Ahead, thick trees blanketed in snow cloaked the glen where Ariel's Mini was now parked outside a rigged-up cabin. My phone, supported by a holder on my dashboard, displayed the locations of the rest of my team, spread around the hillsides, my own a pulsing beat of light on the map.

Silence surrounded me.

All I could see was a pattern.

Larson had started off calm, but yesterday, he'd escalated savagely. There was no demand, no communication, just persistence.

Too well, I knew what had to happen next. He had to take a risk, though it was us here and not the woman he pursued. He'd challenged us, we'd challenged him back. Ariel was safe, protected by teams of people in a public place. Larson only had one option, and that was to come here.

After the cottage and my car, I knew he wouldn't be able to resist the bait, which meant all we needed to do was wait.

him out. If it took all night, I didn't care. If it took a week, I'd be here.

After we'd left the hangar, Ben had pulled me aside and told me not to do anything stupid, but my guess was Larson would take that trophy.

The insight into a fucked-up mind came in handy.

Both of his previous acts had been designed to get Ariel to run. My guess was he'd do something to the cabin which forced her to leave, if she was inside, which limited the risk to him and still gave him the result he wanted.

Follow her, chase her down, spirit her away.

After last night's drama, my guess was he'd lead with fire.

I'd shared my thoughts with the team, and we'd adapted our lying-in-wait process to cover that possibility. Ben monitored two exterior cameras, Valentine the others. Gordain and I were tasked with watching the roads, mine a winding track through the forest. In an hour, we'd switch.

"Check in," Ben ordered over the comms.

"All quiet here," I reported.

Gordain gave the okay, then there was silence again.

"Valentine, do ye copy?" the boss said.

Still nothing.

"Valentine, come in."

I sat up, peering at the map. Valentine's tracker had moved, just slightly, but into a new position.

My pulse picked up a faster beat.

Maybe he had seen something but wasn't able to speak. If that was the case, we had codes to send.

None had been received.

Or he'd seen something and taken off without thinking

it through. He was new to this work, as was I. Hell, this was barely bodyguard work. We were on a goddamn stakeout. None of us knew the rules.

Yet logic dictated he would tell us what he was doing.

I readied myself to go find him. I'd be quicker on foot, as his position was directly beneath mine in the glen, off-road.

With my phone in my hand, I unlocked my door.

Stepped onto the snow, sinking an inch.

"Shite," Valentine said over the comms, his tone full of chagrin. "I was just taking a piss, and my in-ear blipped out. Think it needs charging."

His brother cursed him out. I breathed a sigh of relief, imagining an unsaid quip from Valentine about no one thinking about his dick. If his brother wasn't around, he'd make the joke. Be more casual. But—

A twig snapped behind me, the sound overly loud in the silent landscape.

"Turn around slowly," a man said.

My adrenaline rushed.

Though I'd never heard Larson speak, the American accent gave him away.

I twisted, sighting my enemy ten feet away at the edge of the trees.

A tall and skinny man with fair hair poking out from under a black woollen hat, the rest of his clothes dark, too.

I opened my mouth to alert my team.

Larson lifted his hand, some device clutched between his fingers. He pressed the trigger.

Something hit me hard, slicing through my jacket.

And I dropped like a stone.

# 33

## Ariel

We left the ops centre, letting Lochinvar and his people take ownership again for their training.

I muttered apologies to the people I knew for chewing up their day with babysitting me, then hid out once more in the rec room, Daisy taking a bathroom break and Raphael making a phone call which required him to walk away, frowning.

At a different table, Cameron, Lochinvar's second-in-command, read a book with Zander, his five-year-old son, all while keeping a quiet eye on me.

I sipped coffee and tried to reconcile my mother's confession.

Was she so broken by the actions of men that ownership by a terrible person who loved her was more important than fighting for the children she'd made?

Jackson's mother had blamed and hated her daughter. Mine had abandoned hers.

I'd never understand either of them.

Even as messed up as I probably was, I knew love.

My heart throbbed, missing the man I'd got used to when I'd meant to do anything but.

The chair across the table from me screeched as someone pulled it out.

I lifted my gaze to the head of the mountain rescue team, joining me at my table. "How are ye doing?" Lochinvar asked.

I shrugged. "I've been better."

"It'll be over soon, I promise. These kinds of things have an expiration date." Lochinvar flashed me a rare smile. "Besides, Ava misses ye as her teacher and demanded I help get ye back to work."

I found my own smile. There were so many families around here. Where Cameron had Zander, who was part of a troop of half-wild mountain boys, and a younger daughter who was a little angel, Lochinvar was the father of three girls. His middle child, five-year-old Ava, was one of my favourite students. A big personality, she was happy to boss others around as much as cheer them on. If she fell on the slopes, she picked herself back up and carried on.

I could take a lesson from that.

Sulking over my parents wouldn't get me anywhere.

"I appreciate the advice. You lived through something like this," I said to Lochinvar.

"Worse. He took Cait. I almost lost my mind. If I could've raised an army to protect her, like your lad did for ye, I would've."

I glanced around, suddenly realising what Jackson had done.

I'd been to the hangar any number of times, but today was far busier than usual.

People milled everywhere, wandering in and out of the rec room. Through the open door, they chatted in groups, gazes sliding my way on the regular. Gabe and Effie, Casey and Brodie with one of their kids, Isobel and Lennox.

Jackson had asked them to be here. Not just a few faces, but everyone he could find.

God.

With a few more words of encouragement, Lochinvar left me, and I finished the dregs of my coffee, never alone from my army's company and gaining strength from their care.

Leaving the rec room, I sought Raphael in the busy space, mechanics coming and going, engines roaring, and the bright sounds of people everywhere.

I needed to find out what happened to my brother's training, but on my way to joining him, out on the hangar floor, my phone rang.

Bridgette calling.

Jeez.

Fire lit in my belly. After all her actions had done, and the grief her mother had given me, apparently not even Jackson filling them in on my situation had deterred them.

I wanted to answer and yell at her. Take out all my hurt and worry on an idiotic kid who'd earned a telling-off but didn't deserve the amount of angst I was ready to unleash.

Nor did I want to scupper Effie's business by outraging the parents she relied on for an income. I shook, glaring at the call until it rang off. Then I took several deep breaths, calming myself.

A text sounded.

I jumped to read it.

*Bridgette: I know you're ignoring my call. No one misses their phone ringing. Anyway, we're still away, but my mother told me to apologise and to ask again if you could…*

I stopped reading.

A shout came up across the hangar, someone calling something urgent to Raphael.

Ahead of me by a few paces, my brother stilled.

He spun around.

At his expression, my heart dropped. I stared at him. "What?"

"Ben's office."

He guided me inside and lifted his phone, dialling someone. "Ben, talk to us," he said.

Our friend spoke over loudspeaker. "Can Ariel hear me?"

"I'm here. What's happened?"

Already, I knew it wasn't good. Had that twisting in my gut which preceded news that was liable to hurt.

I tensed for the impact.

"Jackson last reported in thirty minutes ago. We call out every ten. He's been silent since."

"What does that mean?" I burst out. "He missed the call? Why would that happen?"

Raphael strode to a laptop and activated it, tapping in a password to bring up a map, the same as the one Jackson had once shown me.

"I just made it to his last known location," Ben continued.

On the screen, four pulses of light converged in the middle of the forest, miles away.

Raphael pointed at them, quietly identifying each. First,

the two close together. "Jax and Ben." Then the two further away. "Gordain and Valentine."

"You're right on top of him," I said to Ben. "We're looking at the map now. Your tracker is with his."

"I found his phone discarded on the ground."

Oh God, no.

"He's gone?" I uttered.

"There are footprints leading away, though the snow is covering them rapidly. Valentine's tracking them now."

Another voice came in, Valentine's. "I reached a lane. The prints lead to another car's trail."

I squinted, trying to work that out. "He got into another car? Left without telling anyone?"

"Shite. We don't know he left voluntarily," Ben said. "Valentine, are there any other footprints?"

"Possibly. Hard to say with how fast the snow is pitching."

Ice slid through my veins.

"Ben, are there signs of a struggle? Was his car broken into?" Raphael asked.

"Negative," Ben returned. "At least I can't be sure for the same reason as Valentine. It's an open clearing here, so the snow has covered everything. I had to sweep it to even find his phone."

Gordain joined in. "That car has a tracker and a voice recorder. Ben, access it now. Tell us if we're commencing a hunt."

Raphael went pale. "What if he arranged to be picked up because he had somewhere else to be?"

"What do you mean?" I demanded.

My brother shot his gaze to mine. "In the message he left me, he revealed that his mother had tried to call him. Her stepson's hearing had been brought forward to today. She wanted him to be a character witness, but what if he went to do the opposite? To give reasons why that fucker should never get parole?"

"He didn't mention that to me," Ben said.

He hadn't told me about it either, though I knew he wished he'd given evidence against the man originally.

I walked away a few steps, feeling sick.

Then there was what I'd done. Told him it was okay to be obsessed when he'd warned me of how he never wanted to be. How inconsiderate of me. How could I have said that to his face after what he'd been through?

I was still holding my phone, and I shoved it into my pocket.

There was a piece of paper inside.

I drew it out, puzzling at it. I unfolded my list.

Weird. I definitely hadn't grabbed that when we'd fled the tower.

Then I noted a new line, scrawled across the bottom.

*Fall in love with him*, it read.

Jackson had added this. He'd written it and hidden it there for me to find.

My poor heart throbbed. I knew without doubt that he hadn't left me of his own volition.

"He's been taken," I said, turning back.

My brother held my gaze.

"He wouldn't leave any of us. We're his family, and he'd never walk away, not for any reason. He's been taken, and we're going to find him."

# 34

# *Jackson*

A slap hit my face, jolting my head to the left. I groaned, opening my eyes, my whole body aching and every muscle strained.

A man stood over me.

Larson.

I reared up, trying to stand, but my hands were locked behind me in handcuffs and zip tied to my seat. Likewise, my ankles were tied to the chair.

My action tipped me forward. I landed on my face and shoulder before tumbling to my side with a clatter on the hardwood floor.

"For fuck's sake," my kidnapper said. He righted me with a huff of effort. "Calm down. You're still alive, so assume you're useful for now."

I gritted my teeth, forcing my brain to wake up faster to assess the situation.

Memories flooded me. He'd appeared in the woods and Tasered me with a shock of electricity outside my car

Dropped me to the ground before I'd had a chance to move. He'd followed the rules of weapon training—finger on the trigger if you mean business, and don't hesitate.

Somehow, he'd got me here.

I glanced around at the tidy living room, trying to identify the location. Typical comfortable space, with blankets on the back of the couch and family pictures on the wall, no one I knew.

A child in one photo seemed familiar, but I couldn't place her.

Almost as if I'd seen her on a TV show or a video of some kind.

It was still daylight, so I hadn't been unconscious long, which probably meant we weren't far from home. He must've gagged me, too, because fibres clung to my tongue.

My jaw ached from my fall, but it only added to the catalogue of minor aches.

I wasn't badly hurt. Why, I had no idea.

Larson took a seat opposite me. Set down the Taser he'd still been holding and lifted a phone.

"How did ye knock me out?" I asked.

He squinted at his screen. "Blood choke hold."

Compression to the neck, a technique used in martial arts. You clamped down on the person's carotid artery and jugular vein and could render them unconscious in seconds. It didn't even take much effort. It also didn't last long.

"I should've woken up when ye released my throat," I said.

Larson spread his arms. "Sometimes people die from it. Probably mixing it with the Taser was a bad idea. Whatever, it worked for me, and it gave me enough time to carry you to the car. Drugging your ass would've been such a pain."

He was stronger than he appeared. He'd so easily been able to capture me.

I'd wanted this, to come face to face with the man who'd terrorised Ariel, but he had me at his mercy.

I needed to regain control. The rule of thumb was to create a connection and generate sympathy. Kinship with your kidnapper.

"My arms hurt. I think my right one is broken. Can ye unlock the cuffs?" I asked.

He shook his head, his gaze still on his phone. "The fucking camera has crashed. Cheap piece of crap."

"I'm pretty good with electronics. Let me help," I tried.

Larson sighed and raised his gaze to me. "With a fake broken arm? Just be quiet."

He wasn't what I expected.

Skinny and tall with fair hair, as per the CCTV footage we'd seen, but he was also intelligent-looking. No feverish glint in his eyes. No real emotion, except for perhaps slight boredom.

I didn't know who I was reasoning with.

I tried another approach.

"Ye want me to be quiet? After everything you've done? Ye terrorised my girlfriend, tried to kidnap her then stalked her through her friend's house. Ye even burned my fucking car to smoke her out. Doesn't that earn me a voice?"

This got me his attention. Larson leaned on the armrest, regarding me. "I'm here for Ariel, boyfriend, but none of that was to do with me. I didn't touch your car."

"Bullshit."

His blond eyebrows dove together. "Last night, the

explosion across the loch drew me over the water, and I encountered a woman with bobbed hair fleeing the scene with her dog. I guess that's your arsonist, not me. If you need proof, I've got her on camera."

He tapped his phone. Grimaced.

"When it works."

I stared, the description eerily familiar.

Earlier, I'd checked my messages to find one from my mother, sent after I'd ignored a call from her yesterday. She'd been sobbing, telling me the parole hearing for TJ had been brought forward to today. I hadn't listened to the rest.

What were the chances that another bobbed-haired woman had been lurking around here?

Larson grumbled at his phone, and my thoughts swerved in a new direction as another part of his speech registered.

*Across the loch.*

The village was across the loch from Castle McRae and this house had the snug, cottage-like feel of a village home.

So I was in the village. Not far away at all. But where?

A further memory eked in, and I felt like a fucking idiot.

When Bridgette's mother had rung Ariel, and I'd intercepted the call, she'd stated that they were on holiday but there was a problem with the doorbell camera at their home. She'd wanted Ariel to go fix it for their peace of mind, but what if it had been shut down so a stranger could come and go as he pleased?

I'd had it in the back of my mind to go check, but it hadn't been important—the woman and her child weren't due back for a few more days and other matters had taken over. I wasn't about to jump to their commands any more than Ariel would, but I wouldn't leave them unsafe either.

I knew exactly where I was.

All that time, the clue to our hunter's lair had been under my nose.

But that did nothing when I couldn't communicate that to anyone or free myself.

I choked out my words. "But ye don't deny stalking Ariel?"

"If you mean waiting for her to come to me, which is exactly what she's about to do, guilty. That's why I needed you. An incentive to get her ass here, considering she'd hidden so well. You were a guess, but a good one. Besties with her brother but somehow absent from your security team this past week. Where could you have been but squirreled away with her?"

My anger curled in my stomach. Adrenaline rushed where I needed to take this man apart. He'd scared her. Forced her into hiding. Then calmly admitted his method.

I was losing my cool, aided by the fact I felt like I'd been hit by a truck.

A sense of desperation came over me.

"I get it," I spat. "I get that you're obsessed. Ye have been since meeting Ariel at school, but ye can't have her. She'll never be yours."

Larson tilted his head at me. "That's a lot of words from a man in handcuffs with no power in this situation."

The phone he'd been messing with reset in his hand, and he flashed a short smile. He stood, training the lens on me.

"Get ready to say cheese so I can send this to her and bring her in."

My blood chilled.

Ariel could not come here.

She couldn't be anywhere near this man.

"Ye can't have her," I roared. "She's mine. Mine to be obsessed with. And she's obsessed with me as well. I will never give her up."

Larson rolled his eyes. "I'm not interested in her beyond my paycheque, Jackson, so shut the fuck up."

He took the shot and went to send it, speaking as he typed. "Don't alert the cops, yada, yada."

He then lifted his gaze to the window behind me, focusing on something outside.

His features settled into a frown.

"You've got to be kidding me. I haven't even hit send."

I twisted, trying to see. In my peripheral vision, I caught a glimpse of a large group of people on the street. A net curtain hid us, so I wasn't sure that they could see us, but I opened my mouth to shout.

"No, you fucking don't," he snapped.

Larson marched over and put the Taser to my temple. It had a shock point as well as the firing mechanism. At close range, it could give me brain damage.

I closed my mouth, breathing through my nose.

"Now listen up. Whatever assumption you made about why I'm here, you're wrong. I don't give a fuck about Ariel. Aside from this specific use."

"What use?" I didn't believe him.

He stood over me, watching whoever was outside. "I'm not explaining it to you then repeating myself. Lucky for you, your obsession is right outside with a whole inconvenient troop of others."

Ariel had come. And not alone.

I closed my eyes, wishing her anywhere but here.

Larson stooped and collected something from the floor beside me. Then he dragged it over my head and strung it around my mouth. A gag. Tightened so I couldn't speak.

He placed a phone call, somehow connecting to Ariel.

The line was answered, no one saying a word.

"The door's open," Larson told her. "Come inside, Ariel. Bring your brother. Either one of you makes a move I don't like, or anyone outside causes a fuss, and your boy here gets a shock to the brain. Understood?"

To my horror, her voice returned. "Loud and clear."

# 35

## Ariel

"**D**on't go in there," Lochinvar challenged.

On the snowy path outside Bridgette's house, her doorbell cam on the ground by my feet, I felt no cold. Nothing but burning need to get to the man I cared about.

"He's got Jackson," I countered, turning to face the twenty people who'd come along.

I'd brought an army and I couldn't use them.

After the phone call from Bridgette, it had been so obvious where Larson had been hiding. Jackson had told me her mom had wanted a favour—something to do with their house. It had taken me thirty seconds to see how Bridgette had publicised being on holiday on her social media, sharing goddamned bikini shots as well.

What better way to advertise an empty home?

I despaired over that kid. I also wanted to hug her—her risky behaviour had enabled me to find Jackson.

"I have to go in," I insisted. "What other choice is there?"

"We rush him," someone in the group called.

"And he kills Jackson," I concluded. "Every other version of what we could do ends up with Jackson hurt. I can't risk that. I'm going in and hearing him out. It's not like he can walk away with all of you here. Will you stay? Please?"

With reluctance, people slowly nodded.

Raphael took my arm, slowing me. "I'll go first."

I eyed the innocuous entry door and took a shaky breath, my bravado barely holding on. "Let's do this."

As Larson had stated, the lock had been left on the catch. We entered Bridgette's house.

"In the lounge," Larson called.

We stepped inside.

The man I hadn't seen since he'd attacked me in a school corridor years ago stood behind Jackson, one hand on his shoulder and the other holding a device to his temple.

"Let's make this quick," Larson said. "Sit down."

Both of us obeyed. I took in Jackson. The cloth tied around his head to gag him. A bruise reddening his jaw.

No blood. Nothing but anger in his eyes. His gaze met mine, and I wanted to cry from imagining the worst but seeing him alive.

"Send your people away," Larson ordered with a head jerk to the window.

"Why bother? You aren't walking away from this," I said on a breath. I'd meant to be calm, but that was an impossibility when faced with Jackson tied to a seat.

"Yes I will. Even if I don't, he'll send others."

There was no confusion over who he meant.

"What did my dad ask you to do?" I said.

"Exactly this. Get you," he looked between me and Raphael, "both of you together. Your boy here just got in the way. Or maybe I should call him a happy accident." He held up a phone. "As for the ask, Mr West can tell you himself."

Dad's face appeared onscreen. I stiffened, but it was only a video.

"I won't bore you with the preamble," Larson said, skipping on.

Dad spoke. "Of Gabriel, I expect nothing. Your life has been made elsewhere, and I respect your choices. After becoming a father, you'll understand me better, and I expect you'll see my point of view. Family comes first, always. Even so, your absence in my life presents a problem for me. People notice, competitors particularly. They judge me for not controlling my children. Which brings me to Raphael."

At my side, my brother stilled, his gaze laser focused on the video.

Dad continued. "By now, you should have finished your flight school exams, am I correct? Congratulations on your undoubted success. You've made your old man proud, and I'm glad to see your intelligence came from me, rather than your mother. I regret that I had to find out your prowess by subterfuge, rather than from your own lips, but I'll let that slide, considering how useful you're about to become to me."

Jackson stared at my brother. Horrified, I leaned into Raphael like I could protect him from the threat.

Because Dad had just played his hand.

He'd used Jackson to lure me in, but I wasn't his objective. It was Raphael all along.

We'd suspected that from the first call, but the knowledge he'd used me and hurt Jackson to get there burned.

Larson darkened the phone, killing the recording. "What your father hasn't stated is there's a choice. Raphael, you can return to California and assume a position at your father's side. You'll learn the family business and take on more responsibilities as the years pass and his trust in you grows."

"What's the other option?" I said.

Larson switched his attention to me. "You come with me and your father finds another way to pay the debt his kids owe him. Oh, and your friend here will accompany us. Your father has a use for him."

I'd be sold, and Jackson...what? Put into service? Or killed because I'd chosen him.

"No," Raphael said. "He can't do this."

Larson blinked. "Which part?"

"Fuck up our lives."

Larson shrugged. "Don't shoot the messenger. Honestly, I agree with you. Fuck that guy. But I'm just following orders."

I curled my lip. "Don't pretend you aren't deep in this. I know you. Remember what happened in school? You're a sadist."

Larson's eyes narrowed. I'd pissed him off. Good.

But then he heaved a sigh, resting a hand on Jackson's shoulder. He settled his gaze on me. "I feel like I need to apologise for that."

My words dried up.

"In my defence," Larson continued. "I was a messed-up kid. When your father gave me his instruction, I was new to this job."

I jerked forward. "What the hell are you talking about? You were working for my father then?"

He gave a short nod. "He needed someone in the school to watch you, and I got the job."

My history suddenly looked a lot murkier. Memories of Larson following me around adapted. Dad had ordered that?

"Why?" I managed.

"He didn't explain himself to me, the only thing I knew was that I had to scare away any other boys and report back to him if you were interested in anyone."

Briefly, I closed my eyes. "He hired you to keep me away from boys."

Because he intended to sell me off. A teenage bride, virginity guaranteed.

Larson nodded. "Something about keeping you clean, by which I guessed he meant untouched. I figured he was an overprotective father. I didn't have a dad myself, so I accepted it, and his money, at face value. Anyway, I reported to your father that you'd flirted with a boy, and he ordered me to direct your attention onto me."

Hot emotion rushed. "That's why you attacked me?"

I didn't want to believe him.

But my would-be kidnapper had the nerve to look embarrassed. "I made a bad choice. I had no idea what I was doing, and I've regretted it since. If it helps, I'm sorry. I'm not a pervert. I'd never hurt a woman, unless I was paid to."

He said the last sentence with a small, unfunny laugh.

My heart raced.

"What about your tattoo of my name?" I spat, suddenly recalling that fun little detail. "Don't deny it. Justin told us all about it."

"Your name? That fucking idiot smokes too much." He

tugged his shirt aside at the collar, revealing script work.

*April,* it read.

"My mom." Larson shrugged. "What can I say? I'm a mama's boy."

Not my name after all.

Stunned, I sat back.

None of this was going how I'd expected. I'd anticipated a fight, not a sit-down chat. Larson was a psychopath, but apparently a reasonable one. Not that I trusted him for a second.

But what he told us had both reset my thoughts on several things plus given me a better understanding of the depths to which my father would stoop to manage his family.

I didn't know why I was surprised.

Though I'd tried to block out all knowledge of my father, the years I'd spent under his roof were crystal clear in my mind.

The phone calls where he'd threatened and manipulated people to bend them to his will. The meetings in our great room where he'd make deals with scary men, undercutting rivals and casually sabotaging their businesses, bragging about it to my brothers.

There was nothing redeemable about that man.

There was no way I'd let Raphael go back to him.

But that meant I'd have to, and Jackson as well.

Not happening.

Slyly, I gauged the distance between me and Larson, trying to work out if I could spring from my seat and knock him away from Jackson. Between me and Raphael, surely we could overpower him. Then there was a whole host of people outside who could help.

Larson tilted his head. "Don't bother. There's no way you can beat him, no matter what you're considering doing to me. Let me lay this out for you. Mr West knows where you live. He had an idea after you ran from him but didn't bother actively pursuing you until now when it was worth his while. You and your brother are old enough to be of value to him, specifically with Raphael flying. He let you have your teenage years in peace, which he considers a gift, but that time is over. I've passed on your location. If I go silent, he'll send worse men than me. All those folks outside will be in the way. He wants you back, and he'll have you. So make your choice."

The image he painted hit me like a truck.

Dad's mobster friends coming here. Hurting people. Destroying the place I loved.

From his comment about Gabe becoming a father, I wondered if he knew about that, too, or if it had been a guess.

Pure hatred chased away my fear. How fucking dare he?

Raphael stood. "Uncuff Jackson and I'll go with ye."

Larson considered him. "You're agreeing to go back to your father?"

"If that's what it takes."

Jackson gave a growl of unhappiness behind his gag.

I shot to my feet, glaring at my brother. "No, you can't."

"What choice do we have?" His grey eyes beseeched mine. "The cops can do nothing about him, he's paid too many off and he has powerful people in his pocket. You're not going back to that life. It's me Dad wants. He knows that I'm flying."

"Listen to me," I pleaded. "You're not going to sacrifice yourself."

My brother had been fifteen when we'd fled and had already seen too much of blood. Gabe had confessed he was shocked by how well Raphael knew his way around a gun. While I'd sat and listened, Raphael had been dragged into active involvement.

But he was no killer.

He might be a foot taller than me and a year older, but Raphael had none of my bite. He was warm-hearted. Loyal and caring. He'd learned to cook so we could eat well. He'd spotted a soul in need in Jackson and brought him home.

With resignation in every look, Raphael touched his gaze on his best friend. "Besides all that, we know what will happen if he gets hold of Jax. I care about him, I can't let that happen."

"I can't either. I love him," I said quickly.

Raphael's eyes widened then crinkled at the edges. "In a very different way to me, I imagine. Fucking hell, Ariel."

The sound came from beside us, and I snapped my gaze to find Jackson staring at us, hot emotion present in his eyes.

God, what a way for him to hear my feelings about him.

Larson heaved a sigh. "I don't want to interrupt this love-in, but if I go back empty-handed, he'll kill me. So you see, I have an incentive. Make your decision. I've been in this cold-assed country too long."

I took a step forward, hands up. "What if there is another way?"

An inkling of an idea had taken hold in my mind. It relied on Larson listening. Of me being able to pull this off. It was so out there, but fuck my dad. I was furious at everything he'd done, and all I could see was the need to take revenge.

I knew exactly how to do it.

But before I could speak, my brother sucked in a breath

and launched himself across the room.

And a bolt of electricity shot from Larson's Taser, the crackle terrifying.

36

# Valentine

I hated being late to the party. A small crowd gathered at the end of the road in the village across the loch from the McRae estate. I leapt from my car, jogging up to Lochinvar, Ben and Gordain a minute behind me.

Besides Ariel's stroke of genius in working out where to look, Ben had played Jackson's car's video and audio, confirming a snap of sound that could only be a Taser.

It gave us hope that he was alive.

"What's going on?" I barked.

Lochinvar sliced his gaze at the house. "The kidnapper's inside with Jackson. We came here with Ariel, then the fucker called her. She and Raphael went in. She told us to wait."

"For what, exactly?"

A snap of electricity came from the darkened living room in conjunction with a cry.

Fuck waiting.

I barged in, smacking the front door open with my shoulder, striding down the hall to an open living room doorway, others following.

Inside, Raphael grappled with a man on the floor. Larson, I recognised him from his video.

I piled in, no hesitation, Lochinvar at my side. With three of us on him, we rolled the guy to his front and yanked both arms behind his back.

I elbowed him between the shoulder blades for good measure.

He swore but submitted.

Shame, I wanted the fight.

Beside them, Ariel crouched over Jackson, his hands tied behind him, and the chair he was constrained to tipped over.

"Is he okay?" I barked.

Raphael appeared healthy, she was standing, but Jackson hadn't made a sound.

She fluttered over the handcuffs. "I can't get these off. I need a key."

Fear filled her voice.

I jammed my hands into Larson's jacket pockets, hoping I didn't have to go delving into his jeans.

Luck was on my side. I pulled a key out and passed it to Ariel.

She uncuffed Jackson, the silver links falling away. But his legs were still tied to the seat. I took out my knife and nudged Ariel aside so I could slice the plastic and free him, Cameron taking my place with Lochinvar and Raphael, guarding the kidnapper.

Helping Jackson up, I peered at his face, relieved to fuck

that his eyes were open and bright. "Ye good, bro?"

"Fucking peachy." He rolled his shoulders and touched his fingertips to his neck, a welt forming, presumably from where Larson had shocked him.

Ariel gave a soft cry, and Jackson brought her into his arms, holding her close. They dropped to a sofa, my man looking wrecked.

A crowd of people filled the hallway and the entrance to the room, keeping clear so we could move, but all playing witness.

Finally, the two lovebirds were public. Drama much?

I turned back to Raphael who was still pinning down Larson. "Shall I get the cops, or are we burying him in the woods?"

Raphael shook his head. "I have no fucking idea. There's no way to win this."

Yeah, fuck that.

This man had messed with the wrong crew, and I was down for whatever it took to get rid of him.

I had a powerful right hook, a shovel, and zero conscience when it came to shite like this.

His sister spoke behind me. "There might be. But we'll need his help."

She pointed at the kidnapper.

Her brother scowled. "You've got to be fucking kidding me."

"You heard what he said. If it's not him, then someone else will come. Maybe someone worse. I need to end this." She collected the handcuffs from the floor and handed them to Raphael. "Cuff him, then give me a second to work my idea through."

While Ariel found a piece of paper and pen on a side table, Raphael constrained Larson, and I helped right the man so he was sitting against the wall, legs out, hands bound behind his back.

I stared him down. "Ugly fucker, aren't ye? See what happens now the tables have flipped."

He held my gaze. "What Ariel said is correct. I'm the least of their worries."

A chill went through me.

Perhaps I was too used to military ways and zero subtlety, but Larson had kidnapped Jackson after trying for days to catch Ariel. Why weren't they jumping to jail the arsehole?

The others who'd followed me in crowded the hall, muttering.

At Jackson's side, Ariel began scribbling on the page.

I crouched in front of my colleague, turning his head to check on his injury. "Where does it hurt?"

"I'm fine."

"Don't be a fucking hero. What's this?" I glanced over a bruise on his jaw.

"Fell on my face."

"Any other injuries?"

"Tasered, twice," he admitted. "The second one was aimed at my temple but hit my neck."

"Shame. Could've reset your brain," I answered, pressing lightly around the mark to check the blood pressure response.

He gave a weak laugh, letting me take his pulse and watch his breathing. My first-aid training was better than most, but I was no doctor.

"Is he okay?" Ariel asked.

He ran his arm around her. "Unbreakable."

They shared a moment of eye contact, and she resumed her hurried scribbling.

I had no idea what we were doing next. The crowd of people in the house wasn't budging. Ariel held the reins, and we all waited on her.

At last, she put down the pen and regarded Larson. "Now listen to me. I need you to follow my instructions—"

Larson made a sound of disgust. "What don't you get about this situation? You don't have the upper hand. You never did because you're just a girl. Even with all the people you can pull in, it'll never be enough."

Jackson leapt from the sofa, pushing me aside. He ushered Lochinvar and Cameron out of the way then grasped Larson by the lapels, tightening them around his throat. Without ceremony, he yanked the man to his feet and dragged him across the room to kneel before Ariel.

"Shut your mouth and listen to her."

I gave up worrying about his health. My boy was recovering fine.

Ariel smiled prettily. "Thanks for that. Everyone else, I'm going to need you to clear the space. Wait in your cars if you like, but I'll need quiet for what I'm about to do."

There were protests, but Ariel had taken charge, and one by one, everyone obeyed.

Aside from me, of course.

Same as her brother and Jackson. The three of us remained with her and Larson.

Ariel held up a sheet of paper for Larson to see. "Pass me his phone," she said to her brother.

Raphael collected the device from the floor and handed

it over.

Ariel activated the video. Trained it on Larson so only he was visible on the screen. "You're going to read this list," she told him. "Speak clearly, don't hesitate, and if you go off script, Jackson has permission to hurt you."

He squinted at the page and paled. "What is this?"

I was dying to know, too.

"Just read," she commanded, hitting 'record'.

Larson worked his jaw then commenced reading from the list.

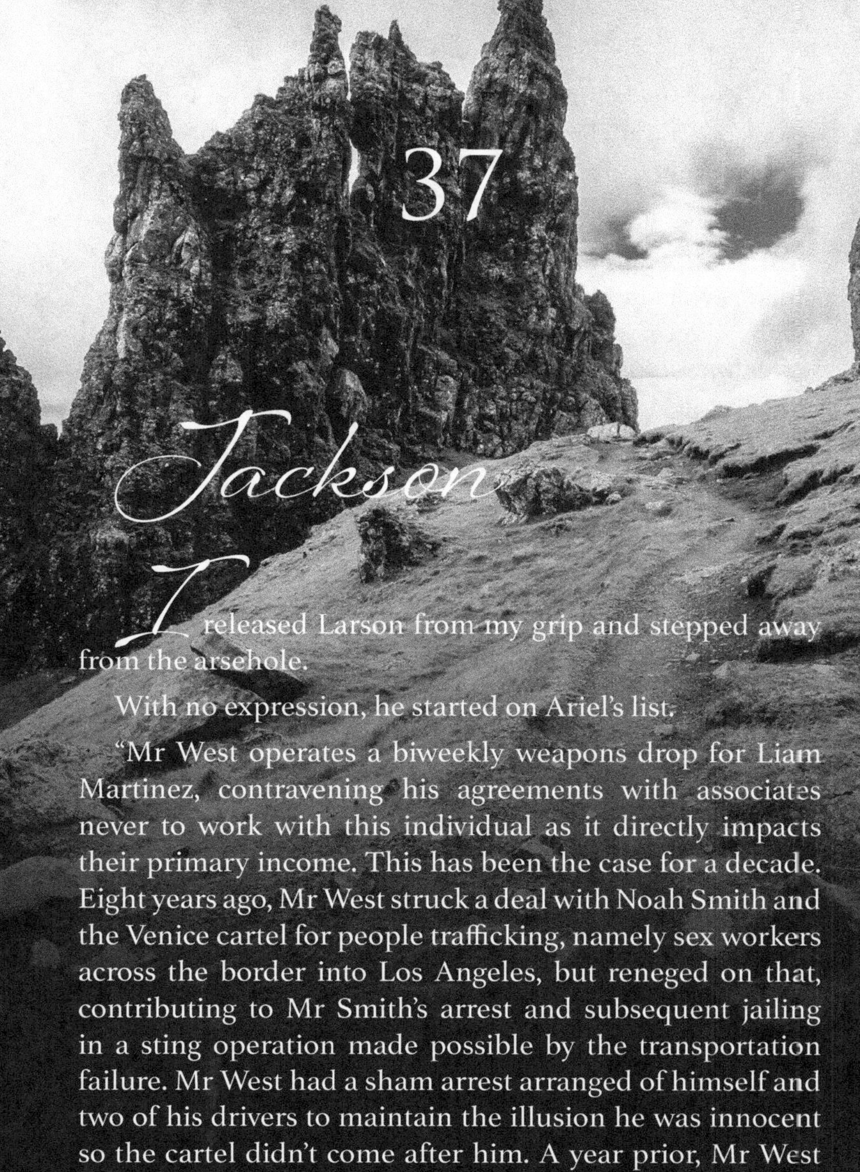

# 37

## *Jackson*

*I* released Larson from my grip and stepped away from the arsehole.

With no expression, he started on Ariel's list.

"Mr West operates a biweekly weapons drop for Liam Martinez, contravening his agreements with associates never to work with this individual as it directly impacts their primary income. This has been the case for a decade. Eight years ago, Mr West struck a deal with Noah Smith and the Venice cartel for people trafficking, namely sex workers across the border into Los Angeles, but reneged on that, contributing to Mr Smith's arrest and subsequent jailing in a sting operation made possible by the transportation failure. Mr West had a sham arrest arranged of himself and two of his drivers to maintain the illusion he was innocent so the cartel didn't come after him. A year prior, Mr West orchestrated a bloodbath between the Seventeenth Street Brotherhood and the Black Fence street gangs by stealing parts of shipments of narcotics one was delivering to the other, while blaming the other party for his theft. Mr West took a cut of payments to Julian Reyes—"

Larson read line after line, naming Ariel's father's associates, politicians, gangs, and accusations of all he'd done to them.

It painted a damning picture.

She condemned her father to everyone who worked with him. Previously, Daisy had released records of her family's dealings to the feds, knowing it would tie them up in legal wranglings and successfully get them to leave her alone.

The same wouldn't work for the West father.

It wouldn't be enough to reveal his crimes because of the number of powerful people he worked with. But revealing how he'd played them off against each other was certain death.

Pride burst through me at her power move.

What a card to play.

Larson reached the end of the list and calmly regarded the camera. Ariel stopped the video, cropped the beginning and end, and held it up to Larson.

"How do you communicate with my father?"

He took her in, his expression unreadable.

Then he relented and indicated a number he'd used.

She sent the video.

"Now what?" Raphael asked.

She took a long, steady exhale. "We wait."

I wasn't just going to sit here and not be able to touch her. Grabbing her hand, I tugged her up and out of the room. At the end of the hall was a small kitchen. I dragged out a stool from the breakfast bar and sat her on it.

"It should be you sitting down," she said. "The whole way here, I thought the worst, that he was going to hurt you, and then he did. When he pressed that trigger, I thought you were going to die."

Her voice cracked. I stood between her legs, loving how she instantly curled them around my back, hugging me to her.

"You love me," I replied.

She lifted her head from where she'd tucked it against my chest, her eyes wide, words on her lips.

But I wasn't done.

I brushed my nose over hers, holding her gaze. "In case it isn't obvious, I'm in love with ye. Like the insane, maniac, obsessed kind of love. It's important to me that ye know I'll never hurt ye, and if ye give me a chance, I'll sum up all the ways and times I fell. I know lists work—"

My offer was cut off by Ariel pressing her lips to mine.

She kissed me, just like she'd done on the street near this house what felt like forever ago. But this time, I'd stopped lying to myself. I held her face between my hands and kissed her back, pouring every bit of sentiment into our clinch while my heart did some crazy shite.

Ariel pulled me in tighter, squeezing my hips between her thighs, careful of the places I hurt.

Instantly, my mind shot to a darker place, where I could shred both our clothes and get inside her. Last night, we hadn't had sex. It felt disrespectful under someone else's roof, even if technically we'd always been in the castle, but a week of sexual exploration made the past eighteen hours feel like a drought.

I was harder for her than ever. Almost grinding against her in my need to be closer.

Nothing felt better or safer than being with this woman. She challenged me, pushed me, and guided me, and now she was midway through saving her family, too. It was a knife's-edge of action, and if she needed to leave this place, I'd follow. I couldn't do anything else.

Someone cleared their throat from the doorway.

We broke apart, breathing hard. I lifted my focus to find Valentine in the frame.

He'd averted his gaze. "Phone's ringing."

Ariel's breath caught. "Already?"

I helped her off the chair, and we hustled to answer the call from her old man.

# 38

## Ariel

Cold confidence infused me while I set up the phone, my brother holding the device and Larson in the video frame. Then I swiped to connect before it rang out.

Dad appeared.

There was silence while he took in who'd answered.

"What was that?" he asked.

I smiled, not that he could see. He was already rattled.

Larson remained silent.

"What. The fuck. Was that?" he roared.

I rounded to stand in front of Larson, forcing him out of my way.

"A counteroffer," I replied.

"Ariel," Dad said with a sneer.

"I got your message. Sorry to be the bearer of bad news, but you can't have me. Or Raphael and Gabe. Or, for that matter, Jackson, who Larson apparently filled you in on, or anyone else connected to me." I curled my lip. "You can't have any of them because they're mine. So I'm telling you now to call off your dog."

Dad steepled his fingers, his expression settling to frosty with a side of patronising. "I admire your spirit, but—"

I spoke over him, not giving him the floor.

"Shut your damn mouth and listen. You'll accept my offer or I'll expose every crooked thing you've ever done. All the ones Larson listed and far more, because trust me, I can bring the receipts for each. I tried to forget your existence, but my memory is infallible, and I was always there. I remember every meeting you held in our house, all the phone calls, every person you wined and dined or dealt with. I can give the dates, locations, and what was said. Every single gang member or crooked politician you fucked over will get my exposé. Daisy's family are in the shit. They'd willingly trade that info with the feds and let the politicians fight over it."

I smiled, the image of the savage daughter he'd accidentally created but neglected to notice.

Then I spoke my killer blow.

"Or worse, I'll feed it to Mom. Isn't that what you wanted? For me to talk to my mother, not my father? I realise now that you were trying to punish her further by reminding her of my existence, but it only made me consider how her man would love getting evidence of how you undercut and sold out people who are far more dangerous than you. And the man your wife left you for is the worst of all. Isn't that why you let her go without a fight?"

His expression had dropped the more I spoke.

Now, he went white.

I held my ground, controlled my racing pulse, and looked him in the eye. "Believe me, Dad, for the sin of underestimating your daughter, I'll do it all with a smile on my face. Now call off your dog. Permanently."

For a long minute, he glared back at me. Breathed through his nose.

Then he stabbed at his phone, hanging up.

# 39

## Jackson

Collectively, we all released a breath. Glanced at each other.

Raphael lowered the phone, turning a puzzled expression on his sister. "He used to say to me that to show fear was the greatest form of weakness a man could display. Worse than that, he'd say to even feel that fear was a sign I was weak."

In the doorway, Ben made a noise of disgust. "That's bull, and the type of toxic shite that winds up with men exploding in emotional outbursts of anger. Fear is healthy. It's a bodily warning designed to keep us safe."

I watched Ariel. "What does that mean that he reacted like that? He was afraid, aye?"

She inclined her head. "I think so. But I don't know what he'll do next. Either it's over, or he'll explode like Ben said, and I've brought the war Larson promised."

Seated on the chair I'd been tied to, Larson waited, unperturbed. The guy had to be a psychopath for how little emotion he showed.

Then his phone dinged with a message.

Raphael squinted at it. "It's a code."

"Show me," Larson asked.

Raphael gave a soft laugh. "No dice. Tell me the code you'd expect him to send."

Larson inclined his head. "To abandon the mission and return, he'd send me my initials, the date, and X."

Ariel's brother held up the phone. "Looks like you're going home."

A conversation started up. A debate over handcuffing Larson and seeing him back to the airport. A question to him over what he'd do with the information he now had. It was only part of what Ariel knew, and in one breath condemned him, as well as giving him power.

The kidnapper shrugged. "I'll decide that when I'm Stateside. Safe to say I can no longer work for your father, so thanks for the unemployment."

It was agreed that Ben and Valentine would ensure he went, with Lochinvar going along for good measure.

With Larson still in cuffs, they left, the majority of the others leaving, too.

Throughout all of the discussion, I only had eyes for Ariel. This was her victory, but she seemed deflated.

Raphael drove us back to the tower, all of us lost to introspection.

This time, he parked outside the front. Eyed the scorched ground and blackened stone where my car had been torched, thankfully removed by someone so I didn't have to look at the wreckage.

The three of us climbed the tower's stairs, the scent of smoke still lingering in the hall, but a sense of safety regained.

In the circular living room, Raphael threw himself into a seat and spoke to his sister. "How did ye remember all of that? So much of what ye said was familiar, that was like opening a box in my mind. One I'd intentionally locked and thrown away the key."

She curled her legs underneath herself. "Probably because he didn't tell me any of it and I was desperate to listen. You were forced to be in the room. I went in there to gain his approval by finding any way to be helpful to him." Ariel's shoulders rose. "I spoke to Willow, and between her and the brief conversation with Mom, it sparked the idea that I could ruin his reputation, even though I'm in hiding. If I spoke about him publicly, revealed his alliances and all that shady shit he'd done, his business world would crumble. And that is more important to him than any of his kids."

"What does this mean for your safety?" I asked. "Could this mean he'll target ye?"

"Larson has that list now, and Dad will be sure to assume I wasn't the only person on the call. I'm not scared of him." She took a deep breath. "I'm not in hiding anymore either. None of us are, I'm just realising. We've been so restricted for the past six years, hell, for that matter, all of our lives. And now? Nothing we can do can make the threat of him any different, so until there's a reason to worry, I'm just going to live."

She reached for me. I'd sat beside her but left space, unsure of how to navigate this thing we'd found.

I hooked my arm around her and brought her close, closing my eyes briefly while I pressed my lips to the top of her head.

Then I regarded Raphael, because I'd crossed a line, and though I'd called him to tell him I'd fallen for his sister, he was my friend, and I owed him a better explanation than that.

His gaze moved between us, and he generated a wry smile. "This is new."

Ariel pulled an awkward expression. "I promise I'm not stealing your friend. We'll have entirely different uses for him."

Raphael barked a surprised laugh. "God, don't make my mind go there. I'm happy for ye. Both of ye. In fact, Jackson, can I assume you'll stay here tonight?"

I hadn't thought beyond the next few minutes all day.

I had no reason to stay over at the tower now. Ariel didn't need a bodyguard with Larson gone, and she wouldn't be here alone anymore.

But her fingers twisted through mine, and my answer was right there.

"If Ariel wants me here, I'm staying," I told him.

"I do," she confirmed.

"Good, because I have somewhere else to be. See me out?" He leapt up.

I frowned but followed, dropping a quick kiss on Ariel once more.

"Raph," she said, stalling his progress. "Did you take your final exam? You didn't say."

My friend inclined his head. "Passed with flying colours, pun intended. Going to grab some clean clothes and I'll be out of your hair."

I smiled at his joke—finally he was giving them back—and trailed him downstairs to the bedroom floor. Raphael entered his room, sorting through his drawers and collecting a pile of clothes that he stuffed into a bag.

"Where are ye going?" I asked.

"Ben and Daisy are moving into the cottage, so there's a room open in Castle Braithar, Ben's old space. I can officially join the bodyguard team now, and Gordain and Ella prefer to have someone live on site. I'm going to try it for a couple of days." He gestured with his head to indicate upstairs. "Ariel deserves her own space, and to fill it with the people of her choice, not a brother hanging around."

I guessed he needed space, too, but I got the sense that Raphael wasn't happy, despite his words upstairs.

"We're celebrating your joining the team," I said. "Beers tomorrow night?"

"Sure, man." He took a heavy breath. "Don't think this face is anything to do with ye. I like that you're dating my sister. There's no one I'd trust more. I've just got some shite going on."

"Talk to me."

"Aye, I will, but not now." He hefted his bag on his back. "Oh, before I forget. Ben handed me this before he left."

He held out my phone, knocked from my hand in the scuffle with Larson outside my car.

"And I have a gift for ye."

I accepted a small parcel from him, the packaging plain, no clue as to what was inside. The gesture had my heart pounding.

"What do pilots take to be better in the bedroom?" I asked, my throat tight.

Raphael paused at the door, a single dark eyebrow arching and his ever-patient expression in place.

"Flyagra."

His mouth opened. He raised his gaze to the ceiling.

Then he was gone.

The door slammed downstairs, and I pulled the tape to open my gift.

It was a little metal dragon, a majestic wee fellow, unpainted, and without a note.

It didn't need one. My best friend had seen the missing parts in me and done all he could to fill them. A home, someone to talk to, and even a hobby.

Fucking hell.

Whatever was bothering Raphael would answer to me.

I carried the dragon into Ariel's bedroom and set it beside her fox, then returned upstairs, tapping out a 'thank you' to my best friend.

Maybe one day I'd be lucky enough to call him brother, but I was getting ahead of myself, and there were problems at hand I needed to tackle first.

As had become common for me, my phone had countless messages and missed calls, several from my mother.

I dropped onto the sofa beside Ariel and collected her to my lap without ceremony. Then I hit 'play' on the voicemail Ma had left.

"Jackson. After all you've done, and you won't even pick up the phone to hear the outcome. TJ lost the hearing. He lost! They consider him to be a danger to the community, and it's all your fault because of your selfish nature."

I smiled and brought Ariel's lips to mine for a kiss.

"Terence has kicked me out," Ma continued. "Call me back. Please. I'm begging."

I killed the call, dropping my head back.

Ariel curled into me. "I'm sorry she said those things."

I wasn't. She hadn't changed, and I'd finally stopped

hoping she would.

"I think she torched my car," I said.

Ariel took a breath and grabbed her phone. Hit the button to place a call, mouthing *Lochinvar* at me. "Hey, sorry to disturb you. Did you get a description of that dog walker your crew member had seen after our scare at Daisy's house?"

She listened, then thanked the mountain rescue leader, and hung up.

"Middle-aged woman, bobbed hair."

I rubbed the heel of my hand into my forehead. "She tried to frighten ye, presumably to get to me. I'm so sorry."

"I'm not. I don't regret a single thing that has happened. How can I when the result is this?"

She kissed me again, and I was half a second from taking this further, heat bubbling under. But there was something I needed first.

"Hold that thought."

I called my mother back and put her on loudspeaker.

"Jackson? Thank God. At last you've seen sense," she said, her voice fraught.

"Good to know TJ's parole hearing failed," I said.

"Good? How can anything about this be good? My husband ordered me to move out. He said he can't be in a marriage anymore when I'm so clearly not on his side. Because of ye I'm homeless. What am I going to do?"

"How did ye torch my car?" I asked.

Silence filled the line.

I continued, musing. "Was it ye alone? Or did your newly ex-husband provide the tools and method? I assume so because from everything I've seen, your default is to follow blindly where he leads. Plus he owns a string of garages, so if anyone knows how to cause an explosion like that, it would be him. How about when ye followed me when I dropped off my girlfriend and then tried to scare her? Was he there, too? Or just your dog?"

My mother didn't reply, only her breathing audible.

"This is the last time I'm going to tell ye to leave me alone. Try contacting me again, or harass my girlfriend in any way, and I'll have ye arrested. As for your miserable life, I get that you're upset, but this is a reality ye created for yourself. Get a lawyer and fight for your share in the divorce. I'd offer my car for ye to sleep in, like I had to when ye kicked me out, but considering ye burned it—"

She hung up on me.

I couldn't bring myself to care.

My family was here, and it was the one I'd found. The team who'd searched for me, the woman and her brother who'd turned their lives upside down for me, the whole host of people from the estate who'd showed up.

But it was to Ariel that I had something to say to now. For her, I'd create my very own list.

# 40

## Ariel

Jackson reached for the side table and collected my notepad and pen. "Write this down, little fox."

I opened a page and clicked the pen, waiting on him.

"Title: How Jackson Fell for Ariel."

I stilled, my heart thumping, but at his gesture, wrote the words.

He continued. "When she roundhouse kicked me in the gut, naked. When she was so brave in kissing me the first time, but braver in telling me off after for holding back. When she had the most unhinged birthday party and created a sex list from it. When I got to work through that list with her and worship her body the way it should be. The very first time I came here and saw her and had to look away."

I jotted down every word but seized up at the last.

"I thought I was beneath your interest."

"I couldn't have been more interested. It's why I couldn't

keep my gaze on ye."

Emotion threatened me. I held it together and poked him in the chest with my pen. "In the car once, you called me a kid."

"While fighting the urge to mentally undress ye."

He leaned in and pressed a kiss to my throat. The sensation spiralled into lust, and I closed my eyes, dipping my head back to give him space to do more.

"Hanging out with her, laughing, grocery shopping together then cooking dinner," he said against my skin and between kisses. "Add to that list: right now in this moment. In every damn moment."

But I'd abandoned my writing. I'd never known anything like what I felt for this man. The trust I had in him, how he felt like a missing part of me.

If he'd been hurt, I couldn't bear it. If we hadn't found him, I don't know what I would have done.

I dropped the notepad and pen to the floor then found Jackson's mouth with mine. We kissed, taking our time to drive each other wild, sliding into wet, drugging kisses while our hands roamed.

Jackson shifted me onto my back on the sofa, then hooked an arm under my knees to yank me lower. I stretched my arms above my head, my top sliding up.

He went still then stooped to kiss my bare midriff.

I stripped my shirt. He did the same with his.

My little fox bracelet caught the light, and I took Jackson's hand and set a finger on it. "What would you say if I wanted you to wear one of these?"

He kissed my wrist. "I'll get one made."

"Obviously I won't track you day to day," I stumbled.

"Only if you were missing."

He knelt between my legs and put his face to mine. "Track me everywhere. Check on me when ye need to. I want ye to feel safe, and I'll never have a problem with ye knowing where I am." He kissed me, going deep. "I intend to feed your obsession. Starting now."

Jackson reached under me and undid my bra, dragging it away and tossing it across the room. He groaned at the sight of my breasts and ducked to kiss each, sucking on a nipple and curling his tongue around it to stiffen it to a peak.

I arched into him, lost in every suck and pull. He continued going, trailing his mouth down my belly and to my jeans. Quickly, they were gone, too, along with my underwear, and that clever mouth of his was between my thighs.

We'd tried all kinds of sex. Different positions, using toys, and all the other things on my list, but all I needed was him.

Jackson nuzzled my clit, pressing a kiss to it before following with a hard suck. I saw stars, surging into his touch. He lifted me with one hand so he could slide his tongue inside me.

"Jackson," I breathed.

"Tell me what ye need. Where did we get to on your list?"

In a rush, I couldn't wait a moment more. I twisted my fingers in his hair and dragged his head up. "I need you inside me. Right now."

He gave a devilish grin. "Close your eyes."

I obeyed, and he moved away, the rustle of material telling me his clothes were being shed.

Then Jackson returned to between my legs, notching his dick to my core.

"I'm so fucking in love with ye," he said and jerked to fill me.

Any words I could summon were lost in a groan.

I reached for him and brought his torso down to meet mine, our mouths connecting, no space between us, as close as two people could be. He made love to me, taking his time and stoking my passion until I was a writhing mess.

I couldn't resist opening my eyes to see him.

That devoted expression, the competent, beautiful man who could've been broken by the world but who'd kept on living. Nothing could be better than what we'd found, the care and love he'd shown and that I'd return. If it took the rest of my life, I would never tire of learning about him and finding ways to make him happy.

Give him the sense of family he deserved. That both of us did.

When I came, it was easily, and with a muttered curse from him and a matching climax where he fucked in deep and held himself hard inside me.

I'd fallen hard for Jackson Reid, and I never, ever wanted to come out.

# 41

# Ariel

Days passed, and Jackson barely left my side, even while I returned to work, joyful in my freedom on the slopes.

He watched on as a muted Bridgette joined my lesson again, her gaze downcast and her attitude gone. I'd spoken to her mother and told her how her daughter's too-much-information posts had clued in a stranger to their house being empty, and that had caused a break-in.

There had been no need to explain more, and I'd left them to take it up with the police. I'd got an apology and a thanks, while Bridgette lost her phone.

The bodyguard team took a long weekend, everyone needing some downtime.

This afternoon, Jackson and my brother had gone out together, their plan to hunt down a new car for Jackson with a couple of test drives, then bring home my Mini for me.

Meanwhile, Daisy and I were hanging out, entertaining

ourselves with messages from our girl group while binge-watching a TV show.

Normal life had resumed.

Well, a normal I'd barely known, but I was thrilled that it had become my reality.

*Casey: We're going to need a ranking of your top-five positions, now you're an experienced lady.*

*Viola: While Ariel's writing that, Leo bought me a new toy! It's called the Rose. I highly recommend it, particularly if other parts are out of action from pushing babies out.*

*Isobel: Searching for it now.*

*Isobel: Ooh, that looks good. Does it rotate? It's like a tongue.*

*Viola: It SUCKS. So. Damn. Well.*

*Effie: Huh. Discreet enough to have on your shelf without anyone knowing what it's for.*

*Casey: Good for nips?*

*Viola: Why haven't I tried that? BRB.*

*Daisy: Oops. My finger slipped, and I ordered one.*

*Viola: That's what she said.*

*Ariel: In no order, from behind over furniture, in the middle of the night, when he walks in the door and we go at it on the floor, same but against a wall, pretty much every other thing we've done, too.*

*Effie: Aw, you're so in love. It's making me so happy. Even tearful. Wait, I'm ACTUALLY crying about you being loved up and getting great sex. WTF?*

*Viola: That's pregnancy hormones for you. Did I mention I'm THRILLED for you? Thrilled. Our babies will be in the same school year, assuming he or she is on time.*

*Casey: Can we get back to this Rose thing? Should I indulge?*

On the shelf, a phone buzzed.

The one we used to talk to our father. In all the times we'd kept in contact with our little brother, Dad had never rung it himself.

I showed Daisy then angled the screen away from her, answering with my heart thudding.

Dad sat in his office with Willow and Azrael on either side of him. All smiled, my father's expression carefully serene.

Tension strung me up tight. Who knew where his mind was at.

"Ariel, my daughter," he said.

I resisted the urge to let my jaw drop. No searching for my brothers, no disappointment that it was only me.

"I came across a discovery I thought would interest you," he continued. "Your mother left jewellery here. Some of it was your grandmother's, originating in Scotland. Pretty pieces, things I believe you'd like and which would suit you. By rights, that now belongs to you."

At my lack of words, because I was truly speechless, Dad continued.

"Willow has it for safekeeping and has even spent some time cleaning it. You can organise with her to have it sent on. Azrael, greet your sister."

My brother gave a shy wave and chatted on about a little league club he'd joined.

I didn't believe for a minute my father had turned a corner, but neither of my brothers had been in clubs, and I had been forbidden from playing sports.

I smiled at Azrael's telling, realising now that's probably why I'd signed up to work for Effie so readily and spent my life outdoors and on the slopes.

After a few minutes of small talk, Willow and Azrael left the room.

My father regarded me. "There are many things I regret in life. You were never one of them, until recently. I was too hasty with you, daughter. And too tough on your brothers, I recognise. All of it, I did out of love for my family and a desire to continue our name. You might not see that now, or understand my methods, but in future, when you have a family of your own, I believe you'll understand me better. I'll leave off by saying now that if ever you want to join the family fold and return to being a West, the door is wide open. You'd be as welcome as your brothers. More so, perhaps. I see the apple didn't fall far from the tree when it comes to you."

Stunned, I dipped my head, acknowledging the compliment. I wasn't about to thank him, but a sense of relief broke over me.

We ended the call, and I looked at Daisy.

"New future as a mob queen?" she asked with a head tilt.

I cracked up, needing the release of laughter like I never had before. Holy shit.

The final piece had fallen into place, and now all I needed was Jackson back with me again.

An hour later, he returned with my Mini, this time bringing Ben up with him instead of my brother. I'd already messaged my family group to tell them what happened with our father, my brothers just as shocked as I'd been. I knew from Jackson's expression that Raphael had told him.

He came to me and dipped me backwards, stealing a kiss. "Proud of ye."

He loved on my lips for as long as was appropriate with an audience, then righted me, a self-satisfied grin on his gorgeous face.

In Ben's arms, Daisy regarded us. "Dinner at ours? We finally have enough kitchen equipment and plates to offer a meal with."

With a quick check for Jackson's agreement, I smiled, buoyant with the ability to go on a date like this. The new normal looked mighty fine. "We'd love to."

The four of us descended the spiral steps of Castle McRae's tower.

"I meant to ask," I said to Daisy. "Did you ever hear back from Mia?"

Her expression brightened in animation. "Yes! I meant to say. She took up the offer for temporary accommodation and should be arriving soon, with her daughter coming a couple of days later. I have my very first staff member!"

I congratulated her, and they climbed into Ben's car and set off.

Jackson offered me the keys to my Mini. I took them, delighted to have my car back.

Over the bonnet, he spoke to me. "What Daisy didn't say regarding her new staff member was that Mia will be moving into the bunkhouse for a few days."

I blinked, wondering how that setup would work. Then again, it had several beds in both of the sleeping quarters, and a roof over her head was maybe all she needed to get away from her unhappy life.

"I know I haven't slept there since," he gestured between us, indicating our shacking up, "but I wanted to check you're happy for me to stay at the tower for a while longer. That means she just has to share the communal space with Valentine, rather than two men she doesn't know. I think she'll feel safer, but if you'd rather have time to yourself, I'll sleep on Raphael's floor."

My heart skipped a beat. "No. I mean, I don't ever want you to sleep anywhere else. God."

Jackson stopped. "What are ye saying?"

I flushed hot, so inexperienced with this but also utterly sure. "Move in with me."

He swallowed, and my insistence built.

"Move in. Bring the rest of your things. Share the space with me and make it your home, too." I rounded the car to get to him. Ran my arms around him and peeked up. "You've been living here on and off for years. If you hadn't been so stubborn at the start, we'd already be there."

He tutted, emotion bright in his eyes.

I smiled bigger. "Oh, and my brother said something to me earlier about you and dragons. That you had his approval to turn his old bedroom into a stable for them. I've no idea what he's talking about, but I imagine it's linked to the one that's buddied up to my fox. If it gets you to say yes, I'm down. Bring on the dragons. Bring on anything it takes."

"An old hobby," he confessed.

"How about you bring that old hobby into a new life with me?"

The emotion was replaced with humour as he gazed down at me in utter and compelling love. "If you're sure?"

"One hundred percent. I've never been so certain about anything as I am about you. But I also need something back." I held up my locket. "This has been empty for too long. I want a twist of your hair to go in here so I'm carrying it around with me everywhere."

Finally, he released his smile. It used to be so rare, but now he wore it often.

"Yes, I'll move in. I don't ever want to be apart from ye again. And if ye want something for your locket, I'll paint ye a pretty little fox."

He boosted me onto the bonnet and kissed me.

I knew where his mind was at: That somehow, he was the lucky one. But as far as I was concerned, Jackson had given me everything, and it was him I'd treasure, and every memory I'd made with him, I'd forever save.

# EPILOGUE

## *Valentine*

Under the hot stream of water, I scrubbed shampoo into my hair, letting the suds roll down the long lengths and over my chest.

I was pissed off with myself and trying to work out what the hell was wrong with me.

The previous evening, in the pub in the village, a woman had come on strong with me. She'd been a pretty lass, a local but not too close, and she'd given green lights all over the place.

I'd bought her a drink. Left my table to chat with her at the bar.

Then at the last moment, I'd got spooked and told her I was engaged. She went running, the smile turning into a sneer—and rightly so.

What the fuck was up with me?

My neglected balls ached for release.

I was a free man and down to fuck, but I'd been unable

to seal the deal.

Maybe it was the fact that both Ben and Jackson were stupidly in love and I was sworn off relationships, so the reminder was right there in my face, generating violent dislike every time I witnessed it. Additionally, my brother was pissing me off more with his frequent attempts to talk. He'd led by asking about my ex.

Really, Ben?

Way to focus on the very last person I wanted to talk about.

I didn't care about Kelly anymore, even if I'd never managed to shake the betrayal of what she'd done. But I also couldn't deny that some part of me was broken now.

I'd wanted a wife. A marriage and kids and a nice house to make into a home.

All that had changed, and I didn't want it back.

Still, I couldn't deny how on edge I was.

I ran my hand down to my dick and started stroking, needing to get off and quickly. In my mind, I summoned a heavy pair of tits to bury my face in and play with.

A weighty, gorgeous pair.

Nipples to suck.

Quickly, I was hard and jerking into my fist, though I was unable to put a face to my mystery fantasy, even as I loved on her luscious body.

Thick thighs. The lass grinding her sweet pussy on my face. And those tits...

The water sluiced down me, heating me further, steam swirling around me.

I was approaching the edge, a climax exactly what I needed.

A voice came from outside the bunkhouse's bathroom. "That's the communal shower room. I'll let you take a look while I grab you some bedding."

The door opened, and a woman peeked through the gap.

Blonde, pretty, curvy as hell. The most amazing tits I'd ever seen.

Breathing hard, I stopped moving, though my dick pulsed in my hand, hard enough to drive nails into the wall.

Her gaze landed on me, and she soaked me in. My interrupter didn't shriek or run. Instead, her cheeks flushed red, and she stared unashamedly, her focus slipping down to my manhood.

I had a flash of the image in reverse. The vision I was offering. A six-and-a-half-foot man with long hair, sopping wet under the shower, and his hefty dick in hand. I knew I was packing, and I wasn't scared to use it.

It could make an intimidating sight.

The woman didn't leave.

Well shit. Hi, honey, welcome home.

I locked her face and body into my mind, filling in the gaps of my imagination so I could return to my dick stroking. It was as if I'd summoned her, a woman who fit every sexual fantasy I'd ever had.

Dropping my gaze to her tits again, I traced the swell and pictured her joining me in the steam, that top of hers yanked down to expose her to me.

I fucked my fist harder.

Her breath hitched.

"Mia?" The second voice returned.

My little spy jumped and slammed the door closed.

Mia, then. My new roommate.

I should feel bad, but from her expression and actions, I hadn't horrified her in the least.

Tipping my head back, I came in a flood with her tits on my mind and her name on my lips.

*The End.*

To read the steamy sex scene Ariel and Jackson had to delay because of the explosion, download their bonus epilogue now.

https://dl.bookfunnel.com/f4dib7t8cd

You can order Valentine's devilishly sexy story-
Take Her from You -
https://www.amazon.com/dp/B0CMJS38FV

# ARIEL'S SMEXY LIST

*Jackson's Number*
*07123 000 123*

Lose virginity fast with straight up missionary.

Full body contact. Moving slow.

Get on your knees for him. Have him go
down on you. Sixty-nine until you're both on the edge.

*Deep throat him with his hand fisting your ponytail.*

Meet somewhere semi-public and get off fast and hard before anyone sees yo

*Wake with him between your legs (give him permission first. obvs.*

*On all fours, head down, doggy.*

In his arms against a wall.

*Reverse cowgirl.*

Blindfolding!

*Car sex!*

*Sexy sex toys.*

*Ass play (but this isn't for beginners).*

*This one's sweet - on his lap, both sitting up.*

Repeat all using toys.

*Sex websites list — get position of the week and try each.*


*FALL IN LOVE WITH HIM.*

Jolie ♡ Vines

# ACKNOWLEDGEMENTS

Dear reader,

We're done with Jackson and Ariel's story! I love a dark horse, and Jackson had so much hidden under the surface. Ariel was exactly the kind of bright spark to fire up the connection both needed.

I had a little help from my reader group in suggesting pick up lines for the women to share at Ariel's party. That was a delightful conversation, and it brought me a lot of joy. Thanks go to Samantha, Shannon, and Rachel for their hilarious contributions.

SECRET CODES (there's one in each McRae Bodyguards book and the answer for each is in the next book)

Ariel's spicy list was a lot of fun to create. Did you spot the notepad picture of it at the end of the story? There's a hidden code on the bottom right of the page that Jackson will text to Ariel for her to guess.

Go find it and have a guess.

Save Her from Me's code will be revealed in my Jolie Vines's Fall Hard Reader Group a week after launch and also at the end of the next book (Take Her from You).

I'll share it in my newsletter, too. You can add yourself here - https://www.jolievines.com/newsletter

Did you spot the code in book one - Touch Her and Die? Guess it here then find the answer below!

Ben hands Daisy his phone and tells her this: "If it locks again, the code is three-two-four-seven-nine-four."

Using the letters on the keypad on your phone (1 – ABC, 2 – DEF etc), you can work out the answer.

I've included it at the end of this letter so it doesn't drive you crazy.

Big thanks go to my readers who have given me the best career in the world by believing in my books. To Elle, Zoe, Emmy, Sara, Shellie, and Liz – you're the best and I couldn't get anything done without you. To Cleo, you make such pretty graphics and beautiful formatting. To Aaron and Addison, Troy and Denise, the audio is fabulous. To my ARC and Street Team, I can't wait for the excitement you always bring. I can already picture the memes over the women's party antics.

Lastly, as always, I thank N&M, my motivation, inspiration, and happiness.

Jolie x


Ben's code spells out DAISYG.

Her surname is Devereux. His is Graham. I wonder how conscious he was of deciding on that last letter.

# ALSO BY JOLIE VINES

**Marry the Scot series**
1) Storm the Castle
2) Love Most, Say Least
3) Hero
4) Picture This
5) Oh Baby

**Wild Scots series**
1) Hard Nox
2) Perfect Storm
3) Lion Heart
4) Fallen Snow
5) Stubborn Spark

**Wild Mountain Scots series**
1) Obsessed
2) Hunted
3) Stolen
4) Betrayed
5) Tormented

**Dark Island Scots series**
1) Ruin
2) Sin
3) Scar
4) Burn

**McRae Bodyguards**
1) Touch Her and Die
2) Save Her from Me
3) Take Her from You

**Standalones**
Cocky Kilt:
a Cocky Hero Club Novel
Race You:
An Office-Based Enemies-to-Lovers Romance
Fight For Us:
a Second-Chance Military Romantic Suspense

# ABOUT THE AUTHOR

JOLIE VINES is a romance author who lives in the UK with her husband and son.

Jolie loves her heroes to be one-woman guys.

Whether they are a brooding pilot (Gordain in Hero), a wrongfully imprisoned rich boy (Sebastian in Lion Heart), or a tormented twin (Max in Betrayed), they will adore their heroine until the end of time.

Her favourite pastime is wrecking emotions, then making up for it by giving her imaginary friends deep and meaningful happily ever afters.

Have you found all of Jolie's Scots?

Visit her page on Amazon and join her ever active Fall Hard Facebook group.

www.ingramcontent.com/pod-product-compliance
Lightning Source LLC
Chambersburg PA
CBHW072045190726
48294CB00005B/1409